'*A Loyal Traitor* is a thoroughly gripping spy thriller. Tim Glister puts the reader at the heart of the Cold War and captures the high-stakes paranoia of the era brilliantly.'

Adam Hamdy, author of *Black 13*

'There is a ruthless female killer at large, sightings of a Soviet submarine and ambitious KGB officers fomenting audacious coups. All this and references to Harry Palmer and *The Day of the Jackal* cram the stage with scenery before a climax at the Royal Opera House.'

The Times, thriller of the month

'*A Loyal Traitor* is an accomplished and atmospheric spy novel with an original protagonist and a burning question at its heart. Considered and entertaining. I was drawn in from page one.'

Charlotte Philby, author of *A Double Life*

'Stunningly authentic, masterfully plotted and brilliantly composed, this is historical thriller writing at its very best.'

Matthew Richardson, author of *The Insider*

'Original, gritty and compelling, *A Loyal Traitor* cements Glister's reputation as a master storyteller. Fans of John le Carré will love this!'

Awais Khan, author of *No Honour*

'Intelligent, involving and gripping... The jigsaw pieces of the complex plot are picture-perfect.'

Choice Magazine, hardback of the month

'The plot is fast-paced, with plenty of tension and action.'

'It is incredibly satisfying reading a follow-up that not only matches but surpasses the original... This is superior stuff. A lean, intelligent espionage thriller skilfully rendering not just the messy truth of Cold War operations, but the intimate emotional toll of such work.'

'Tim Glister is creating such an elegant and vivid style of his own. This is another pitch-perfect portrayal of a Cold War crisis. Glister creates a distinctive and fascinating thriller, which I hugely enjoyed.'

'A brilliantly convoluted plot with layer on layer of subplot at every turn.'

PRAISE FOR *RED CORONA*

'Relentless and sleek. This pitch-perfect debut – a gripping espionage thriller in the vein of Charles Cumming, Tom Rob Smith and Mick Herron – signals the arrival of a remarkable talent.'

A.J. Finn, author of *The Woman in the Window*

'Catchy title! Actually, *Red Corona* has nothing to do with viruses, but the space race in 1961… An entertaining, not to say nostalgic, espionage thriller.'

The Times and *Sunday Times* Crime Club

'A thoroughly engaging spy thriller that had me gripped from start to finish and left me desperate for more!'

S.J. Watson, author of *Before I Go to Sleep*

'Thrills by the bucket… An entertaining blend of Le Carré-like in-house establishment rivalries and sheer propulsive action reminiscent of Len Deighton.'

Maxim Jakubowski

TIM GLISTER

A GAME
OF DECEIT

**POINT
BLANK**

A Point Blank Book

First published in Great Britain, Australia and the Republic of Ireland by Point Blank,
an imprint of Oneworld Publications, 2023

ISBN 978-0-86154-171-3
ISBN 978-0-86154-170-6 (ebook)

Typeset by Geethik Technologies
Printed and bound in Great Britain by Clays Ltd, Elcograf S.p.A.

This book is a work of fiction. Names, characters, businesses,
organizations, places, and events are either the product of the author's
imagination or are used fictitiously. Any resemblance to actual
persons, living or dead, events, or locales is entirely coincidental.

Oneworld Publications
10 Bloomsbury Street
London WC1B 3SR
England

PROLOGUE

It was Barend Visser's curiosity that killed him.

He wasn't supposed to die. He was supposed to see the world.

For the last two years he'd crewed small cargo ships out of Rotterdam. Short hops across the North Sea to Britain, or slightly longer jaunts, edging the tumultuous Atlantic to the calmer waters of the Mediterranean. But never further.

The M.S. Tasman was going to change that. It was going to take him across vast oceans to far-off lands. To 'see what's out there', his father had said with the resigned enthusiasm of someone who had finally accepted that their son wouldn't be satisfied with the sedate wonders of the Zeeland peninsula.

Visser was hired on a Wednesday, and the Tasman was due to be loaded and sail early the following Tuesday. That gave Visser time for a final visit home to Ritthem, and one last Sunday stroll with his father along the banks of the Westerschelde to the low, angular ruins of Fort Rammekens. For most of his teenage years Visser had hated these walks, their repetition every weekend reinforcing the stultification of country life. However, this weekend he found the familiarity comforting, a memory he would be happy to carry with him across the globe because he no longer had to live it over and over. He also enjoyed the boterkoek that his father produced once they were back at the house – an early celebration for the twentieth birthday they wouldn't be able to celebrate together in a few weeks' time.

The Tasman was the largest ship Visser had ever been on, over four hundred feet long, with five gleaming white decks above the hold that was capable of carrying almost six thousand tonnes of cargo, and a crew of almost fifty men.

Tuesday was an efficient, exciting blur. The first leg of the ship's long journey was to be a light one – its belly was quarter-filled by mid-morning, and it left Rotterdam on schedule.

In stark contrast, its stop at Gibraltar, the tiny British outpost at the mouth to the Mediterranean, was rushed and everyone on board, including Visser, was drafted in to make sure that all the crates and containers that needed to be taken off the ship were, and everything that was due to be loaded onto it made it aboard before they left again.

After five hours of strenuous effort, the hold was over half full, all paperwork had been signed off, and the crew was preparing to leave port, eat some food and get some rest. However, before Visser would be able to head to the mess or his bunk, the chief mate ordered him to double-check every single piece of cargo against the ship's manifest.

Visser knew this was a rite of passage he had to endure as the youngest and newest member of the crew, so he didn't argue. It was also an opportunity to prove his diligence.

It took him almost another two hours of clambering and cross-referencing to work his way through everything and confirm the cargo was all where it was supposed to be. Until he reached the final section of the hold, where he discovered a discrepancy: two crates that should have been loaded in Gibraltar weren't there. And it wasn't that they were somewhere else, or stacked in a way that made them look like they were missing. There was a large, clear gap between other crates where they were supposed to be.

Visser went to look for the chief mate and report the problem. He found him in the mess, playing cards with three other crew members who had clearly worked on the Tasman long enough to be on sociable terms with its second-in-command.

He handed the manifest to the chief mate and pointed to the gap in the column of thin, neat ticks he'd marked down the right-hand side of its pages.

'You're sure?' the chief mate asked after several seconds of quiet contemplation.

The man was almost fifty years old, and he looked like he'd been at sea for most of them. He wore an officer's uniform, but the deep tan and hard skin on his lined face and thick forearms betrayed a long career below as well as above deck.

Visser nodded. The chief mate was silent for another moment, then a wide smile spread across his face.

'Well, that's their problem,' he said. 'The dock was clear when we left, and if something's not there it's not our fault we can't load it.'

The next few days sailing across the Mediterranean were uneventful, the quiet time between ports when duties were easy, light, and didn't get much in the way of Visser's new favourite hobby of staring over the prow of the Tasman *at the horizon and imagining what was beyond it.*

The ship put in at Piraeus, but only briefly, the changeover of cargo small enough to not need Visser, who was off-shift, to help with it. He offered, but the chief mate sent him back up to his bunk almost as soon as he appeared in the hold, telling him half-jokingly that there was a difference between taking on extra work and taking other people's, and that only one of the two would make him friends on a boat like the Tasman.

Visser worried if he'd been too eager, if after making a good impression after Gibraltar he'd now singled himself out for the wrong reasons. But then his concerns were replaced with barely contained excitement as he finally reached a latitude and longitude he'd never passed before: the entrance to the Suez Canal.

Suez was the gateway to the east, the hundred-and-twenty-mile shortcut that had been hewn straight through Egypt to the Red Sea so ships didn't have to sail all the way round Africa to reach the Indian Ocean. It was the furthest point to which Visser had ever travelled. It was also, he suddenly felt, a point of no return.

The Tasman *reached Port Said on the Egyptian coast just before nightfall, but it wouldn't enter the canal until morning. Most of the crew took the opportunity to catch up on some sleep, but Visser's mind and body refused to rest.*

He paced up and down the dark deck, trying to exhaust his limbs, then counted stars for twenty minutes. Neither worked, and he resorted to aimlessly wandering through the ship, eventually ending up meandering through the cargo hold.

The hold was never completely silent, but in the middle of the night with the Tasman's *engines running low and the sea on the other side of the hull calm, it was unusually quiet.*

Visser wondered if this solitude might be what finally pushed him to sleep, but then he reached the very end of the hold and saw something that shouldn't have been there.

Two things, in fact. The crates that hadn't been loaded in Gibraltar.

He leaned over them, peering at their labels in the gloom and racking his brain. Had he miscounted after all? Had someone found them and moved them to where they were supposed to be when they'd stopped off in Greece? Or had they been taken on there?

Visser heard a cough behind him, and looked up to find the chief mate, haloed under a lamp, looking down at him. Visser stood up, suddenly feeling guilty for being in the hold.

'Couldn't sleep?' the chief mate asked.

'No, sir,' Visser replied.

'First time through the canal, right?'

Visser nodded. The chief mate smiled.

'I remember mine,' he said. 'That strip of water stretching out ahead of you with nothing but sand dunes on either side. It all feels like it goes on forever.'

Visser felt his shoulders relax as he pictured the image the chief mate had described. The other man looked past him, at the two crates.

'You solved your little mystery,' he said.

Visser followed the chief mate's gaze, turning to glance at the crates again. He was about to say 'yes, sir' again. But before he could, the older man smashed the outer edge of a rigid hand into his throat.

Visser staggered backwards, grabbing at his neck and trying to breathe through his crushed windpipe. He stumbled and fell to his knees, doubling over as his face started to turn purple.

He stared up at the chief mate, his eyes begging for help, but all he saw was a hand coming towards him again, this time to slam his head against the bulkhead.

Visser's body was still just clinging to life as the chief mate dragged him by the armpits through the hold and up onto the deck. But, unconscious and with only the barest amount of oxygen reaching his lungs, he was unable to put up any sort of fight as he was tipped over the side of the boat, or to stop himself from drowning within seconds of splashing into the sea.

JUNE 1967

CHAPTER 1

Everybody runs.

Guilty or innocent, it doesn't matter. If someone feels like they're being chased, they'll bolt. It's just a case of how fast, how far, and how much damage they'll leave in their wake. The trick, Richard Knox reminded himself as he lingered fifty yards behind the man he'd been tailing across Bloomsbury for the last hour, was to not let them know you were even following them in the first place.

Knox's mark was called Dr Hamish Rabe. He didn't look like one of Britain's most celebrated molecular biologists, but then research scientists tended not to parade round with their institute and academy medals dangling from their necks as they ran errands on random Tuesday lunchtimes in summer.

He was also innocent. And it was Knox's job to keep him safe.

So far, that had involved Knox spending several hours walking in loops around the enormous university building just off Gower Street, of which Rabe's laboratory occupied the whole basement, occasionally snatching furtive glances at its pristine whiteness through knee-high windows and wondering which of its compass-point doors the scientist might emerge from. And the last sixty minutes not letting him out of his sight.

Rabe might not have been festooned in ribbons, or draped in a crisply pressed lab coat, but he'd been easy to spot when he'd finally appeared. Partly because the upper reaches of Bloomsbury were quiet, its university students either deep in revision or exams or, if the papers were to be believed, flocking to San Francisco wearing nothing but flowers in their hair for a debauched and drug-fuelled 'summer of love'. But mostly because he was roughly six foot seven tall and had completely alabaster skin, a mop of shockingly red hair on the top of his head, and an equally bright moustache across his upper lip. He moved in a slow rhythm, his rake-thin arms reaching out of his rolled-up shirtsleeves and swinging pendulously as his body swayed slightly from side to side.

As Knox watched him clambering his way through a crowd of schoolchildren that had streamed messily and noisily out of the British Museum and onto Great Russell Street, it seemed to him that Rabe almost belonged to another species altogether. He was like a giraffe picking its way through a herd of warthogs, or an alien come down to Earth to observe humanity and decide whether or not it should be annihilated. That second analogy wasn't entirely farcical because, according to James Holland, the head of MI5, who had briefed Knox in person first thing this morning, Rabe was on the verge of wielding such awesome power.

'Microbial genetics,' Holland had replied when Knox, sitting opposite the director general in his office on the fifth floor of Leconfield House, MI5's Mayfair headquarters, had asked him what made Rabe important enough to warrant round-the-clock security. 'He's developing a new kind of adaptive pesticide that has the potential to revolutionise agriculture on a global scale and eradicate world hunger, or make Agent Orange look like gritting salt.'

Neither biology nor farming were Knox's forte, but he was well aware of Agent Orange – the most viciously destructive of a whole rainbow of chemical compounds the American Army had spent the last six years spraying over the jungles, fields, and people of Vietnam, Laos, and Cambodia, to devastating effect on all of them.

However, it wasn't just Rabe's apparent quest to either save or destroy the planet that meant he'd spent the last week being constantly followed by Watchers, MI5's leg men, and now Knox, without his knowledge.

MI5's Pipistrelle listening devices had recently picked up a spate of concerned conversations among members of the international intelligence agencies that operated in London about a series of unexplained deaths and disappearances within their scientific communities.

A leading French biologist had evaporated into thin air on their way home from a conference in Brazil. A West German experimental physicist had had a heart attack two days after climbing the Schneck-Ostwand in the Allgäu Alps. A prominent American chemical engineer had seemingly decided to drive across several states in the middle of the night and plunge into the Pacific off Highway 1.

So far, though, nothing untoward had happened to Britain's scientists, and Holland wanted to keep it that way.

'We're keeping it out of the press,' he'd said. 'And so is everyone else while they try to work out if it's all a coincidence or something's afoot. No need to spook our brilliant minds unnecessarily.'

Unfortunately, the Service's analysts had yet to find any concrete links between the dead and the missing, or definitively conclude that there were no connections at all. So, while they continued their search, everyone else was on clandestine protection duty.

Rabe paused for a moment on Bloomsbury Street, waiting for a couple of taxis to pass before he crossed over into Bedford Square and continued on his way back to his subterranean lair. Knox slowed his own stroll in response, and took the opportunity to affect a quick change to his appearance, slipping his grey linen Hardy Amies blazer that had been folded across his right forearm back over his cream polo shirt.

He was sure he was less conspicuous than Rabe, but he also knew he was rusty. It was nearly a year since he'd been on an active assignment like this one, and almost the same since he'd been in the city for longer than a quick visit to Holland's office, or his own next door to it.

He hadn't made any mistakes yet. The handover with the anonymous-looking Watcher who had followed Rabe into the city from his home in Richmond had been seamless. Since then, Knox had secretly accompanied his mark round a bookshop, where he'd spent ten minutes surveying the latest releases, into a large, busy, and unseasonably cool cafe that served enormous sandwiches filled with meat carved from roast joints, and waited discreetly as he ducked into a dry-cleaners only to leave empty-handed a minute later.

Knox had momentarily wondered if there was something nefarious behind that brief stop – was the cleaners a cover for making contact or relaying a message? – but then he'd reminded himself that just because most of the people he knew were spies that didn't mean everyone was. It was more likely the man was just checking to see if some shirts had been ironed early.

It wasn't until Rabe was in Torrington Place, a few hundred yards from his lab, that Knox let his concentration slip and got too close.

The side street was much quieter than the main road they'd turned off a few seconds before, and they were the only pedestrians on it. So, when Rabe instinctively glanced to his side before crossing over to the opposite pavement, his eyes naturally fell on Knox. He didn't run straight away, but Knox could tell from the subtle stiffening in the swing of Rabe's arms as he started walking again that he'd been made.

Then Rabe started to accelerate, and Knox's suspicions were confirmed.

He crossed over Torrington Place and into a little mews. After a few more yards his fast walk became a jog.

Rabe never looked behind him, so he didn't see Knox lingering at the entrance of the narrow lane, waiting for the scientist to realise he was racing towards a dead end, or notice his shadow swear under his breath when he disappeared down a hidden cut-through that led out to another road.

Knox sprinted down the mews, almost missing the thin, sunless gap between buildings Rabe had turned into, and then repeatedly banged both his shoulders against its old brick walls as he pumped his arms and legs to try to make up the distance between them.

Knox could have kicked himself, both for letting Rabe notice him and for giving him a head start, but he didn't have the luxury. He had to catch up. At least there was no longer any need or point pretending that wasn't what he was doing.

He emerged just in time to see Rabe turn again, this time down the side of the ornate, spired cruciform of University College Hospital.

Knox had guessed that Rabe would race back to the safety of his lab, but he'd sped straight past it.

Knox continued giving chase, feeling the old familiar sting from the scar that ran across the top of his head, which throbbed whenever he exerted himself. Then he felt a second one in his chest. He told himself it was a stitch, and that it was pure coincidence that it was coming from the exact spot where he'd once been shot almost through the heart. He pushed through both sensations until they faded.

Rabe's long limbs made it look like he was moving in slow motion, even as he got faster and faster. Knox hoped he was about to burn through the adrenaline that had helped him get so far so quickly. However, the scientist kept his impressive pace as he reached the top of Gower Street and careered straight over the double lanes of Euston Road.

There was a blare of horns as cars and vans swerved to avoid Rabe, then, a few moments later, another one as Knox dodged a double-decker only to almost be mown down by a black cab.

Rabe finally turned his head and made eye contact with Knox as he reached the safety of the pavement. Even from a distance, Knox saw the look of fear flash across the other man's face.

It occurred to Knox that maybe some of the country's most intelligent scientists had noticed what had been happening to their international compatriots after all.

Of course, there was no reason for him to be scared of a member of MI5, but there was also no way for Knox to convince him of that fact until he caught up with him. So Rabe kept going east, putting even more distance between the two of them, before veering north between the stumps of the old Doric arch that had once stood in front of the entrance to Euston train station.

Knox swore again, more loudly this time.

He knew that if Rabe made it onto an intercity train before he got to him and persuaded him that he wasn't actually in any danger – at least from Knox – MI5 would have to ask the Transport Police for help, and he'd have to tell Holland that he'd made a mess of a simple job.

But Rabe didn't head for the mainline station's entrance, gallop through its concourse and down any of the long ramps that led to its platforms. Instead, as Knox watched, his red hair lurched towards a completely different set of lines and tracks: the Underground.

CHAPTER 2

Knox dashed through the ticket hall and down into the Tube station's complex knot of tunnels, at last gaining some ground as Rabe began to slow down. Knox didn't know if it was because the scientist was starting to run out of energy, or didn't know where he was going, or wanted to avoid the attention of the shuffling midday commuters that surrounded him. He was just glad he hadn't lost him, and that they were now in very familiar territory.

After years of training and active shadowing operations, Knox, like every MI5 officer, knew the Tube network like the back of his hand. Alongside Pipistrelle, its labyrinthine passageways were one of the Service's greatest surveillance assets. Wherever Rabe went underground, Knox would have the advantage.

Rabe reached a Northern line platform, and, a few seconds later, so did Knox. Then, as if on cue, a Tube train arrived. It was old stock, its red paint dull and faded, its wheels rickety, and its doors slow to open. Few people got off, which meant it would have been easy for Knox to close the gap between him and his quarry with one last burst of effort. But he hung back, pausing next to the open mouth of a carriage vestibule just in case Rabe leaped on at the last moment.

However, the scientist kept striding down the platform as the train slowly and noisily pulled away. He reached the end just as the final carriage trundled into darkness, and Knox wondered if he was planning on jumping down onto the tracks and following it into the tunnel. He didn't, but he did vanish – through a small service door directly in front of him that his body had blocked from Knox's view.

Suddenly Knox was sprinting again towards the door he could now see was completely flush with and the same colour as the wall it was built into, asking himself why on earth it wasn't locked, and how the hell a molecular biologist knew it was even there.

He yanked the handle open, stepped through, and almost immediately fell up a set of yellow-edged stairs on the other side.

The staircase was lit by a string of dim emergency lights, and its tiled walls were smeared with grime. It was colder than the platform, and the air felt different, stale with dust yet charged with electricity too. It was also quieter, so Knox had no trouble making out the scientist's footsteps ahead of him.

When he reached the top of the stairs, he saw a curve-roofed passageway stretching out in front of him. It had just enough kinks in it that Knox didn't have a clear line of sight down its whole length. But, although he couldn't see Rabe, he could still hear him.

He called out his name, hoping the sound of it reverberating round him might surprise him enough to make him pause, but his shoes kept pounding the dirt-caked floor somewhere in the distance. It wasn't until Knox began jogging down the tunnel and adding his own rhythmic echoes that the scientist seemed to change his mind and his footsteps stopped.

Knox moved cautiously. He doubted he'd find Rabe waiting for him under one of the weak spotlights, so he didn't want to miss any nooks or crannies he might be hiding in. After about thirty yards he spotted one, slowed to a silent halt, and realised that despite all the dim twists and turns he knew exactly where he was.

The Euston mainline station had been a building site for most of the sixties, its old Great Hall demolished along with its arch so it could be enlarged to accommodate rising passenger demand. The same was true below ground.

The new Victoria line was due to pass through Euston next year, and the ticket hall Rabe and Knox had run through was a replacement for one of the two Underground stations that dated back to when the Northern line was two railways, run by separate companies. However, not every remnant of the past had been erased, and Knox was now in the middle of one of them: the old interchange corridor that ran between what were now the Northern line's Bank and Charing Cross branches.

A few feet to Knox's side a ticket booth was embedded in the wall – a tight, dark space just large enough for Rabe to have folded himself up into.

'There's no need to hide,' Knox said towards the shadows.

Then he lunged through the slim, cream-tile-edged opening, and grabbed at nothing.

A deep rumble filled the corridor, dislodging a fine shower of dust from its roof, as a Tube train passed through a tunnel nearby. And then another sound. Not the repetitive thudding of feet but a single, metallic clattering.

Knox set off again, making his way further along the passageway. Until he hit an abrupt turn, signalled by the word *Psycho* appearing directly in front of him, emblazoned across the wall in vivid red letters. A poster for the film that had been released the year before the interchange had been closed, which no one had bothered removing. Knox passed more – a bright pink illustration of people floating next to a futuristic submarine, an advert for a long-since staged Christmas production of *Puss in Boots* at the Theatre Royal, and several more promoting cheap day trips – all in remarkably good condition.

He continued on, reaching a second sharp turn and, after that, another staircase. However, unlike the one that had led him up to the interchange corridor, the top of this one was completely bricked up.

So far, Knox had been grudgingly impressed with Rabe's skill for evasion. But he was fairly sure the other man couldn't walk through solid walls. He must have missed another hidden door somewhere. He doubled back, checking both sides of the corridor even more carefully than before, and found it in the middle of the second straight, positioned frustratingly perfectly between light wells, and camouflaged even more by the advert for *Coronation Street* pasted over most of it.

This one took a sharp shoulder to open, and revealed another completely different environment – filthier, colder, louder, and windy.

Knox was now in a ventilation shaft.

There was a faint glow from the surface opening of the wide, circular shaft several storeys above him. But most of the light came from beneath him, cast upwards through the grilles in the ceiling of the Tube platform below. More grated metal extended across the centre of the void, and Knox could see Rabe on the far side of it, struggling to reach a ladder bolted to the shaft wall, which, for some reason, ran up the length of the shaft ten feet to the side of the walkway.

The amplified screech of a Northern line train arriving covered Knox's steps until he was halfway to Rabe.

'Please,' Knox called out, 'I'm on your side.'

The scientist clearly didn't believe him.

'No you're not,' Rabe replied, Knox finally hearing his broad Highland Scots accent for the first time.

Then he climbed up onto the walkway's railing, trying to balance on it and stretch out at the same time.

If he managed to get a hand on the ladder and haul himself up, there was no way Knox would be able to follow him. He'd just have to hope he could make it back out of the station and up to the surface before Rabe emerged wherever the shaft let out.

However, that wasn't going to happen, because as another sharp shriek echoed up the shaft, the scientist's left foot slipped off the rail and he lost balance and plunged down through one of the grilles.

CHAPTER 3

After Rabe's broken body was gently scooped up off the platform floor it had crashed into and stretchered away, Knox returned to Leconfield House.

He went straight up to his office, where he prepared his report on the disastrous turn his operation had taken, and waited to be summoned next door for a dressing-down by Holland.

And he kept waiting.

Then, after several hours spent staring alternatingly out of the window, at his desk, and at his watch – a 1956 Omega with a silver body and tan leather strap – Holland's secretary, Miss Albury, phoned to tell him that the director general wasn't going to be coming back from the lunch at his club that had 'run over a tad'.

Knox decided to go home.

The fifth floor was quiet when he stepped out of his office, even though he was technically knocking off a little early, and the lift he took down to the underground car park didn't stop at any other floors on the way, which was also unusual – but Knox told himself that both these oddities were more likely the result of most of headquarters being out on their own protection details than people purposefully steering clear of him.

However, he couldn't explain why Holland's dark green Bentley S2 wasn't parked in the space next to his gunmetal-grey E-type Jaguar. Holland wouldn't have taken it to Ockham's, his club on Mount Street, because it took less time to walk there, and if the director general's lunch really had turned into the kind of uncharacteristic afternoon his secretary had so indelicately implied, he would have taken a taxi home to Highgate.

Knox didn't drive the short distance to his flat on top of Kemp House in the middle of Soho. He went to his other home – the one that wasn't his, but was where he'd spent almost every day of the last year – Rabley Heath in Hertfordshire.

As he headed out of the city, Knox brooded over the day. He thought about Rabe. Not about the sound of him smashing through the ventilation-shaft grille, or of his bones breaking, or the screaming and shouting that had followed from the people who had been minding their own business on the Tube platform, but the strange, hard certainty of the few words he'd said to Knox. How was the scientist so sure he wasn't there to help? Did he know something Knox didn't? Or was his response simply the result of cold terror?

He also thought more about Holland. The director general had been Knox's mentor for almost twenty years, and Knox his closest confidant for the same. And yet he couldn't shake the feeling that his boss was avoiding him. The message from Miss Albury had been a flat-out lie. But why? Had Rabe been a test to see if Knox was ready to take on more active duties, and he'd failed so badly the director general was too ashamed to even berate him in person? Or was something else going on? He hoped for the latter.

The evening was bright as Knox left the A1 just north of Welwyn Garden City and transferred onto the quieter country roads that would lead him the rest of the way to his destination, but he felt like he was driving under a cloud.

Rabley Heath was a mongrel manor hidden away in an ancient forest. A crenellated Jacobean hall with Georgian wings and a modernist ballroom bolted onto its rear. A family home that had been commandeered by the government during the war and then left to decay, partly under Knox's supervision, until its owner had returned from the dead a year ago and started repairing and rebuilding it.

Knox turned past the small white-painted gatehouse he'd stayed in while he was the place's sole custodian, and up the driveway. There were no other cars on the gravel circle in front of the grand, arched front door, but Knox knew the property's one other resident would be in, because at this time of day he always was.

Jack Williams was Knox's oldest friend. But for the last year, Knox had been his jailer and his interrogator.

While the rest of Britain had been catching their breath after the end of World War Two, Holland had persuaded Knox to join MI5 and Knox, in turn, had recruited Williams. They'd risen through the ranks together for a decade, then Knox had sent his friend on a mission that had ended in his death. Or, at least, so everyone had thought until he'd suddenly appeared outside a CIA compound in the Caribbean thirteen months ago.

He'd been the victim and unwitting agent of Line Z, one of the KGB's most secret sections, which specialised in a particularly effective combination of sledgehammer-like mind control and scalpel-sharp brutality.

Williams had almost wreaked havoc on MI5 once he'd been brought back to London, but he'd been stopped before the plan Line Z had forced him to enact reached its devastating conclusion.

Holland had accepted that he couldn't be blamed for his actions, but had also decreed that he needed to be contained somewhere far away from the public until he'd fully recovered from what he'd been through, been comprehensively debriefed, and proved that he was no longer a risk to national security. Knox had suggested taking him back to Rabley Heath, and the director general had agreed.

So, while Williams had tried to restore his ancestral home to its former glory, Knox had attempted the same with his friend's head, helping him rediscover his old self while also unpicking the litany of plots and assassinations he'd been forced to take part in, and extracting every last piece of information that might help the Service in its never-ending battles with its enemies on the other side of the Iron Curtain.

Williams had been a willing captive, but after a year under house arrest his trove of intelligence had been completely mined and Knox knew that, like himself, he wanted to do more than just keep going over and over the horrors he'd endured.

Knox parked his car, did his customary loop of the grounds, checking that the estate's stone walls were still keeping the forest more or less at bay, then walked across the lawn to the back door that led to the house's cavernous kitchen. He was joined halfway across the grass by a flash of mottled fur that raced ahead of him.

'Slow down, Stinky,' he called out, 'I'm coming.'

Knox didn't know the cat's real name, or if it belonged to anyone in the tiny village that had slowly built up beyond Rabley Heath's gates over the last four hundred years, but it never failed to appear whenever he arrived at the house, demanding a saucer of milk, which was always dutifully supplied.

Knox opened the door to the smell of cooking, and recognised the deep aroma of shepherd's pie. Williams had brought the kitchen up to working order once it had become clear his incarceration was going to last longer than he and Knox could survive on cheese on toast and coffee from the gatehouse. It was the heart of Rabley Heath, the core of its strange domesticity.

'Any idea what this is?' Knox asked Stinky as he poured out the cat's drink on one of the long marble slabs that ran round the edge of the room, pointing at what looked like a large bolt of mouldy fabric piled at the other end of the counter.

The cat ignored him.

'You could at least pretend to be curious,' he said as he put the pint bottle back in the fridge.

When he shut the door again, he found Williams stroking the cat and staring at him with an amused look on his face.

'Thank God you're not talking to yourself, old man,' he said. 'There's only room for one lunatic in this asylum.'

Ten minutes later, Stinky was gone and both men were leaning against the counter with a bowl in front of each of them and a half-demolished casserole dish of meat and mashed potato between them.

Rabley Heath had a dining room, but it was designed to seat twenty people, not two, and there were no upcoming soirées booked in the house's empty social calendar, so it was fairly low down Williams's list of planned renovations.

'Are you going to explain that?' Knox asked, pointing again at the mound of fabric.

'The family crest, I think,' Williams replied, between mouthfuls. 'Went exploring up the eastern turret this morning and found it.'

'Is it safe up there?'

'Only put my feet through a couple of rotten steps and a bit of the roof.'

Knox frowned, the image of a tumbling body flashing in front of his eyes. Williams was now in much better shape, mentally and physically, than when Knox had first seen him gaunt and malnourished on a bench in Regent's Park after seven years apart, but he still didn't like the idea of his friend putting himself in any kind of jeopardy when he wasn't there to keep him safe.

'What about you?' Williams asked. 'How did the big day go?'

Knox sighed. 'Not well.'

As he finished the last of his pie, he explained how badly things had gone with Rabe and his maudlin suspicions about Holland's absence from Leconfield House.

When he was done, Williams's face darkened.

'Sounds familiar,' he said, snatching up their dishes and dumping them in the sink.

When he turned back to face Knox, his mouth had turned into a sad smile, and there was no humour in his voice.

'I could be out there helping. I've told the Service everything I know about Line Z, proved I can be trusted, but I'm still stuck here, with no idea if I'm an asset or an embarrassment.'

Knox couldn't argue. Williams's frustrations were entirely legitimate. They also snapped him out of his own navel-gazing, because though he was right about their similarities, he wasn't about their scale.

Knox had had a bad day, and might well have another one tomorrow, but even if he did, it wouldn't compare to the limbo he knew Williams would wake up to. His best friend's pain didn't make him feel better about his own, but it did stop him from indulging it too much.

CHAPTER 4

The next day, Knox was back at Leconfield House early, after an even earlier coffee with Williams and a promise to discuss the future of his incarceration with Holland.

This morning, the director general didn't keep his deputy waiting, and Knox was summoned next door barely five minutes after he'd reached his office.

Holland was sitting behind his expansive mahogany desk, polishing his gold-rimmed glasses with a small square of chamois, when Knox stepped into the wood-panelled sanctum he'd ruled over MI5 from for almost a decade.

As usual, the only thing on the desk was whatever Holland was dealing with at that moment, and right now that meant Knox's report on the chase through the Euston tunnels.

'Quite the adventure yesterday,' Holland said by way of invitation for Knox to sit down.

'Yes,' Knox replied, lowering stiffly into the chair across from the director general.

Holland put the cloth back in a drawer, and his glasses on his face. 'Your man Rabe is conscious.'

'That's good to hear.'

'The doctors think he'll make a full enough recovery eventually, though he may well wish that wasn't the case.'

Knox couldn't stop his left eyebrow from rising.

'You were right to be sceptical about him running,' Holland continued, tapping the manila folder in front of him. 'While he was doped up on morphine overnight I had some Watchers give his house a discreet once-over. They found duplicates of his research going back five years.'

Knox shrugged. 'Scientists can be rather cautious. Perhaps he was worried about his lab burning down.'

'They weren't filed neatly away in an office,' Holland replied, letting the obvious implication hang between them.

Relief pricked at Knox. He hadn't hurt an innocent man after all. In fact, he'd uncovered a possible traitor. And it was unlikely that Holland was going to drag him over the coals for doing so. He felt his back and shoulders ease a few inches.

'Do we have an idea who he's been supplying, or if anyone else on his team is involved?' he asked, jumping ahead to what he assumed would be his next set of orders.

Holland shook his head. 'The official line will be that he suffered a terrible accident, which is true.'

Knox couldn't imagine there wouldn't be some sort of investigation beyond questioning Rabe when he was in a fitter state. If his pesticides could be used for destructive as well as humanitarian ends, then MI5 needed to know what sort of danger the country – and possibly the planet – might be facing.

'What does Whitehall think about it?'

'A little bluster, but not from anyone we need to pay much attention to.'

Knox noted Holland's uncharacteristic evasion, just like he'd sensed it yesterday. But, before he could ask why his superior wasn't being his usual candid self, the director general stood up and announced they were almost late for a meeting Knox didn't know he was supposed to be attending.

'White has something to show us,' was all the detail Holland offered up by way of explanation.

Knox and Holland took the lift down to the research and development department, which had been run by Malcolm White for as long as Knox had worked for MI5. They rode in silence, and they stopped a floor early. Knox wondered if White's fiefdom had extended in his prolonged absence from Leconfield House.

The lift doors opened onto a long corridor, just like the fifth floor only with more doors running along its sides. Holland strode over to the third door on the right and opened it without knocking. Knox followed him through.

Inside was not a small office. Every partition on this side of the building had been removed, creating a single large space. In the middle of it was a very big, free-standing glass box. And inside that was White.

Knox turned to Holland as they walked over to the strange construction, and opened his mouth to say something. But the director general gave him a look that made it clear he shouldn't.

The box had two doors lined up perfectly with each other, and Holland and White opened them both simultaneously. As Knox was ushered inside he saw that the walls were almost three feet thick and made of eight panes of glass – the whole thing was octuple-glazed.

'Sorry about all that,' Holland said to Knox, once they were all inside the box and both doors had been silently swung back shut. 'But you'll understand in a moment.'

'At least as much as we do,' White said, beckoning them both over to a small table that looked, like the three men, as if it was hovering above the maroon-patterned carpet.

There was an hourglass standing on the corner of the table, almost drained of sand. White turned it over. Then he picked up a tiny black box that was lying next to it, less than half the size of a fingernail, and showed it to Knox and Holland. 'This is the next generation of Pipistrelle.'

'Very impressive,' Knox said, squinting slightly to try to make out any notches or seams on the miniature box's matte black surface.

'Larger range, longer life, broader bandwidth,' White replied.

'And still completely undetectable by radio and magnetic sweeps,' Holland added. 'Total audio surveillance, and the only way anyone would have a clue it was listening to them was if they actually saw it.'

'Sounds like you've worked another miracle, Malcolm,' Knox said, which earned him a huff from the R&D head as he swapped the box for a photo – a square of cracked plaster with a small black square nestled in the middle of it.

'Unfortunately, someone beat me to it,' White said. 'A clumsy clerk put their elbow through a partition wall in the Bank of England two weeks ago and found this.'

'Not one of your engineers getting curious about the price of gold, I take it,' Knox said, which elicited another huff, and another photo.

The second image showed another minute black square, this time nestled in a small, hollowed-out groove in the back of what looked like a piece of wood panelling. Knox didn't recognise the wood at first glance, but he was very familiar with the desk it had been lying on when the photo was taken – it was Holland's.

'When did you remove this?' Knox asked White.

'We didn't,' he replied.

'Because that would let whoever planted it there know that we're on to them,' Holland added. 'Hence me being rather less than forthcoming with answers to your questions upstairs.'

'How long has it been there?' Knox asked.

'We have no idea.'

Knox tried to imagine how many conversations in Holland's office had been listened in to, how many official secrets had leaked from the very centre of the nation's intelligence apparatus. The audacity of whoever had done this was incredible, and the scandal it could cause was unfathomable.

'We haven't been able to trace any repair works or gaps in security that would explain it.'

Few people in the Service had clearance for the fifth floor, and even fewer were able to access Holland's office when the director general wasn't there. Knox was among them, so was White, and Miss Albury. Beyond that there were only a few heavily vetted members of the cleaning staff, and the engineers who regularly swept the whole building.

Despite the nature of Knox's profession, and the years he'd spent hunting moles and traitors, he always preferred to think that everyone who worked for MI5 was as loyal as he was. He didn't like the possibility that someone from among its ranks was behind this – even the idea that some foreign agent had somehow managed to transport themselves into one of the most secure areas of Leconfield House without leaving any trace was better than the possibility of betrayal by one's own.

'We only discovered it after taking most of my office apart, very slowly, and quietly,' Holland said.

'And we've found five more,' White continued, pre-empting Knox's next question and finally letting a fortnight's worth of irritation show in his voice. 'Two in meeting rooms, two in the School Hall, and one in my lab.'

'Which prompted this little renovation project,' Holland said.

'It was a rush job,' White said, pointing to the hourglass that had now deposited almost all its sand in its lower half. 'It's soundproof, but it's also airtight.'

'We're under siege,' Knox said.

'A touch more than usual,' Holland said. 'But White's already become quite the expert at generating enough chicken-feed for our junior officers to chat about over their desks and lunches. And while we work on getting our hands properly on one of the bugs, anything of major significance will have to be discussed in here, quickly, or outside Leconfield House.'

CHAPTER 5

Knox and Holland's next destination was the rose garden in the south-east corner of Hyde Park, a short walk from Leconfield House along Curzon Street and through the Park Lane underpass.

It was a fine morning – one of those bright, warm days that tricked Brits into thinking summer had arrived before the inevitable spate of late-June downpours – so the two men weren't alone as they weaved their way through the intricate pattern of pink, white and red flower beds. But none of the other strollers ever got close enough to them to hear their conversation, and the bushes they passed were too low for anyone to crouch in and point a parabolic microphone their way. The park was open ground but, for the moment, less exposed than MI5 headquarters.

Knox was relieved there was now an excuse for the director general's evasiveness, but not about the reason itself. He was also surprised by Holland's demeanour. White's frustration was understandable. Pipistrelle was his creation and after years of keeping the strictest, tightest control of every device that had been deployed in the field and the priceless intelligence they had all gathered for the Service, someone had managed to get ahead of him. Holland, however, betrayed no signs of anger at the idea of Leconfield House being infiltrated and infested.

A year ago, Knox had wondered if the director general had been about to retire, finally giving in to the stalemate it felt like the Cold War had been fought to. Now, however, he seemed energised by this new challenge. Eager, almost, that someone was shaking things up. Knox just hoped it wouldn't end with MI5 coming crashing down.

'Do you think there could be a connection between Rabe and this?' Knox asked as they looped the small fountain of Diana, the Greek goddess of hunting, unable to resist looking for some link between the two major events of the last twenty-four hours.

'Possibly not him specifically,' Holland replied. 'But perhaps the larger issue we're having with our assets going missing.'

'The Russians?'

'No.'

Knox was surprised by the definitiveness of Holland's reply, considering how squarely kidnapping and bugging sat within the KGB's usual modus operandi.

'You seem very sure of that,' he said

'The *rezident* told me himself.'

That response almost made Knox stop in his tracks. 'You met with Bakulin?'

Oleg Bakulin had been the KGB's resident-designate and bureau chief in London for the last decade. Like Holland, his identity was officially secret and, also like Holland, known by every intelligence operative in the city and most on the planet.

Bakulin was a titan of the espionage game. He'd survived Stalin, Khrushchev, and the current troika of Brezhnev, Kosygin and Podgorny by both being very good at his job and never taking unnecessary risks. Knox couldn't remember any occasion when two spies as senior as him and Holland from opposite sides of the Iron Curtain had met face to face to exchange information – or at least would admit to it.

'When?' he asked, struggling a little to keep his voice even and quiet.

'Yesterday afternoon,' Holland replied, revealing what he'd really been up to at Oakham's. 'They appear to be having the same problems as we are, at least as far as people going missing.'

'It could still be a play. Has anyone else confirmed?'

'For once, our enemies are being more forthcoming than our allies. No one's saying much, but everyone's concerned.'

Knox was all too aware that the sheer size and fractal, bureaucratic nature of the KGB meant that it was easy for its right hand to have no idea what its left one was up to. He'd been caught up in the Soviet Union's intelligence agency's internal plots and power games before, and on each occasion had felt like a pawn permanently three moves behind. However, Bakulin couldn't have approached Holland without approval from the highest levels, and if what he'd said had convinced the director general then that should be enough for him as well. Unfortunately, that also meant they needed to find another suspect.

'Bianchi and Moretti somehow?' Knox asked, thinking about the two long-dead Italian physicists and the plot six years ago by Nicholas Peterson, an MI5 traitor, to sell a version of Pipistrelle to the highest bidder.

Holland shook his head. 'White assures me nothing they managed to achieve could possibly have led to this, no matter who else might have got their hands on their calculations.'

Knox ran through the short list of other likely possibilities he could conjure up in his head. 'China?'

'Mao seems determined to get rid of all his finest minds by himself, but this might be the work of some department in the PLA or CID we don't know about.'

It was just over a year since the start of the Cultural Revolution, Mao Zedong's latest attempt to cement ultimate power over the vast population of the People's Republic of China by purging the nation's bourgeois and intelligentsia. So far, reports suggested it was working.

However, like in most countries, politics was only one of the levers of power. The People's Liberation Army and the Central Investigation Department, which included China's equivalents of MI5 and MI6 within their broad auspices, were both formidable organisations. And, while the People's Republic and the Soviet

Union were no longer on friendly terms, the latter had helped the former establish its military and intelligence infrastructures. It was entirely possible that one of them had also developed its own version of something like Line Z, which was now trying to apply Mao's ambitions on a global scale.

'I assume Six is looking into it,' Knox said.

'They are,' Holland replied.

'And are they sharing?'

'Not a lot.'

They paused for a moment at the western edge of the garden, letting an elderly woman pushing a double pram pass them before turning back east. Knox glanced under the two hoods, expecting a pair of infant grandchildren, but instead saw two small, sleeping dogs tucked under lace blankets.

'It's a shame we can't go poking around Beijing,' he said, returning to a subject that was somehow less bizarre than what he'd just seen.

'Quite,' Holland replied, his voice a fraction quieter than it had been. 'But you could take a look over the border.'

It took Knox a moment to process what the director general had just suggested.

'Hong Kong? Wouldn't that be stepping on Atwood's toes?'

'It would, and frankly I think he could use it,' Holland said.

Dominic Atwood was the MI5 security liaison officer stationed in Hong Kong. He'd been there for as long as Knox could remember, and while he was a stalwart of the Service he wasn't one of its stars.

'But we've also been afforded a rather convenient cover that he won't be able to complain about. Lord Reeve's daughter has got into some sort of trouble out there and the Home Secretary has asked me to send someone to retrieve her.'

At any other time, being told to chaperone a peer's wayward daughter halfway round the planet would definitely sound like being sidelined to Knox, but considering the real instructions behind the order he understood why the director general wanted to send him. And the prospect of getting out in the field properly, with an important mission, excited him. Still, with what he now knew about what was happening on MI5's home front, he wondered if Holland didn't need the people closest to him nearest him.

'Laing would jump at the chance to get over there,' he said.

Simon Laing had been an SLO, like Atwood, until a KGB provocation in Canada had cut short his deployment after just six months. He'd been stationed at MI5 headquarters since. Knox knew he was eager to escape London.

'Laing is the only person getting anything close to cooperation out of Six at the moment. I don't want to lose what little headway he's made with them on Line Z by pulling him away. And I need someone who I can be sure couldn't have had anything to do with what's going on in Leconfield House. Someone I can trust completely.'

Knox let himself take the compliment, and enjoy the adrenaline that he could already feel swirling through him – until he remembered the other thing he needed to discuss with Holland.

'What about Jack?' he said.

'Williams will be looked in on while you're away,' Holland replied.

'He's one of our most valuable assets. I don't think we should be leaving him alone given the current situation.'

'You'll only be gone a few days, and I'm entirely confident he can take care of himself. He has the scars and the body count to prove it.'

Knox knew the director general was right, at least about Williams's ability to physically protect himself, but he was also sure his best friend wouldn't react well to being abandoned by his only companion at sudden notice.

'He could come with me. He might be familiar with the territory, and it would give him the chance to show he's ready to return to active duty.'

Knox didn't know if Williams had ever actually been to Hong Kong – the colony was one of the few places that hadn't come up in any of their long conversations about what he'd done in his seven missing years – but it was a punt he was willing to take to persuade Holland that he shouldn't just be left in Rabley Heath.

'I understand your concern, but I need him to stay where he is,' Holland said, his voice taking on a tone that made it clear Knox shouldn't press the point any further.

CHAPTER 6

Knox spent the rest of the day in his office, calling in the latest reports from Hong Kong – and despatches from several other SLOs stationed in colonies and Commonwealth members as cover lest Leconfield House's record archives had also been bugged – and then his evening having a very awkward conversation with Williams.

There was no toasting to Knox's adventure, no joking about him being hurled straight from the frying pan into the fire, no reminiscing about old missions together, or unlocking of hidden memories over the suet-crust mince and onion pie Williams had made for them. Just disappointment and what felt like shallow excuses.

Knox didn't mention that MI5's headquarters had been compromised, but he did share Holland's theory that Chinese elements might be behind the Service's other major problem, and that there was no evidence of Russian involvement. He hoped that assuring his friend that Line Z didn't seem to be connected would soften the blow of him being left to stew in Rabley Heath alone while Knox was off gallivanting in Asia. It didn't.

'So I'm not an asset or an embarrassment after all,' Williams said as he got up from the kitchen counter, leaving Knox to tidy up. 'I'm bait.'

'I'll only be gone a couple of days,' Knox replied, trying not to sound too apologetic.

He wanted to stop his friend from stalking out of the kitchen and into the depths of the house, tell him that wasn't what was happening and that the director general actually wanted to keep him away from danger. But he couldn't, because Holland's responses to his own queries about Williams's security had made it impossible for him to reach any other conclusion than that one himself.

For a brief, concerning moment, as he watched Williams disappear through the doorway, another motive occurred to Knox – that Holland was using this opportunity to test Williams's loyalty once more and maybe even push him back into the wild. It sat on him, stealing the early night he needed as he lay in his bed in what had once been a guest suite on the first floor of the house, listening to the place creak and groan around him, and only disappeared when he was dashing back through the kitchen shortly after dawn and saw a small note Williams had left propped up against the rolled-up flag that was still on the counter: *Good luck old man – I'll have this flying for your return.*

Now, Knox was in the lounge at London Airport, waiting with other bleary-eyed passengers for the 8 a.m. BOAC Boeing 707 that would take him to Rome, Tehran, New Delhi, Bangkok, and finally, twenty hours after departure, Hong Kong.

He'd ordered a coffee, which was yet to materialise, though he'd decided that was probably for the best – avoiding caffeine would make it easier for him to catch up on some of his lost sleep in the air.

Knox had read about various different ways of tackling jet lag: don't drink, drink a lot, stay awake for the whole trip, switch to your destination's time as soon as you get on the plane. He'd tried all of them and had settled for listening to his body – if he was hungry he ate, if he was thirsty he drank, if he was tired he slept.

He appreciated the relative solitude jet travel offered – little was expected of him when he was thirty thousand feet in the air. Once his plane had taken off on its first leg he'd be free to dream, daydream, and go over the parameters of the two missions he was being sent on in whichever order he preferred.

The first one was straightforward enough. Lady Penelope Reeve, daughter of Lord Trevor Reeve, the old Labour MP turned peer who had helped pass the Wages Councils Act after the war, had taken her family's left-wing leanings a little too much to heart and gone to Hong Kong to support the pro-communist protests that had been rumbling on there since the spring of 1966. Now, her political fervour had got her arrested and her father wanted her home before she got into any more trouble, or caused him more discomfiture in the corridors of the Palace of Westminster.

The second one, however, was going to be trickier.

Knox had always been curious about Hong Kong. The countries and cities he'd visited for work over the years had all tended to be versions of Britain and London. Hong Kong was different. It was more of a melting pot, a crossroads where West and East met and folded over and round each other. That made it enticing but also unfamiliar ground.

It was still a crown colony, so technically under MI5's jurisdiction. And, as SLO, Atwood could have been its intelligence king. Yet he'd never claimed the crown. He'd apparently been content to let the Special Branch of the Hong Kong Police take the lead on domestic security for decades. Even when SIFE, Security Intelligence Far East, which had coordinated MI5 operations across Asia out of Singapore after the war, was disbanded in 1963 he hadn't used the opportunity to persuade the Service to shift its focus and resources one and a half thousand miles north.

Atwood had fought in the Asian theatre, and had been SLO in Hong Kong ever since it had been taken back from the Japanese in 1945. Twenty-two years was an unusually long tenure in a posting that was normally given to promising new recruits on a fairly regular rotation – especially considering that according to his service record Atwood had achieved very little of note.

Knox had to believe that he would at least know the lie of the land, but also felt fairly sure that he wouldn't be able to rely on him. Which meant that, as his flight number was finally called, he couldn't stop himself from suddenly feeling a little apprehensive about flying off into the unknown, alone.

CHAPTER 7

The anxiety that niggled at Knox refused to fade.

The first leg of his flight, to Rome, passed in an increasingly uncomfortable blur. And so did most of the next one.

He tried to doze, but bursts of turbulence over the Adriatic and Sea of Marmara made his attempts fitful and stopped him from drifting off properly.

As he gazed out of his window down at the vast stretches of empty Turkey thousands of feet beneath him, a land that had been one of the planet's greatest trading routes until capitalist ingenuity had taken humanity to the skies and ploughed a canal straight through the Arabian desert, he tried to work out what was causing his unease.

He hoped it was just a ghost of his old fear of flying. Knox's formative experiences with planes had not been positive. He'd lived through the Blitz in London, then served in France after the Normandy invasion. For a long time, the sight or sound of a plane above had made him instinctively look for the nearest place to take cover. And whenever he'd got on one he'd imagined it being strafed by Messerschmitts or shot out of the sky by a hidden Nazi artillery battery. But then he'd spent most of the first half of the sixties travelling to increasingly far-flung destinations on Service business, an exposure therapy that had helped him get over his nerves. However, he'd barely left Rabley Heath in the last year, let alone the surly bonds of Earth. So, perhaps he was just out of practice and simply needed a few more hours to get used to soaring through the sky in a jet-propelled metal tube again.

Of course, he knew that wasn't actually the case. It wasn't ancient concerns that were really bothering him. It was more current ones.

He knew that whatever might happen in his absence, Williams would be able to take care of himself, and that whoever might decide he was too tempting a target not to try to abduct or attack would come off much worse after an encounter with him. But he still didn't like leaving his friend alone.

Likewise, while the nature of Knox's job often involved operating independently, without all the facts, and against unknown agendas, it was also over a year since he'd done anything like what he was about to.

At least there was something he could do about that before he landed in Hong Kong.

After his mid-flight meal had been served – a beef wellington accompanied by a reasonable Côtes du Rhône and followed by a generous slice of tarte Tatin – Knox ordered a gin and tonic and started thumbing his way through the latest edition of *The Economist*, which had been waiting for him along with his tickets at the BOAC desk at London Airport.

In the middle was a section no one else who had bought this particular issue of the magazine would read. It was an overview of recent political and social developments in Hong Kong, drafted by an MI5 analyst, designed to look like a normal *Economist* article, and slipped into Knox's copy overnight in Leconfield House.

He read through the three spreads quickly once, then again more slowly, absorbing all the overt and obscure details that had been included. He was equally impressed by the analysis and shocked by how little he knew about the colony's present situation.

He remembered the short-lived protests from April the previous year after the Star Ferry – the main public connection between Kowloon and Hong Kong Island – raised its ticket prices. And he could vaguely recall hearing a few flippant radio reports on something similar happening this spring, when a plastic-flower factory had fired some of its workers. However, he had no idea of the true scale of civil unrest this seemingly minor event had prompted.

There'd been roving demonstrations across the colony throughout May. Sympathetic protests had taken place in Beijing, and the British diplomatic residence in Shanghai had been broken into and ransacked. Then, on 22 May, thousands of people on Hong Kong Island had marched up Garden Road to Government House to demand that the colonial government improve working conditions, and had ended up clashing violently and bloodily with police.

The Garden Road incident prompted a series of measures by both Britain and the People's Republic that were outwardly intended to calm the situation but, in the view of the article's nameless author, were more likely to end up forcing the colony's leftist workers even closer to their comrades over the border, and possibly even result in open conflict between the two countries.

The first was the declaration of a temporary, week-long curfew on Hong Kong Island – the first since the Japanese occupation. The second was Beijing's announcement of the closure of the British mission in Shanghai and the expulsion of its diplomat, Peter Hewitt. And the third was the despatching of the Centaur-class aircraft carrier HMS *Bulwark* to the colony.

Knox agreed with the anonymous analyst. These decisions were blunt, reactive, and they lacked intelligence.

The final few paragraphs of the article formed a coda that could be read as either vaguely amusing or faintly terrifying. As with most political issues, this one's flames were being fanned by the press, and the latest set of headlines had reached a hyperbolic level, referring to 'bloody debts', 'towering crimes', and 'fascist authorities' on both sides.

As had so often been the case during Knox's career, an infinitely more complex and serious situation lurked beneath Holland's composed understatement. Hong Kong was balancing on a precipice, and it was clear to Knox that not enough was being done to stop it from toppling off the edge.

Beyond that, the Service's reputation was at stake. Of course, the director general bore ultimate responsibility for everything that was done in MI5's name, but it was Atwood's job to stop things getting to this point and he'd failed woefully. Knox was now convinced that the SLO didn't need his toes stepping on so much as a kick up his rear. And he was more than happy to be the one who delivered it.

CHAPTER 8

The builders had been told to be late and loud. And they were happy to oblige, mainly on account of them being very handsomely overpaid to do both.

Connell & Sons didn't normally take work at such short notice, and they weren't usually hired by well-spoken men in carefully pressed mackintoshes who appeared unannounced at their yard in Mile End minutes before they knocked off for the evening. But trade had been a bit slow for the last month, and the job being offered to them sounded too easy – and entertaining – to pass up. Plus, they were given half of their extremely generous compensation up front in the form of fifteen crisp ten-pound notes, which were handed over along with a typed-up formal schedule of works on headed paper and an accompanying additional list of simple but also slightly odd instructions to be followed in order to get the rest.

As requested, the yard's eponymous gaffer and two of his workmen, who were not his sons, arrived at the trade entrance of the Bank of England on Lothbury shortly after nine o'clock in the morning. Their dark blue, snub-nosed Bedford CA van had been given a quick clean and polish before the short drive between the next-door but far-removed realms of the East End and the City. Its engine, however, which was in desperate need of a tune-up, had been left to cough, splutter and pop.

The security guard, a gaunt man in a stiff, dark uniform who gave off the air of an officious pallbearer, tried to wave the van away from his post — a tiny glass-fronted office not much bigger than a phone box tucked in the narrow gap between the curve of the entrance's old stone arch and its more recent pair of heavy metal doors. Then, when the two young workmen hopped out and started unloading their tools, he called out to them to move along.

Connell, who probably had a good twenty years on the guard, dangled the schedule out of the driver's window and told him, in an accent a few shades rougher than his natural cockney, that they'd be doing no such thing.

The guard snatched the paper and scanned its contents as the older man got out and joined the other builders pulling oil- and dust-stained canvas holdalls out of the back of the Bedford.

'I don't have any record of this work,' the guard said.

'In charge of renovations, are you?' Connell replied, eliciting snickers from his colleagues.

The guard attempted an imperious glare, but Connell ignored him, and after a few moments he retreated to his station to retrieve the logbook that would prove that regardless of how legitimate the paper he'd been given appeared, the builders weren't supposed to be there. Except that it didn't. Impossibly, the list of deliveries and arrivals he'd checked less than an hour ago now included the three men currently blocking the pavement. He checked the ink — it was as dry as all the other entries, and written with the same pen, and there were no signs of a page having somehow been torn out and replaced while he'd not been looking.

It was a mystery but, with the logbook and the schedule of works matching, one that was no longer his to solve. It had now surpassed the limits of his responsibilities. So, instead of stepping back out onto the street and continuing to argue, he called through for a porter, unlocked one of the large double doors, and ignored the three men as they strolled through it, bags slung over their shoulders.

The builders' destination was an office on the fourth floor of the bank. Its occupant, a junior regional director, also had no idea that he was going to be visited by them this morning, and took very clear umbrage at the sudden interruption of his working day by three men in shirtsleeves and flat caps.

Umbrage turned to outrage as two of the men began clumsily moving a bookcase away from a wall, sending volumes of neoclassical theory and Keynesian analysis tumbling onto the carpet, while the third pulled a sledgehammer out of one of the large bags that had been casually dumped just inside the door.

'Now, wait just a minute,' the director said, getting up from his desk.

'Remedial works. Scheduled and paid for. Got to be done,' replied the older of the two men carrying the bookshelf.

Then he nodded at the wall and the third intruder swung the blunt, bulbous end of the hammer straight through it.

'This will not do,' the director exclaimed, marching out of the room.

However, whatever higher power he had planned to invoke to stop the abrupt remodelling of his office apparently denied him, and the three builders were left to get on with their job in peace – which involved completely demolishing the entire plaster partition apart from a specific two-by-two-foot square that they had been instructed to remove intact.

It took them half an hour to take down the wall. Then, while one of the workmen tidied the rubble into sacks and prepared the space for another partition to go up in exactly the same place as the one that had just been destroyed, Connell and the other younger man carried the salvaged section of plaster back down to the Bedford.

It was a fifteen-minute drive past Mansion House and over Blackfriars Bridge, to an alley off the Elephant and Castle roundabout, where, as arranged, the man in the mackintosh from the previous evening was waiting for them in a Ford Transit van containing a large copper-lined box and another wad of ten-pound notes.

CHAPTER 9

Hong Kong sprawled out beneath Knox. A dense, orderless tangle of buildings, streets, and alleys split in two by the wide gash of Victoria Harbour, itself clogged with boats of all shapes and sizes heading in random, chaotic directions.

Knox had heard that the descent into Kai Tak airport was one of the most breathtaking in the world. As he got closer to landing, he wondered if that was because of the towering peaks that surrounded the city or because arriving planes circled so closely to the high-rises that sprang up taller and faster in Hong Kong than almost anywhere else in the world that it felt like one of them might shear a wing clean off at any moment.

Below him, Knox could see the past and future frenetically tumbling over each other – the alabaster-white colonial buildings in their pristine grounds, the ancient temples with their dark-red tiles, and the more recent monuments to commerce that rose above both, crowned not with flags, statues, or religious symbols, but enormous logos for Schaeffer, Longines, and Coca-Cola.

The Boeing banked sharply, so Knox was almost looking straight down through his window as it passed over a particularly tightly packed cluster of buildings. There were shacks built on top of roofs, balconies bolted at odd angles, walkways suspended between structures, and laundry attached to every dangling wire or railing.

Then the plane turned once more and began a final approach over the harbour. Waves rose up on both sides of the 707 and for a moment Knox wondered if he'd imagined the runway he'd seen sticking out from the Kowloon side of the city on a knife-like spur of reclaimed land and the pilot was about to ditch into the water. But then he felt wheels connect with firm ground, and suddenly the plane was sedately taxiing towards its gate.

A few minutes later, he was walking through customs. He saw families, lone travellers, people in the uniforms of various spiritual and social ideologies, and could hear English, Cantonese, Mandarin, and countless other languages.

As he neared the arrivals hall, he started to look out for another type of person – one who might be looking out for him.

Atwood had been informed of his impending arrival. Depending on how lackadaisical the SLO was, that could mean someone had been sent to meet him or that word had slipped out to any of the allied and not-so-friendly intelligence agencies that operated in the city. Holland had assured Knox that, for once, the Russians weren't an active participant in the game he'd asked Knox to play, but the local KGB might still take an interest in what he might get up to. Likewise, if the Chinese were behind the abductions and disappearances he had to assume they'd be paying attention.

His suspicions were rewarded almost as soon as the hall's wide doors opened. Over the heads of people hugging, shaking hands and handing over luggage to chauffeurs, Knox spotted a twenty-something Hong Konger in a light-grey suit with a thin black tie hanging loose around his open-buttoned neck leaning against a tall column. He wasn't rushing to anyone, or constantly checking the arrivals list in case he was too early or too late to meet a loved one or client. He was just waiting.

The young man looked thoroughly bored, casting his gaze lazily across the throng. Knox turned away before they made eye contact, but could still see the man straighten in his peripheral vision and start towards him. Whoever he was, Knox wanted to test him – and himself. Evasion was as important a skill for a spy as shadowing, and Knox wanted to reassure himself that he still knew all the basics.

Knox drifted away from the man, slowly, making it look as if he was simply following the stream of people around him. He sped up and slowed down, abruptly sidestepping one slow-moving group and then lingering behind another. It worked. The man got closer, but always battling the current Knox was riding.

Then the crowd started to thin and Knox was forced to improvise. He ducked behind another wide column, then tripped the last of a line of porters laden with bags, prompting a domino fall as the poor, innocent man tumbled forward.

It was a cheap tactic, and it made it clear to the other man that Knox was well aware that he'd been made, but it was also effective. Voices erupted in anger and apology as bags were grabbed at and righted. The crowd slowed, bunched up again, and provided enough of a distraction for Knox to fall into step with two pilots who were also using the commotion to get out of the airport ahead of the throng.

He was lucky again with the taxi rank outside. There was only one person ahead of him at the front of a long line of red, green, and yellow cabs.

A heavily tanned and visibly drunk couple in bright, Hawaiian-print shirts appeared behind him just as it was his turn to tell the elderly man who apparently controlled the cars where he wanted to go. Knox let them go ahead. He doubted they – or the driver of the taxi that was supposed to have been his – were actually cunningly disguised enemy agents, but the young man in the suit still hadn't emerged from the arrivals hall, so he could afford himself a few extra moments of precaution.

As the couple's cab raced off and a new one screeched to a halt in its place, Knox took off his jacket, in part to effect a quick change of appearance, but mainly because he'd started to feel the humidity of the city.

'Star Ferry,' the driver repeated as Knox sat in the back seat and glanced behind him towards the terminal exit.

'Yes,' Knox replied. 'Quickly, please.'

A nod, and the taxi leapt forward, out of the airport car park and into Kowloon.

Knox expected to stay on the wide road that led away from Kai Tak. Instead, the driver turned off it as soon as he could into a sequence of narrower streets that felt like deep, man-made gullies, strung with telephone cables and weather-worn shop awnings.

Knox briefly pondered whether he'd made a tactical error and had let himself be kidnapped. But as the taxi swerved round a cluster of cyclists and barrelled through a pedestrian crossing, horn blaring and sending people scattering, he realised the only danger he was in was from the driver's desire to be the loudest, fastest thing on the road.

The taxi twisted its way through Kowloon, taking sudden corners whenever the driver spotted a lumbering truck making late-morning deliveries or a bus pulling away from a stop ahead of them. Then, like a bullet blasting from a gun, it burst out of an alley and onto the esplanade that ran along the mainland side of Victoria Harbour and led to the Tsim Sha Tsui Star Ferry pier.

The driver pulled up in front of a clock tower, and pointed up at the large, four-sided face. 'Next boat in two minutes.'

Knox thanked the man, overpaid his fare, and went down to the green-and-white-painted ferry that was, at least in part, responsible for his presence in Hong Kong.

The short journey across the narrowest part of the strait offered another spectacular view of the city. Now its peaks rose up all around Knox, creating extra dimensions and perspectives that he sailed through.

Leaning against the outside rail on the semi-exposed upper deck strung with lifebuoys, he watched Hong Kong Island get closer as tall-sailed junks, flat-bottomed sampans and pristine pleasure yachts danced their ways deferentially around the ferry. Even the hulking slab of HMS *Bulwark* gave a wide, respectable berth, keeping its distance from the harbour's long-reigning queen.

Knox couldn't imagine ever complaining about the cost of his ticket to cross the strait, but then he reminded himself that he was viewing it through the eyes of a tourist with a very healthy expense account, not someone who had to make the journey twice a day, every day, in all weathers and conditions.

Back on dry land, he hailed another taxi from a rank in front of the ferry pier on one side of a very neat square of imposing governmental buildings and headed west, from the grand buildings of Central to the less impressive and shabbier ones of Sheung Wan, the district that had been the site of the first British occupation of Hong Kong Island in 1842.

Bonham Strand was a sequence of ground-floor bakeries, hole-in-the-wall restaurants and shops with shelves piled high with what Knox guessed were a range of dried delicacies from the South China Sea but which all looked to him like monstrously sized pigs' ears.

His cab pulled over halfway along the street, and he waited until it turned a far corner before he strolled over to the peeling black-lacquered door of number ninety-nine. The building directory listed several companies on its higher floors, including Avalon Logistics on its uppermost level and Jura Maritime Transit Incorporated immediately below it. Knox pressed the buzzers for both in order, letting whoever would be listening to them know that he was a bona fide visitor and not someone looking to peddle their wares or enquire about shipping rates.

After a brief pause, the door opened and he made his way up to MI5's Hong Kong Station.

CHAPTER 10

The lift was a tight fit. It was also slow, dark, and hot. Knox had thought he'd made the smarter choice in opting for it instead of taking the stairs to the top of the building. But it felt like he'd voluntarily climbed into an oven. The humidity was worse too – the sides of the small carriage Knox's shoulders rubbed up against were slick with damp.

He found himself holding his breath, imagining he was on a midwinter tramp across the Hertfordshire countryside as he willed the lift to speed up to its destination. When it finally stopped, he flung the door open, then threw a hand out to grab it before it clattered against a wall or swung back on him.

Knox stepped out into a short corridor of faded maroon-painted plaster lit by brass wall lights that looked like they were missing paintings under them, and pushed a few strands of stray hair that had fallen over his forehead back across his head.

He heard feet on the stairs as he walked the few feet to the door of Avalon Logistics, and just before he knocked on it the man from the arrivals hall appeared. Knox offered him a wry smile. He received an irritated glare in return as the man stormed past him and into MI5's local headquarters, leaving the door wide open behind him.

Knox followed the man, and did his best to disguise his shock at what he discovered on the other side of the door. He knew it wasn't just individual intelligence operatives who needed effective covers. But the office he'd just entered looked like it really did belong to a logistics company – and one that was very much on its uppers. Shelves were laden with mismatched boxes, unoccupied desks were piled high with newspapers and unopened correspondence, and bins overflowed with crumpled papers and greasy wrappers. Knox couldn't imagine any kind of order hiding under the chaos, which either meant Atwood and his team were true masters of camouflage or they were dangerously unprofessional.

The SLO was nowhere to be seen. The only other person in the office was the man from the airport, who had slumped behind a desk in the far corner of the room and was staring fixedly at the slow-moving fan bolted to the ceiling – which made Knox curious about just who had let him into the building.

Knox took a few more steps towards him, but before he could choose between asking him where his boss was and suggesting he show a little more respect for a superior officer who had already outmanoeuvred him on home soil, a doorway Knox hadn't noticed tucked between two bookcases opened and Atwood appeared.

'Ah, our European sales representative has arrived,' he said, crossing over to Knox and almost knocking over a yellowing pile of *South China Morning Post*s as he held out his hand for him to shake.

The man's voice was mirthful to the point of flippancy. And it was loud – louder than a spy's should be. In fact, nothing about Atwood was as it should have been. The crumpled suit that stretched across his corpulent frame was a bright, garish blue. His nose was a telltale map of burst blood vessels. And the rest of his skin was an unhealthy, milky beige sheened with glassy sweat, apart from the edges of his receding blond hair, which were raw with untreated sunburn.

He didn't give off any signs that he might be the local station chief of an intelligence agency. Again, Knox wondered if he was looking at a lord of disguise or a minor talent long gone to seed on Her Majesty's Hong Kong dollar.

'Knox,' he said. 'Richard.'

'Of course, marvellous,' Atwood replied. Then he nodded at the other man. 'And I trust you're already acquainted with our young Mister Charlie here.'

'Afraid I gave him a bit of a runaround on the way in from Kai Tak.'

Atwood grinned. 'Did you? Well, let that be a lesson to him. Anyway, welcome to our operation. Not quite the luxury or manpower of headquarters, but we get by and do our best. Now, you must be famished. I know I am. It's been a while, but one assumes BOAC in-flight meals still aren't up to much. Let's go find some food. Charlie, you can watch the shop as your penance. Come along, Richard, we don't want to get caught in the lunch rush.'

'Gravy's almost as good as your mother's, isn't it?' Atwood boomed, seemingly intending the compliment to go directly from his mouth to the restaurant's cooks rather than be passed on to the kitchen by a waiter.

Atwood had been talking constantly since Knox had followed him out of the office of Avalon Logistics and back down into Bonham Strand.

'Used to be much closer to the harbour,' he'd said, gesturing along the street, 'but old Governor Bonham had a passion for expanding the Empire by pulling land up out of the sea. Not the only one, mind you. That runway you came in on didn't used to be there, and it'll be getting even bigger soon enough. Smart, of course, and rather amusing. Every time our neighbours beyond the New Territories complain about our presence, we make the colony a few square feet larger.'

They hadn't gone to one of the nearby dim sum or noodle restaurants. Instead, they'd taken a busy double-decker tram smeared with adverts – 'the best way to see how the city works' – east towards Garden Road, the street that pro-Chinese protestors had recently marched along. They sat close together on narrow wooden seats on the top deck, level with the enormous signs that hung off the sides of almost every building they passed and were made up of hundreds of small bulbs that would put on the city's famous light show when the sun started to go down.

Then they rode another tram up the side of Victoria Peak, racketing along at a forty-five-degree angle – 'a marvel of British engineering' – to a stone and beam restaurant that looked like it belonged more on the top of a Swiss alp than an Asian one, and which served exclusively English cuisine.

Atwood had ordered a full Sunday roast and a bottle of red wine for himself. Knox, finding the array of stews and hot pies that made up the rest of the menu unappetising in thirty-degree heat, had opted for the same, but with a small cold bottle of a local beer.

Atwood had then proceeded to monologue for the duration of the meal, covering almost the entire history of the colony until this very moment. All of Knox's attempts to interject had been batted away. The only brief interruption he'd managed was to try to get some insight on the recent unrest, which Atwood had dismissed as 'a storm in a green teacup'.

So, he now didn't bother correcting his dining companion by informing him that, as his parents had died when he was very young, Knox had no idea what his mother's gravy tasted like. He simply nodded and waited for the man opposite him to run out of small talk.

When he finally did, the switch was so swift Knox almost missed it. One moment, Atwood was telling him that the restaurant had once been a shelter for the sedan-carriers who used to transport the colony's residents who considered themselves too good for the tram to the top of the peak. The next, he was joking about the 'rebellious daughter' who had brought Knox all the way from Mayfair.

'I imagine she'll be in for it once she's back home,' Atwood said. 'Not that she can be having much fun now.'

'Her father seemed more worried than angry,' Knox replied, clutching onto the shreds of cover Atwood had torn through, 'and relieved that he'd caught me the night before I flew out. When can I look in on her?'

'Whenever you like, I suppose. The lads down at Victoria Prison are pretty accommodating when asked nicely.' Atwood pierced the last potato on his plate, and continued to talk as he ate it. 'And I know what you're thinking. Victoria Harbour, Victoria Peak, Victoria Prison. Technically the north shore of the island is the City of Victoria. Hardly imaginative, but easy to remember.'

Knox hadn't been pondering the tactics Britain's empire-builders had used to curry favour with their monarch. He'd been thinking about what sort of state he might find Lady Reeve in.

'Was jail really necessary?' he asked, putting his own knife and fork together.

'Afraid so, especially after the last few weeks. The police don't want to be seen as lax.'

Their plates were cleared, and a few minutes later two unordered coffees were delivered. Atwood's was accompanied by a snifter of whisky.

'They know you here?' Knox asked, his question mostly rhetorical.

'Come as often as I can,' the other man replied. 'Most days if I could. But that depends on the season. Can't be coming up to the peak if a typhoon is on the cards.'

So, as well as being loud and indiscreet, Atwood was also a creature of habit. His actions were predictable. Knox had a vision of upending the table between them and finding a whole range of well-maintained bugs stuck to its underside.

The Moscow Rules were an informal list of techniques for spies operating in the most hostile territory on the planet – the Soviet capital – but they were also the essentials of good trade-craft, which should be used no matter what the environment. They were a checklist against assumptions, complacency and guard-dropping: suspect everyone, always maintain your cover, never fall into habit.

It was clear to Knox that Atwood followed none of them. And he was increasingly less willing to believe it was in the service of some grand ruse. No, he thought, the Hong Kong SLO wasn't a potential ally for the next few days, he was a liability.

Atwood poured his whisky into his coffee, swirled them together, then looked across the restaurant to the door.

'Speaking of not being lax,' he said.

Knox twisted to follow his gaze and saw a woman striding towards them. Her black hair was cut in a short, severe bob, her dark suit was immaculately cut, and her eyes were focused on Knox and Atwood. Knox guessed her age hovered somewhere close to thirty.

He turned back for an explanation, and found that in the last few seconds Atwood had drained his alcohol-laced coffee and got to his feet.

In a couple more, the woman reached them.

'May I present Captain Madeleine Zhou,' Atwood said, edging around the table so it remained between him and the new arrival.

Knox detected the change in the other man's tone. He couldn't tell if it was an echo of irritation or fear, but it certainly wasn't positive. Atwood did not like Madeleine Zhou, and even though she hadn't said a single word yet, Knox guessed the feeling was mutual.

'Our Special Branch liaison,' Atwood added, his voice a few decibels quieter, but still loud enough to reveal the identity and job title of one of Hong Kong's counter-espionage officers to anyone in the restaurant who cared to listen.

Now Knox understood the animosity he'd sensed. As a member of Special Branch, Zhou's job was to do everything Atwood was supposed to. And she was doing it at not far off half his age.

Knox looked up at her. She gave him a curt nod.

'She'll help you with your little problem,' Atwood continued, attempting an abortive chuckle. 'So if you'll excuse me, I'll be on my way. Things to be getting on with and all that.'

The SLO proceeded to shuffle out of the restaurant, leaving Knox to introduce himself and settle the bill.

CHAPTER 11

Knox's descent from the peak was more unnerving than the one into Kai Tak. Once he'd counted up enough dollar bills to pay for lunch, he'd followed Zhou out to her waiting car. It was a Mercedes, black, and it looked like it had clocked up several thousands of miles on Hong Kong's tight streets and steep hills.

Zhou drove like an American pursuit cop. The road down was narrow. It was intended, Knox remembered as she sped through another hidden corner and barely avoided colliding with a giant tree root as hanging vines dragged across the roof of the car, for rich people in single chairs, carried by exhausted coolies. Not the kind of four-seat horse-powered mechanical beasts to which the word sedan now usually referred.

The semi-jungle quickly bled back into the city and soon enough it was bamboo scaffolding, absent-minded pedestrians, and white-gloved police officers in traffic pagodas that Zhou was dodging with her quickfire turns of the Mercedes' steering wheel.

Where Atwood was slow, Zhou was fast. And where he babbled and rambled, she only spoke to give precise answers to direct questions. Knox pondered if this was a fundamental part of her character, her way of navigating being a Hong Konger working for one of the colony overlord's levers of power, or if she just resented Knox invading her patch and imposing on her time.

'Have you read Lady Reeve's arrest report?' Knox asked as they passed a cinema covered in rerun posters. Michael Caine stared through faded black-rimmed glasses at Grace Chang dancing a mambo.

'Yes,' Zhou replied.

'Anything in it that wouldn't have made it back to London?'

'I haven't seen what you were sent.'

Knox suppressed a smirk. Cooperation between spies was always a delicate game. Even more so when they were on the same side. It added extra layers of competition and suspicion. Tipping your hand could gain you an advantage, or lose you one you didn't know you had. Zhou was playing sensibly, going by the book and not giving away anything she didn't absolutely have to. Still, Knox couldn't resist pushing her a little further.

'Did she do anything to warrant being thrown in prison?'

'She attended a protest. She was told she would be arrested if she didn't disperse. She refused to.'

Knox accepted defeat. Zhou was a spy, but she was also police.

Zhou avoided the few marked-out spaces in front of Victoria Prison's main entrance, instead pulling in to park on the far side of a nearby junction. A sensible, simple piece of tradecraft – they couldn't disguise the fact that they were visiting someone in the jail, but they could make it look a little less like they were there on official business.

They crossed back over the junction on foot and through the gate and up the slope that ran alongside the prison's two-storey red-brick administrative building into a wide square that was bordered on its opposite side by a taller, four-level white stone complex lined with balcony corridors.

The colonial-style architecture with its pitched roofs and carved masonry gave the impression that they were standing in a palace courtyard, military parade ground, or exercise yard. But Knox knew this space had been designed for far darker activities. The physical health of prisoners had never been top priority for the Empire's jail-builders. Open spaces as old as this one weren't there for inmates to stretch their legs and get some fresh air. They were for public executions.

A prison officer in a highly starched short-trouser and shirt uniform with a matching cap and single braid across his shoulders marched out to meet them. Zhou spoke to the man quickly and quietly in Cantonese, and he escorted them through an arch at the bottom of the white stone building into a narrower, darker courtyard and into a second, identical cell block.

The difference between what the prison looked like outside and in was stark. They walked down bare corridors lit by wire-caged bulbs, and past solid metal doors, with thin observation slits cut in them at eye level. Every window was barred, and every corner and staircase was guarded.

They climbed two flights of stairs, the officer leading them banging on any door he heard mumbling behind, until they reached Lady Reeve's cell.

Knox expected to find the peer's daughter terrified and remorseful, or furious and belligerent. Curled up in the corner of the small room, pretending she wasn't trapped inside it, or pacing back and forth across it, irate that she was. But she was neither. She was lying on her thin, cushionless bunk, her body rigid and her eyes staring unblinkingly at the ceiling.

For a moment, Knox thought she was dead, until he saw her chest slowly rising and falling and her lips fluttering ever so slightly. She looked both older and younger than he had imagined.

'Lady Reeve, can you hear me?' he asked.

She didn't answer. Her eyes didn't flicker. Her breathing didn't quicken. It was as if she had no idea they were there.

Knox glanced at Zhou, who looked at the officer. They all seemed as confused as each other by her lack of response.

Knox stepped over to the bed and gently nudged her shoulder. She didn't flinch out of her stupor.

'Lady Reeve,' he repeated. 'Penelope. My name's Richard. Your father's sent me to help get you home.'

Still no reaction.

He leaned down, checking her over. She looked a little under-nourished, though not worryingly so. Her fingernails were grubby, but no more so than he'd expect after a few days in jail, and not caked in blood, dirt, or anything else. And the crooks of her elbows felt a little rough with sweat, but there were no telltale marks that she'd been injected with something that would have turned her catatonic.

He moved even closer, his ear barely an inch from her mouth, and realised that her lips weren't simply moving with her breath. She was whispering something. But even so close he could only just make out what she was saying.

One two-word phrase over and over.

'Blue Peacock.'

Then she screamed. A loud, high-pitched wail that deafened Knox and sent him stumbling back across the cell. And she started to move too – her arms suddenly flailing, her eyes squinting and opening wide in total, unrestrained despair.

Zhou rushed over, pinning her in place before she could break a wrist smacking against the wall or twist onto the floor, and the officer shouted something out into the corridor.

By the time Knox had recovered his senses and joined Zhou, holding Lady Reeve's legs down, another man had arrived. His uniform was slightly different from the other officer's – a subtly lighter shade of khaki. He didn't look surprised by the scene he'd walked in on. He produced a small box from a satchel that hung across his chest, removed a syringe from it and plunged its tip into Lady Reeve's neck as his colleague held her head steady.

It took a few seconds for her writhing to calm, her breathing to even out, and her eyes to close. Now she was definitely sedated.

Knox and Zhou looked at each other again, both silently asking what had just happened.

CHAPTER 12

Knox watched the sun dip and the whole city turn into one huge Piccadilly Circus. His hotel, the Waylian, was in Mid-Levels, a short distance from Victoria Prison but a world away from it.

It was modern, with classical touches – as if a Roman architect had been given glass and steel to play with. Every window was recessed in a deep Pantheon-esque square that blocked the glare of the setting sun without sacrificing an inch of the evening view. And from Knox's, he could look down on the knots of streets beneath him on Hong Kong Island and across the twinkling harbour to the rainbow gullies of Kowloon.

It reminded him of his flat in London, perched atop Kemp House on Berwick Street in the centre of Soho. Knox had bought it six years ago precisely so he could gaze out over his home city. For Knox, height was synonymous with perspective. But it was over a year since he'd spent more than a few minutes in Kemp House on his rare trips into the capital from Rabley Heath – just enough time to open some windows for a quick circulation of stale air or pick up any post that hadn't been redirected or collected by a Watcher on one of their midnight security rounds.

From this remove, and behind thick, sound-dampening glass, Hong Kong didn't seem like it was primed to explode. But then, if things were always as they appeared on the surface Knox would have needed to find a different job. He turned his gaze over to the west just as HMS *Bulwark* began another slow transit of the harbour, putting on its own light show laden with heavy under-tones for everyone to watch.

The Waylian wasn't Knox's original booking. He'd had another reservation, made for him by Leconfield House, at an older, grander hotel closer to the harbour. But he'd always planned on switching when he reached Hong Kong, partly because he couldn't guarantee that Atwood's vetting of local properties was adequate, and partly because of taste – the Service tended towards estab-lishments full of brocade and overly ornate woodwork, neither of which Knox was particularly partial to.

The choice of the Waylian had also been a way to build a bridge with Zhou.

After they'd been shepherded out of Lady Reeve's cell, she'd had another rapid conversation in Cantonese with the officer and the man who was either a prison doctor or nurse in the corridor.

'They say she was lucid this morning,' she translated, 'and that they don't know what was wrong with her. The sedative they've given her is the standard dose for difficult inmates. It lasts eight hours, so you won't be able to talk to her until the morning. I will speak to their superiors about this.'

Knox nodded, inwardly questioning the bluntness of prison medicine that involved injecting people before establishing a diagnosis as Zhou rattled off one last sentence at the other men.

'Do you suspect foul play?' she asked when they were back in the Mercedes.

It was the first direct question she'd asked him, and his response was economical. He didn't tell her about the words he'd heard Lady Reeve whisper. He wanted to hold on to that card for the moment, in case he needed to play it later.

'I can't imagine why there would be any,' he replied.

'We will find out if there was. Now I will take you to your hotel.'

'Actually, I was wondering if you could recommend one.'

'Did Atwood not arrange your accommodation?'

'He did.'

Knox detected the tiniest curl in the corner of Zhou's mouth, the smallest lowering of her guard. It was a relief, a first step to having an ally – certainly for dealing with the Reeve situation, and possibly for the other parts of his mission too.

Zhou didn't ask him about his preferred style, or what amenities he might desire, she just drove him up to Mid-Levels and pulled up under the wide slab of white concrete that jutted out from the front of the Waylian to protect its arriving and departing guests from the worst of the city's heat and rain, and told him, 'This should be sufficient.'

Before Knox got out of the car, he asked Zhou one more question. 'What was Lady Reeve doing at the protest in the first place?'

He knew London's theory, but he wanted to see if someone closer would have a different perspective.

'I don't know,' was her professionally non-committed response. 'Some of the city's international residents agree with them. It's reasonable to assume she did too.'

No new insight, then. But her answer did make Knox think about the people who had rushed from Britain to Spain to stand up against Franco in the thirties. He could appreciate the urge to fight for an ideology – he did every day – but it was easier for him to understand when it was about stopping the rise of fascism rather than trying to spread communism.

The hotel was more than sufficient. Knox checked in, made a brief call in one of the expansive, black-marble-floored lobby's private phone booths, sending a coded message that would eventually reach Holland about his change in accommodation, and went up to his suite, in which almost every surface and object was a shade of white or grey.

He swept for obvious bugs, showered, and then ate an early, light dinner in the hotel's restaurant.

After that, he thought about heading out and exploring some more of the city on foot. Maybe finding a rooftop or basement bar for a few drinks – another old habit he hadn't been able to indulge in much over the last year. But his body revolted. It was tired – the kind that meant it would be a bad idea to stray too far from a bed. So he settled for studying the city from above, picking out its landmarks and trying to memorise the most obvious routes between them.

He also briefly mused over what might have happened to Lady Reeve and what Blue Peacock could mean. But he stopped himself from indulging in too much conjecture – there'd be time enough for it in the morning when he was rested and his mind was sharper, and Zhou might have more information to share.

So, he stood at the window watching daylight fade for another twenty minutes. Then he moved to a low, white leather chair for another ten. Then the king-sized bed.

CHAPTER 13

Simon Laing had grown to hate going south of the river. He knew he had to, and he understood how important his trips were supposed to be to the safety of the nation. But that didn't mean he also didn't think they were a waste of time.

When he'd first been told by Holland that he'd be taking on a newly created liaison role with MI6 in the wake of the previous spring's events, he'd embraced it as both a sign of redemption for the single misstep that had put a black mark at the very beginning of his service record and an opportunity for further advancement, either within MI5 or even perhaps its sister intelligence agency. Yet, after a year of weekly meetings and endless exchanges of heavily edited mission reports in stale, empty rooms, his promotion felt more like a punishment.

Six, Laing was convinced, still resented the Home Secretary's command that it was to cooperate with Five on working out just how much havoc Line Z had wrought – and probably continued to wreak – across the West. Especially as it had been abundantly clear that the British foreign security service had had no idea that this particular department of the KGB had even existed until Holland brought it to their attention.

In the intelligence game, even the closest allies competed to know the most and wield the greatest power. Laing had never expected Six to be completely open with its secrets or share everything it discovered that could be linked back to Line Z – MI5 wasn't and didn't – but it irritated him that what little they did hand over was done grudgingly and by a rotation of extremely disinterested agents.

By its very nature, London was a stopover for Six agents, a temporary purgatory between international postings in more exotic locations. Ironically, the promise of getting out of Britain had been what originally tempted Laing to join Britain's domestic intelligence service. He'd been offered a position in Canada, a Commonwealth nation Five claimed a degree of jurisdiction over, and had become one of the Service's youngest SLOs, sent to Ottawa almost as soon as his clearances had been approved. But then the Russians had tricked him into causing a minor but still embarrassing political incident and he'd been sent back to London with his tail between his legs after barely six months. He'd worked hard to redeem himself, but he knew how long rumours and reputations lasted.

So, as certain as Laing was that Six didn't think much of their joint project, he was also fairly sure they didn't take him seriously either. Which meant that as he sat at a grey table in a grey room on the fourteenth floor of Century House, MI6's headquarters on Westminster Bridge Road, he had no idea if the person he'd already waited twenty silent minutes to meet would be someone he'd encountered before or a total stranger – only that they'd most likely be rather dismissive of the information he'd brought with him from Mayfair.

The folder he held in his left hand was another reason for him to be irritated this morning. Particularly the thinness of it. People were disappearing in mysterious circumstances that Laing had spent the last year working out bore the hallmarks of Line Z operations. But while almost every other MI5 officer had been put on some form of protection duty, he'd been sent to Lambeth to deliver a single-sheet report about a four-year-old failed provocation in Abu Dhabi intended to embarrass the leaders of the Trucial States into abandoning their oil-based alliance, that had been squeezed from the messiest recesses of Jack Williams's brain a month ago.

Even Richard Knox, Williams's keeper, had been brought back onto active duty and almost immediately despatched to Hong Kong on the kind of mission Laing craved. Of course, Knox was one of the Service's most senior officers and the director general's closest deputy. And, the quiet abruptness of his departure suggested Holland had sent him on something more than a simple escort job that was probably several grades above Laing's clearance. But still, it was all enough to almost make him drop his eyes from the room's high windows and half-view of the city and gaze at his navel.

Eventually the single door to the room opened and a man stepped inside. He was new, at least to Laing. Older than the people he'd met with previously, and he matched his surroundings – his suit was grey, and so were his hair and skin.

The man didn't introduce himself. He just sat down opposite Laing and nodded at the folder. Laing, feeling no need to make up for his counterpart's lack of niceties, slid it over and watched as he opened it.

'I think it might be time to put that wolf of yours down,' the man said once he'd scanned the paper inside.

The Wolf had been a myth, and a mistranslation. Six, like most other intelligence organisations that paid attention to quiet rumours and conspiracy theories, assumed that Line Z's Volk programme, which Williams had been a very unique offshoot of, was named from the Russian for *Canis lupus*. Five, however, knew it was actually from the German, and meant 'folk' – a reference both oblique and obvious about the programme's size and reach, and an almost jokingly parochial term for a group of highly trained, murderous and occasionally brainwashed psychopaths. This was one of the pieces of information the Service had never seen fit to share, and normally it provided Laing with a little amusement, but not today.

The other man abruptly got up, leaving the folder on the table. 'This isn't useful,' he said, his tone suddenly hard.

As Laing watched him stride out of the room, probably never to be seen again, he felt like he should defend the intelligence that he himself had thought was little more than worthless up until a few moments ago. He should make a stand on behalf of the Service and his professional honour. But he couldn't.

Laing also couldn't resist heaping more meaning on the man's curt statement. It wasn't just the report that wasn't useful – neither was he.

CHAPTER 14

Williams ran every morning. His sleep had improved over the course of the last year, but his dreams were still not an entirely pleasant domain. Demons lurked in them, eager to torment him whenever his unconscious resolve faltered. He'd become an early riser.

When he'd first returned to Rabley Heath, he'd barely been able to walk the grounds or visit every dilapidated room in the house without feeling his joints ache and his head spin. But as soon as he was able, Williams had thrown himself into renovating and restoring his ancestral home, and the results were visible on both the building and him. His sinuous muscles had become less strained, his face was no longer a hollow mask, and his clothes fitted him again. He was now stronger than he'd ever been, and found he had energy to burn. Hence the running.

He'd started in the new year, when the trees that lined the estate were bare and the fields that stretched between it, Knebworth and Hatfield were stubby and brown. His first excursions were short sprints, a mile down the country lane that stretched away from the house – which was almost entirely in view from Rabley Heath's upper levels in case Knox felt the need to keep watch on him – and back again. By June, he could easily cover eight to ten miles a day, and in good time, loping round fields tall with crops and along overgrown wooded paths.

He always returned to Rabley Heath, but he also always paused for the briefest moment at the furthest point he reached. It had become a daily act – his choice to go back to the cage he'd let Knox put him in.

Williams knew his best friend wouldn't be waiting for him when he got back to the house this morning, but it still surprised him a little when he stepped through the door to the kitchen and wasn't met by the smell of a pot of freshly brewed coffee.

He glanced at the clock he'd hung above one of the counters to help him track his runs and realised it was later than he'd thought, and that his mid-morning dose of caffeine could wait until he'd completed another ritual.

He went upstairs to his bathroom, turned his shower on, stripped off his running kit, and began counting the scars and marks that covered his body.

His exercises and the house repairs had helped with his mental as well as physical health. Almost, in fact, as much as his long conversations with Knox about the brutal, dehumanising torture Line Z had put him through and his complete lack of responsibility for the horrific things the rogue KGB division had made him do. Sometimes it felt as if his brain hadn't been washed so much as completely flushed, and he would never be more than an echo or shell of the man his best friend wanted him to be again. But the running and rebuilding calmed him, gave him structure, focus. And on good days he felt closer to peace than he had thought he might ever again.

Yet, each morning he still read the map of damage that had been etched into him, totting up its peaks and troughs. It was his way of remembering what he'd been through, what he'd survived, and what he was capable of. Today, he reached seventeen before the steam from the shower fogged the mirror.

When he was clean, dry, and dressed, Williams went back down to the kitchen, made his coffee and carried it through to the large drawing room he'd usually drink it in with Knox. However, as his best friend was currently on the other side of the world, instead of chatting about the latest news bulletin from the radio or piece of gossip from Leconfield House he indulged in something he normally only did on the rare occasions Knox went into London for the day.

He walked over to the enormous fireplace that filled almost half of one of the room's walls, turned on the Zenith record player he'd installed in it along with a pair of large Tandberg speakers, put a record of Italian operas on the platter, lined the needle up with the first aria, and turned the volume as high as it could go.

Music blasted through him and filled the house. Strings stretched down its corridors and horns and drums filled its rooms. Williams listened as Maria Callas sang of her doomed love for a Roman proconsul, and then about another suitor whose life was at the mercy of an evil baron. It was another kind of therapy – the overwhelming, overpowering rush of being faced with something insurmountably larger than yourself, like standing on a deserted beach, staring out at a vast churning sea, or on top of a mountain, hundreds of miles from civilisation.

Once he'd finished his coffee, he returned his cup to the kitchen, accompanied by a tenor singing over and over about winning the hand of his love, and made his way up to the eastern turret.

Despite his frustration that he was still under house arrest even without a guard, he intended to make good on the promise he'd made to Knox in place of a goodbye. It was time the Williams family crest flew above Rabley Heath again, which meant he needed to check if any more steps on the narrow staircase up to the turret roof were on the verge of collapse.

After a quick inspection, he counted up that he needed to replace eleven boards and six pairs of supports. He already had a workstation set up in one of the nearby empty bedrooms, so set about sawing new stairs and struts from the planks of timber he'd ordered from a local merchant a few weeks ago. For the first hour, his grunts and the cracking of old wood being pulled up were drowned out by music, but eventually he got tired of going down to the record player to turn over LPs and ended up working in silence, with just his occasional curses at miscalculated cuts reverberating through the house.

The work consumed Williams. He lost track of time, and it was only when he had hammered the last fresh board into place and felt his stomach cry out that he realised he'd worked through lunch and hadn't eaten any breakfast either.

Then, as he stepped out of the turret, he realised something else too. The atmosphere of the house had changed.

Williams had spent so much time in Rabley Heath that he knew it beyond intimately. He could feel its moods and sense the subtlest changes in its airflows and pressures. Even when Knox was far on the other side of the vast building, Williams always knew exactly which room he was in. And now he was suddenly sure that someone else was in the house with him.

He froze on the spot – he also knew where all of Rabley Heath's loose floorboards were – and thought about who it could be.

He wasn't expecting any deliveries. He knew MI5 was going to send someone to check in on him, but that they were unlikely not to call first. And there was no way Knox had already come home. That meant whoever it was was either a curious rambler or lost stranger, or that Williams's worries about being used as bait for an attack by Line Z or another malignant force were well founded after all.

He slowed his breathing, rose up onto the balls of his feet, and began to move down the edge of the corridor, towards the old servants' staircase that led to the ground floor. He paused at the top of the stairs, then again halfway down, checking his sixth sense and working out exactly where the other person was.

They were in the kitchen.

Williams didn't have a weapon, but he didn't really need one.

He steadied his heartbeat and slowed his movements even more as he crept to the kitchen door. Then he dived through it, his eyes scanning half the room in the split second before he landed on his shoulder and rolled onto his knees behind the centre counter.

When he came up onto his feet, ready to face off with whoever had come to pay him a visit, there was no one there. No assassin. No KGB active measures team. Just Stinky, sitting next to the oven hob, tail wrapped round his feet, staring at him.

CHAPTER 15

Knox woke early, and so did the rest of the city – if it had ever actually gone to sleep. Through the window he'd returned to for a morning view, he could see activity buzzing beneath him as clouds blew across the sky. Knox was no expert on Asian weather systems, but he hoped they weren't the first signs of a tropical storm.

Today he felt rested, refreshed and energised. His milk-run mission had turned into its own little mystery, and he wanted to solve it.

He resisted the urge to walk over to the slender desk opposite his bed, pick up the phone, call Rabley Heath and tell Williams about the events of the last twenty-four hours. It felt odd not to be sharing his morning coffee with his best friend. But Knox was conscious that, given Williams's mood when he'd left London, such a call might be interpreted less as filling him in and more as rubbing it in. It would also be very much against operational protocol. Out in the field, Knox's lines of communication back home were limited to short messages via Hong Kong Station or direct to Leconfield House. And, considering the situation there, anything Knox sent in – even in heavy code – would have to appear so regular and prosaic in both content and timing that it couldn't possibly arouse any unusual interest.

No, for the moment Williams would have to be satisfied that no news about Knox was good news – until the Service told him otherwise. And likewise for Knox. He had to trust that all would be well at Rabley Heath in his absence, and hope that he wouldn't find a note waiting for him in Bonham Strand at some point telling him it wasn't.

He did, however, call room service for a second pot of strong, black coffee, and showered while he waited for it to arrive.

Once it had and he was dressed, he went downstairs and found Zhou leaning against the bonnet of her Mercedes, waiting for him. She didn't look happy.

'Lady Reeve has been moved,' she announced, pulling herself upright and opening the driver's-side door.

'Under whose orders?' Knox asked, walking round to the passenger side.

'No one's,' Zhou replied.

Knox climbed in next to Zhou as she turned over the engine. She pulled away from the hotel entrance.

'Explain.'

'I went to check on her this morning and talk to the prison governor. He wasn't there and neither was she. Her name was on the overnight transfer list to Stanley.'

Knox wasn't familiar with the precise details of how Hong Kong's prison system worked, but he couldn't imagine that moving a politically sensitive prisoner who was due to leave the colony would happen without some sort of authorisation.'

'Who approved that?'

'As I said, no one. The list is procedural. Drawn up based on capacity at Victoria.'

Knox frowned. He was all for building bridges, but he also needed to remind the captain that even though he was operating in her jurisdiction, he was the more senior spy, and should have been consulted before any actions were taken or questions asked, not after.

'I should have been there with you,' he said. 'Where is Stanley?'

'On the southern tip of Hong Kong Island.'

'And what exactly is it?'

'A high-security facility. It normally houses smugglers, murderers, seditionists.'

Knox was sure the woman he'd seen in the cell in Victoria didn't fit the first two of those categories, and he doubted she could seriously be considered part of the third either.

'Men and women?' he asked.

There was a slight pause before Zhou replied, 'Not usually.'

It was a minor concession, but it was also a sign that Lady Reeve's transfer wasn't so standard, and that Knox's mystery had developed an extra layer.

He didn't ask any more questions, and they continued on through the city in silence. Zhou dipped down into Central and east to Wan Chai, weaving through the traffic with one foot firmly on the accelerator and never even hovering over the brake pedal, before turning south along a road that had a stadium on one side – Hong Kong's famed Happy Valley racecourse – and a vast, stepped cemetery cut into a hill on the other side, an alabaster auditorium that gave the dead the best seats for the derbies.

The Mercedes climbed up through Wong Nai Chung Gap, the small cut through the island's middle ridges, leaving the congestion of the city behind and beneath them. Once more the narrow road they were on became edged with jutting rocks and leaning trees, and Zhou sped up, hurtling through blind, overgrown corners. And, like yesterday, Knox wasn't sure if she was simply impatient to reach Stanley and find out why Lady Reeve had been sent there, or just to collect her, officially hand her over to Knox, and be done with both of them.

The road began a long decline, and soon the sea was filling the view through the windscreen. They reached a bay on the southern side of the island. *Repulse*, a blurred sign informed Knox.

Zhou finally slowed down as they entered the small town that lined the bay, following the curve of its beach. Knox looked out to sea. It was mostly calm, no high waves that might forecast an approaching typhoon. Mostly, apart from the churning wake being left by three long, thin canoes, each brightly painted with grimacing, rearing heads at the front and crewed by at least fifteen people furiously digging wide oars into the water.

'What are they?' he asked, at last breaking the quiet of the car.

'Boats,' Zhou replied.

Knox turned to her, one eyebrow raised. She let out a silent sigh.

'They are practising for the Dragon Boat Festival. It commemorates the death of Qu Yuan, an ancient poet who committed suicide when the emperor he'd remained loyal to even in exile was betrayed by the untrustworthy allies he'd abandoned Qu Yuan for. He drowned himself in a river. The locals raced out in boats to save him. They failed.'

It wasn't the happiest reason Knox could think of for a festival, but how many others with equally dark origins were celebrated around the world? Humanity had a long-established fetish for honouring death and destruction.

'When is it?'

'Monday. There will be races in Victoria Harbour and all around the island. And parties.'

'The kind of thing that might bring people together and make them forget their recent troubles?'

'Hopefully.'

They left Repulse Bay, and headed back into partial jungle for a few more miles before they reached Stanley. This town was smaller, more of an overgrown village that happened to have a sprawling high-security prison and old military fort clustered on the headland south of it.

They passed another cove, filled with the kind of flat-hulled boats locals fished from and lived on, tied together in short rows sticking out from the land.

Then the Mercedes crawled its way through the multiple checkpoints and barriers that restricted access to the jail, a new call being made at each one to confirm Zhou and Knox were allowed to proceed to the next.

Eventually they made it through the final gate and into the near-empty car park.

Just like at Victoria, before they'd made it inside out of the late-morning sun they were met by a man in uniform, who also spoke rapidly to Zhou. However, unlike yesterday their conversation was in English rather than Cantonese.

Knox could follow it, but he didn't understand it.

Lady Reeve was dead.

CHAPTER 16

Lady Reeve didn't look much different in death than in life. Her skin was as pale, as tight across her features. Her hair as limp. Her eyes as vacant. The only real distinctions were that her lips no longer moved, her chest didn't rise and fall, and she lay on a mortuary slab instead of a cell bunk.

The jail doctor's dismissiveness was the kind of professional detachment that came with seeing death on a daily basis. The man's uniform was not as crisp as the ones Knox had seen in Victoria Prison. He was in his late sixties, and he spoke with a faded West Country accent. Knox wondered how long he'd been stationed so far from home.

The doctor reported that there were no signs of bruising around her neck or skull fractures that might have suggested an attack or sudden, violent determination to kill herself. He also couldn't find any indications of recent injections other than the sedative from the previous afternoon. The only possible clue he'd identified was a thin smear of tacky liquid that had run down the left-hand side of her mouth and chin. But that could have just been the natural expulsion of bodily fluids after death, a little more viscous than normal because of dehydration. He estimated her time of death anywhere between when she'd arrived in the middle of the night, and when her body had been found by the junior officer who had been sent to her cell with some breakfast two hours ago.

Knox asked about testing for foreign substances. He was told the medical bay wasn't equipped for that kind of work. The cause of death among inmates was usually very obvious – a shiv through an artery, a shove down a staircase with hands tied, a massive overdose of whatever drug was currently being smuggled inside by a Triad to be tested on desperate men to see how much provided temporary escape from life and how much would make it permanent.

A full post-mortem would give a more satisfactory answer, but it would have to be done in a hospital mortuary, not a prison one. Knox doubted that would happen. The Reeves were Jewish – a faith that considered invasive examinations of dead bodies a desecration. Lord Reeve's desire to know what had happened to his daughter might trump his religious beliefs, but he'd at least need to be asked first, and the time it would take to get an answer might render the exercise pointless anyway.

A transfer to Queen Elizabeth Hospital in Kowloon was arranged, just in case. Papers regarding custody of the body were filled in, and then Knox and Zhou left.

'How did she find the time to die?' Knox asked once they were back on the road and the prison's dull, squat blocks and high wire fences were receding behind them. 'She should barely have woken up.'

'She could have had a delayed reaction to the sedative,' Zhou replied, the tone that crept into her voice suggesting she thought the possibility unlikely. 'Or she woke up earlier than expected and ingested something she had with her in Victoria or found in Stanley.'

Knox imagined the poor woman coming to, not having any idea where she was or how she'd got there. Would the shock and disorientation have been enough to push her over the edge?

He thought of a third option, one he imagined Zhou had also come up with but wasn't prepared to voice without more evidence – someone had used the opportunity of Lady Reeve being sedated to kill her, maybe even arranging for her to be shifted to Stanley to do it. Knox didn't say it out loud either, but he did decide to tip his hand a little.

'Does the phrase "Blue Peacock" mean anything to you?' he said.

Zhou took her foot off the accelerator for the first time in fifteen minutes. Knox thought at first it was a response to what he'd just said but then realised it was actually a reaction to the appearance of Repulse Bay ahead of them after the last fast, blind corner. The water was even calmer now and for a moment the sun dazzled off it like glass. The boat racers were gone, their practice done or suspended while they found some shade for lunch.

Zhou continued to slow down as they re-entered the town.

'No,' she replied finally, as they approached what out in the coastal suburbs probably passed for a midweek traffic jam – two bright-green taxis behind a red double-decker bus that had somehow been transported to Hong Kong direct from Shaftesbury Avenue or Charing Cross Road. 'Where did you hear it?'

'Lady Reeve,' Knox replied. 'She was whispering it over and over in her cell yesterday.'

'You didn't tell me then.'

'It didn't seem relevant,' he replied, meaning almost that. 'Now I'm not so sure.'

'*Lán kǒng què.*'

'Sorry.'

'Blue Peacock.'

'Does it have any significance?'

'Peacocks are traditionally associated with dignity and power. Blue symbolises immortality and prosperity. But it can also represent spring and wood.'

'Sounds pretty open to interpretation.'

'It could be a drug. Names like that have been used since the Opium Wars. Codes used by the Triads to attract customers and confuse us. A new strain of marijuana, opium, or something stronger.'

Knox mulled over the possibility. He'd read enough digests from the Met about the psychedelics and tranquillisers that were making their way from the trenches of Vietnam and hillsides of Afghanistan to the streets of Soho. The Triads of Asia and mafias and gangs of Europe and America were all part of a dark economy that stretched around the globe. He'd also been privy to plenty of reports about abortive and successful drug development programmes by the world's governments, militaries and intelligence agencies – experiments to test the limits of human stamina, resolve, and control – which also tended to come with their own coded names.

'Where would she get something like that?'

'In Hong Kong?' The question was rhetorical and laced with the most overt sarcasm Knox had heard from his new temporary partner. 'The doctor was correct about inmates being used as guinea pigs. We do not have the resources to stop it.'

Zhou lost patience with the slowness of the vehicles in front of them. She dropped down a gear, floored the accelerator, and overtook the taxis and the bus.

'But I will investigate,' she continued. 'And send you a report for you to read in London.'

'I appreciate the offer,' Knox replied. 'But the daughter of a lord has died while she was effectively in both police and Service custody. I'm going to have to gather at least some answers before I go back.'

'Then I will help you do that.'

Zhou dropped Knox off in Sheung Wan, two corners away from Avalon Logistics, so he could send an initial report to Leconfield House and update Atwood.

He was able to do one of those things. Atwood was out to lunch and Charlie, once again, was manning the shop solo.

Knox found him in his chair in the corner, feet up on his desk, face set in a bored sneer. He didn't look happy to see Knox, but he didn't take it too personally. It was possible Charlie was still feeling sore after Kai Tak, but Knox sensed that that small indignity was just a drop in the ocean of the man's petulance. He seemed like the kind of person who would sulk whether he was carrying the world on his shoulders or nothing at all – the type who hated work and the absence of it in precisely equal measure.

Perhaps with the right amount of encouragement and opportunity he'd be able to prove he was capable of more than Knox had seen so far. Perhaps not. Perhaps he was destined to just be a surly errand boy.

As part of its cover, Hong Kong Station sent out daily messages via phone, telegraph, and letter. They were mostly fictitious, and mainly delivered to empty offices in quiet backstreets of other cities. But not all of them.

Knox composed a coded telegram and stood over Charlie as he sullenly sent it on its way to London.

Then Knox went clothes shopping.

On Zhou's slightly surprised recommendation, he hailed a cab and let it take him to the Daimaru department store in Causeway Bay. It was an unusual start to an investigation, but it was clear he was going to have to stay in Hong Kong longer than he and Holland had anticipated and he wanted to acquire some local camouflage.

After an hour spent picking out lightweight suits, shirts, and jackets, which were duly couriered to the Waylian, Knox headed back to Sheung Wan.

This time, Atwood was in his office, and this afternoon he was wearing a faded yellow suit that had once been either white or a more vibrant shade.

Knox explained what he and Zhou had discovered in Stanley. He omitted any mention of Blue Peacock to avoid the possibility of the SLO spreading word of it about over drinks somewhere before he'd had a chance to establish with a little more certainty what it might be.

'Poor soul,' Atwood replied, slouching back in the chair behind the desk in his private office, which was as disordered as the rest of the station. 'What a sorry misadventure. I suppose you'll be heading back home, then. Double shame that you'll miss the Dragon Boat Festival. It really is quite the spectacle.'

'I won't be leaving just yet,' Knox replied, to a look of genuine shock from the other man. 'I'll be helping the police with their investigations for a few more days.'

An odd smile spread across Atwood's face – part scheming child, part dismissive parent. 'You think murder's afoot? Think she spurned a lover or some Triad boss? If it's the latter you may find the trail has already gone cold.'

'The who can come later, if there is one. I'll settle for establishing a little of the how and why at this point.'

Atwood's brow furrowed and he nodded slowly, as if Knox had just said something exceptionally profound and he needed a moment to wrap his head round it. Then his eyes lit up with realisation.

'In that case,' he said, his smile returning, 'I'll leave you in Zhou's capable hands. Good hunting, man, good hunting.'

He didn't get up or reach out a hand to be shaken, but Knox half expected him to do both. As he left Atwood's messy inner sanctum, it was with the distinct impression that the SLO didn't anticipate seeing his London guest again and that whatever Knox would be doing from this point forward would have nothing to do with him.

CHAPTER 17

Irina Valera loved the moment before sunrise. Those few, last seconds of darkness when the temperature managed to dip a couple more fractions of a degree and the silence that surrounded her somehow grew even deeper, until rays of light pierced the gaps between the arêtes and frost-shattered ridges, and the mountain's dawn chorus began.

It had taken her a great deal of time to realise that she could feel such a positive emotion, and even more to accept that she should without guilt. But at long last she finally had, so almost every morning for the last year she had trekked up through overgrown wildflowers, snowdrifts, and the odd temporary river caused by a midnight deluge, to the spot where she was now standing to wait for the arrival of the sun and the signal of another day of freedom.

The peak Valera was atop didn't have a name. It was lower than the others around it, which, she guessed, meant all the explorers and cartographers who had passed through the Colorado Rockies had decided it didn't deserve one. More fool them, she also thought, because it was its diminutive stature that made it the perfect place to watch the sun stream into the valley beneath it and shimmer and dance across the eternally calm, glassy surface of the lake at its base.

The ring of higher summits that surrounded the little mountain also created an almost impregnable wall from the outside world. Here, Valera was safe as well as free.

She'd stumbled on the mountain, the lake, and a small, abandoned cabin nestled where the rock and water met twelve months ago, after wandering the United States for almost four years, a legal but homeless alien, always searching for somewhere to stay for longer than a few days or weeks, and constantly watching her back.

When Valera had arrived in America in 1961, it had been under CIA escort. She'd been welcomed with open arms by the authorities because she was one of the world's leading radio physicists, had defected from the Soviet Union, and was going to help the West breach the world's atmospheric barrier and issue in a new era of global communications – and orbital surveillance.

She'd done what she'd promised, and so had her government handlers, even when she'd gone to them after a year of working with NASA's best engineers at the space agency's Langley Research Center in Hampton, Virginia, and told them she wanted to leave.

'Your citizenship's all arranged and there's enough money in your bank account so you never have to work again,' Phinneus Murphy, her CIA liaison, had said between chain-smoked puffs of cigarettes at the end of their last meeting in her office in Langley. 'But we're also keeping your name on the door in case you decide you want to.'

After she'd told him that was unlikely to happen, he'd handed her a crisp green passport with her photo inside and asked her to do him a favour and let him know if she ever planned on taking a trip abroad. It was a half-joke, and she'd given Murphy the smile she knew he wanted, along with her thanks and a brief, stiff hug.

Then, without any further goodbyes, she'd headed off into the depths of North America to try to make good on another, older promise.

She'd made this one in her previous life, to her son, Ledjo, when they'd lived under the strict control of the GRU, Soviet military intelligence, in a secret, closed city called Povenets B in Karelia near the Soviet Union's border with Finland. She'd told him that one day they'd find a place where they could while away long summer days in a rowing boat on a quiet lake in peace – their reward for two lives filled with hardship.

The bright, hope-laden images of the two of them sailing and fishing together that Valera had conjured up had stopped both of them from giving in when there wasn't enough power to heat their draughty, prefabricated housing unit or enough food to stop their ribs sticking out through their skin. And they had driven Valera to never give up on finding a way to break through the Iron Curtain and flee Russia.

But, in the end, she'd only been able to keep this promise for herself.

She'd gone up and down both coasts, hoping to find anonymity and inspiration among the millions of souls inhabiting their metropolises, then criss-crossed the country's endless plains, ancient forests and lifeless deserts, taking buses, trains, hitch-hiking, and sometimes just walking on her quest. She travelled light, a small, child-sized rucksack across her shoulders containing a couple of changes of clothes and an extra pair of boots. She'd learned very quickly that in America, if you needed something you could always buy it, and that even if her accent drew suspicious looks her money was still as good as anyone else's.

Valera had reached Colorado the previous summer, after spending the spring in the Sierra Nevada. She'd found plenty of lakes in the mountain range that stretched half the length of California, but so had a lot of other people – every road and shoreline was busy with tourists. She needed to search somewhere bigger, vaster, with more geography for her to get lost in.

She hitched a ride from Reno across Nevada and half of Utah to Salt Lake City, then two more across another state border to Grand Junction and, finally, a small, low-slung mining town called Paonia.

Paonia had a lot of churches within its meagre limits, and even more trailheads beyond them. And its God-fearing residents were happy to keep to themselves, or at least to mostly ignore a stranger passing through. After an undisturbed night as the sole guest of the town's only motel, Valera spent a day poring over local maps in its tiny library until she found one hiking route that appeared to lead nowhere. The next morning she set out on it.

The path was overgrown, invisible in places, but after three hours it led her to the narrow, rock-strewn ravine that was the only way to and from her nameless mountain and its lake. As soon as she saw them she knew they were where she wanted to stay, and when she found the abandoned two-room log cabin with an upturned boat lying in the long grass in front of its unlocked front door shortly before nightfall, she moved in.

Once she was sure no one was going to try to evict her from her new home, she'd cleaned it out and tidied it up, shooing bugs out of crevices, washing bedlinen and dusting the cabin's surprisingly well-stocked bookcases and empty kitchen cupboards.

Slowly, with the changing of the seasons, Valera became a more familiar face in Paonia. She couldn't abandon the world entirely. She needed to go to the bank, the hardware and grocery stores, and occasionally stay in the motel when the evening weather turned against her before she could make it back to the cabin. She wasn't exactly embraced as she made her increasingly regular nine-hour round trips to buy supplies and provisions. But she was tolerated, accepted, and not run out of town – which was enough for her.

Sometimes she drew a little more attention than she wanted – Paonia also had an abundance of single men – but she never courted it. Valera had no interest in developing any new relationships, romantic, sexual, or platonic. She'd convinced herself she was beyond such concerns, that she was content to be nothing more than a mysterious mountain hermit. That she was living a simple, honest life, and that she hadn't turned herself into a lonely ghost who was trapped haunting her own dead dreams.

After a few minutes of sunshine she could feel the air round her heat up and decided to start back down into the valley, which had already quietened as its other residents also got on with their mornings.

As she so often did, she imagined Ledjo gambolling and galloping ahead of her, throwing up dandelion seeds in his wake or trampling buttercups under his feet, swelling her heart and breaking it at the same time.

It was six years since she'd lost him, the same length of time that she'd had him. Sometimes she wondered what he might look like now, a twelve-year-old on the cusp of teenagerhood – would he be lanky from growth spurts or still waiting to blossom? Would he look like his father, a man who had barely been in Valera's life and never in Ledjo's? Would she still see herself in his face? – but mostly, she pictured him as the innocent child with almond-shaped eyes that dazzled with excitement and adventure despite all the sadness they'd seen.

She imagined him leaping over the small, steep stream lined with blue columbine and silky lupins in front of her, turning to giggle and beckon her to race him down the rest of the hill. But when she hopped over the thin ribbon of water he'd faded into nothing and she was alone.

Valera let out a silent sigh and continued on her way, turning her mind to more practical matters – calculating how much longer her stores would last. She might now live in a land of plenty, but old habits died hard. She knew exactly how many tins and jars of food were squirrelled away in the kitchen. It was Friday, and she reckoned she would be fine until at least Monday.

That meant that she could spend the day on the lake, keeping up her English with one of the novels she'd inherited and lazily gazing at the odd cloud that drifted across the high blue sky.

However, as she reached the group of pines her cabin stood behind, she realised that today wouldn't be another calm day in her quaint, remote existence. It would be the end of it. Because she could spy wisps of smoke rising above the treetops. And, when she knelt down and peered past their trunks, she saw a raging fire consuming her cabin.

CHAPTER 18

Knox went for a walk, and ended up in a small riot.

He knew how crucial it was for a spy to absorb the fundamental rhythm of any environment they operated in – understand the local context, what was normal and what wasn't. And despite his rapid criss-crossing over Hong Kong and afternoon shopping trip, he was acutely aware that he hadn't managed to get a feel for the base tone of the place yet. Now he had the time to put that right.

Knox left 99 Bonham Strand and sauntered along to a star-shaped junction, where he turned left, then left and left again, which brought him back to the same crossroads. He lingered for a moment, watching to see if anyone had followed him on his little circuit, or was waiting, doing their best to look inconspicuous, in case he returned.

He couldn't spot any tails, obvious or otherwise, so he continued on to the next junction, where Bonham Strand split into Queen's Road and Wellington Street. Feeling more like a soldier than royalty, he took the latter fork.

After a few hundred yards he passed a gap between two neon-covered buildings that was clogged with market stalls and heavy with the scent of cloves and peppers. It wasn't an alley but a dead end, in constant shadow thanks to a dense lattice of bamboo scaffolding that covered it a few feet above head height. Knox couldn't imagine another building squeezing into the tight gap, but the nervous looks on the faces of all the vendors suggested that they could, and that it might happen at any moment.

After a few more paces, Knox reached another junction, this time with Peel Street. As he wasn't a natural politician, he was about to carry on and see where Wellington would lead him, but what was going on in the side street drew his attention and he paused. There were no hawkers, but there were lots of people, loitering in small, silent groups. An eclectic mix of native Hong Kongers, local Asian transplants, and migrants from further afield. They didn't look anxious. They seemed angry, and like they were waiting for something.

It only took a few seconds for Knox to discover what that something was. A large police van approaching from the direction he'd come a few moments earlier, which, he guessed, was carrying leftists to Victoria Prison.

He watched the person closest to the crossroads send a chain of nods up Peel Street, and then thirty-odd protestors poured into the road, blocking the van's path.

Shouts went up in English and Cantonese, and the more bold in the crowd started hitting their fists against the side of the van. The police in the driver's cab didn't react, which only served to encourage the banging to turn into pushing the van from side to side.

After two minutes of rocking, the van's rear doors opened to cheers from the throng. But whoever they had expected to be inside wasn't there. Instead, they were suddenly face to face with twelve police officers – who might have been outnumbered but were considerably better armed.

Knox was curious to see what might happen next with this abrupt shift in the situation's balance of power, but he also realised that he didn't look all that different from some of the protestors and could easily be confused for one of them.

He glanced behind him and backed up a few paces, which meant he didn't see if it was a police officer or a protestor who escalated things.

Suddenly jeers turned into screams, rotten fruit, bricks, and anything else anyone had to hand were being thrown at the van, and bullets were being fired into the air.

Then the police were down on the road, spreading out into a line that cut through the crowd and starting to push the people caught on the wrong side of it – including Knox – into Peel Street.

People tried to hold their ground, hurling more multilingual abuse and anything they could grab off the ground, but the police kept pressing forward and eventually the protestors started to retreat.

Knox doubted he'd be able to convince the row of officers to his left that he was technically on their side, was working with Special Branch, and should be allowed on his way. He was equally sure that if anyone on his right overheard him try they wouldn't appreciate it; they might assume he'd been sent by the police to infiltrate their ranks and focus their rage on him. He also imagined any attempt he might make to play peacemaker between the opposing factions would be futile. So, he settled for letting the crowd carry him away with them.

Until another line of police appeared at the end of Peel Street.

In an instant the overriding feeling emanating from the protestors changed from rage to fear. They were suddenly hemmed in on all sides, trapped in the bottleneck of the narrow street with nowhere to go.

Everyone began frantically searching for an escape route, their earlier boldness replaced by the terror that they might find themselves carted off to prison if they didn't. Or that the police might start lowering the aim of their guns to chest or head height.

Knox pressed himself up against a wall, feeling along it for an unnoticed door or window he could clamber through. He caught sight of someone else doing the same thing across from him, a hood hiding their face and their head tilted down as if they were studying the ground for a possible way out.

And then they disappeared.

They dipped below the shoulders of the people closest to them, and didn't pop up again, either in another part of the crush or miraculously beyond the police.

Up until now, the tension consuming the city had been mostly invisible to Knox. While it had been fascinating to witness it flaring up at close quarters, he decided he'd seen enough of it for one day and elbowed his way over to where the hooded person had been. He looked at the thin strip of pavement beneath him and saw a hinged delivery hatch embedded in it.

Knox shoved a Caucasian man with hippy-ish hair out of his way, reached down, opened the hatch, and climbed down the short ladder that led to a low-ceilinged basement storeroom.

He expected more bodies to tumble down behind him, but as he looked up he saw the hatch swing shut above him and heard a loud clanging as the thick metal sheet fell back into its recess, followed by the shuffling of feet across it.

Knox found a doorway that led to a winding corridor, which in turn brought him to a staircase and a foyer. He checked himself over in the reflection of the front door of the building he now found himself in. And the city through the glass – it looked perfectly normal, as if everyone strolling along the pavement were entirely oblivious to what was going on just a few feet from them, or they were consciously choosing to ignore it.

He straightened his clothes, smoothed down his hair, and checked that his watch was still in one piece. Then he stepped back outside, casting only the most casual and disinterested glance at the police officers blocking the exit of Peel Street.

CHAPTER 19

Valera was running again, leaving everything behind. She only had a few dollar bills scrunched up in the chest pocket of the plaid shirt she'd pulled over her shoulders for the walk up the mountain and then tied round her waist on the way back down. Her passport, the rucksack she'd carried with her all the way from Povenets B, her books – they were all burning, disintegrating into nothing.

She'd crouched behind the copse for a frantic, paralysed minute, trying to work out where the inferno had come from. She hadn't lit the stove when she'd woken up, and there was no other way for a fire to break out in the cabin accidentally. That meant this had happened on purpose. An attack. But by whom? And, more pressingly, did whoever they were think she was inside, suffocating or burning to death, or about to crash through one of the small, thick windows? Or were they hunting her, using the flames to draw her out or force her towards the one way out of her now-shattered idyll?

She'd wondered if she should stay where she was, lie flat and try to press herself down into the grass and soil, or find another, denser cluster of trees and shrubs where she could watch the valley without being seen until dark. She knew the ravine path well enough by now to make it through blindfolded. But she'd decided that would just delay the inevitable, and maybe cost her the chance to get away before whoever was after her realised she was gone.

So, she ran.

Valera didn't head for Paonia. After she'd made it through the sheer-walled pass without being shot, stabbed or having a boulder dropped on her, she'd offered up a curt thanks to a God she didn't believe in, and muttered an admonishment to herself for becoming so lax that she'd never stashed an emergency escape pack in one of its deep fissures. Then she'd turned west, skirting the edge of the town she'd now never step foot in again.

She walked for hours, following the road that led out of the Rockies, but always with a couple of hundred feet of ground between her and the wide strip of cracked tarmac. The mountains fell away, browns and greens turning to sun-bleached dirt, and she was quickly out in the treeless open, exposed – but at least that meant no one would be able to sneak up on her without her spotting them first.

Just after 9 a.m. Valera reached the town of Hotchkiss. She didn't stop for breakfast. Instead, she kept following the highway as it continued to descend through the ancient worn plain of the Gunnison River.

Hour after hour, the temperature rose, shimmering the dry horizon and constantly, cruelly taking her mind back to her dazed, stumbling trek through the endless pools and bogs of the Karelian tundra after her escape from Povenets B. The ghost of the rucksack she'd kept hidden and full of emergency supplies for herself then weighed on her shoulders, and the smaller one that had been meant for Ledjo pulled invisibly on her arms.

She drifted closer to the road, to stop her from losing sight of it, and so she could study the faces of the few truck drivers who passed her. They all looked bored, oblivious to anything other than what was directly in front of or behind them, or mildly surprised when their gaze strayed to the side and they noticed her staring at them with suspicious eyes. None of them seemed murderous.

As the sun hit its zenith, Valera tried to distract herself from the heat of its rays, which she now hated, and her idiocy for not daring to stop in Paonia or Hotchkiss for at least a bottle of water, by theorising about who had set fire to her home.

Had the CIA suddenly got spooked, thought that she really was planning on skipping the country and used one of the fleet of spy satellites she'd helped them put into orbit to find her before she could? Or was the GRU seeking revenge at long last for letting her slip out of their grip?

Valera didn't much like either prospect. But she told herself that it didn't really matter which one of them it might be. She didn't need to know who had come after her. She just needed to keep moving. Find somewhere even more remote where whoever they were wouldn't be able to track her down. Somewhere no one would even think of looking. Somewhere she wouldn't let herself start thinking of as home. Somewhere it'd be easier to leave if it turned out she hadn't hidden well enough again.

After another hour, her mind started to play tricks on her.

She didn't see Ledjo racing ahead or lagging behind her. She saw every other trauma from her past instead.

It was subtle at first. A few shadows dancing around the edges of her eyes that could have been cast by eagles soaring above her – except there was nothing in the bright blue when she squinted up to look for them. Then a strange, low maze appeared, a series of awkward, lumpen shapes she had to step round, but which disappeared as soon as she did.

Her brain turned a distant truck horn into wailing sirens, and she ducked down, suddenly terrified of debris flying past her and tearing her skin to shreds, or a missile falling from the sky and obliterating her.

Neither happened. But she stumbled forward, hands skidding in the dirt and transporting her back to digging through rubble, tears ready to flood down her cheeks, and scratching between frozen cobblestones, desperately searching for anything she could use to feed, warm or protect herself.

Valera climbed back up onto her tired, unstable legs, steeled herself and tried to regain some kind of rational composure.

She forced herself to ignore everything she could see and feel apart from the ground beneath her. She strode through the twisted girders that materialised inches in front of her feet to trip her up, and refused to cower from the flames that licked at her fingers one moment or shield herself from the blizzard that blasted her cheeks the next.

Valera didn't know if it was her stubbornness or exhaustion that finally won out, but eventually all the horrible fantasies fell away and she was left with just grim reality and still many more miles to walk.

CHAPTER 20

Laing's new role afforded him a diminutive office on the third floor of Leconfield House. He knew most of the Service's lower-ranking officers coveted his private little space – a desk that didn't have to be shared, a window he could open at will, a door he could shut whenever he wanted. But what they interpreted as the trappings of promotion, he saw as him and his work being tucked away, out of sight and out of mind.

This feeling was compounded by yet another morning of having very little to do. A single item had been added to his agenda from two floors above – checking in on Jack Williams – but even that wasn't urgent and could wait a few days. So, Laing had a choice to sit and stew or fill his time trawling once more through the archives, searching for old evidence of Line Z's work. He opted for the latter, and decided he'd do it in the School Hall.

The wide, open-plan space was quieter than normal, with most of its regular occupants out shadowing or guarding assets, but there were still a few heads bent under desk lamps, deep in thought, or huddled together in conversations Laing might eavesdrop on or even briefly join. In addition to the opportunity for human contact the School Hall offered, which he reluctantly admitted to himself he needed from time to time, Laing had found over the last year that the clerks were a lot quicker to deliver records here than to individual offices.

Most of Laing's research into Line Z had focused on the last decade – the period during which MI5 could be absolutely sure the

KGB department had been active. However, there was no reason to believe that it hadn't existed for as long as the entire Soviet intelligence apparatus. He decided that today he'd take a look at the early fifties, when the victorious allies of the Second World War were still deciding just what kind of enemies they'd become to each other.

He requested the index of key Service operations spanning 1950 to 1953, intending to read through their precis, and then go through the less important ones – the forgotten oddities and unclosed cases the Volk programme seemed to thrive on.

However, before the clerks could deliver the first tranche of reports, Laing was distracted by something that sounded utterly and totally ridiculous.

'And it can't be pine martens?' a voice to his left said. It belonged to a man who looked only slightly younger than Laing, who was perched on the side of a desk two rows over from him.

'Apparently not,' the occupier of the desk's chair replied.

Both men were struggling to keep their voices level.

'Mink? Weasels? Otters?'

'The orders say it has to be stoats.'

'Poor little buggers.'

'If it's any consolation, they won't know we've strapped bombs to them. They'll just be merrily wandering around Suffolk somewhere, and then they won't be.'

Laing couldn't resist walking over.

'Do we have an exploding mustelid problem?' he asked.

'White's latest big idea,' the sitting man replied. 'Supposed to save us all if we get invaded by the Russians.'

'The great stoat resistance,' the other added, finally giving in to laughter.

It sounded like a joke to Laing. And he decided it had to be. But he also thought he should probably make certain that it was.

The research and development department was busier than the rest of Leconfield House, but it still wasn't exactly a buzzing hub of activity. Instead of the surprisingly passionate conversations of professional scientists, the dominant sound when Laing entered was a combination of the low thrumming of the Atlas mainframes – the enormous computer stacks that processed all the information Pipistrelle collected, and anything else that was uploaded into them – and their ever-whirring cooling fans. There was also no sign of White.

Laing couldn't imagine that the Service's chief brain had been sent out into the field. He had to be somewhere in the building.

A crash behind him made Laing spin round and discover an engineer, who had clearly misjudged the exact dimensions of a doorway, attempting to scoop up several lengths of dark plastic tubing.

'Where's the boss?' he asked as he reached down to pick up one of the longer pieces.

'Upstairs,' the engineer replied, before glancing up at him.

Laing could tell from the flash of fear that crossed the man's face that 'upstairs' was more information than he was supposed to give to someone outside the department. He guessed it didn't mean White was meeting with Holland on the fifth floor.

By the time the engineer had wrangled his tubes enough to stand up, Laing was already halfway up the stairs that wrapped round Leconfield House's lifts to the floor immediately above the research and development department, which, he realised, he'd never been to before. He had no idea what was on it. What he found was a long, silent row of signless doors.

He knocked on the one closest to the stairs. No one came to open it. He tried the second and got the same lack of response. After there was no answer at the third door he tried the handle, and the door opened to reveal something even more farcical than an army of kamikaze stoats careering across the countryside – Malcolm White, hunched over a tangle of metal coils in a large, see-through glass box.

As Laing got closer to the giant cube, he realised that White hadn't registered his presence, and that he was completely absorbed by what now looked like a large copper coil magnet. Next to it he could see a small hourglass that had almost run out of sand.

He waited for White to pause and stretch out his back, then he knocked on the glass. If the other man let out a surprised sound at the unexpected intrusion, Laing didn't hear it. He watched as White spun round, realised who had disturbed him, scowled, then tried to wave him away. Laing didn't go. Instead, he pointed at the timer, waited for White to glance at it, and saw his scowl deepen.

White opened the door on the inside of the box, then the one on the outside, and gestured at Laing to keep his mouth shut. After nearly a minute of awkward silence, he beckoned him inside, shut the doors again, and turned over the hourglass.

'Did Holland send you?' he asked.

'No,' Laing replied.

'Damn.'

'What's all this?'

'A soundproof box.'

'I gathered that much. Why?'

'Because of that,' White said, pointing at the rings of copper. Or, more precisely, at the tiny box nestled on a miniature plinth in the middle of them.

It looked to Laing like a Pipistrelle bug. But he knew that if it was there'd be no reason to construct such dramatic precautions around it. It must be something else.

'Is it also the reason for the nonsense I'm hearing in the School Hall?'

White huffed his affirmation.

Now Laing frowned at the grim implication. He wanted to know how bad the situation was. How much of Leconfield House had been compromised? And who had managed to penetrate the Service's security so effectively? But he imagined if White had had the answers to any of those questions, they wouldn't currently be chatting inside a hermetically sealed box. He settled for asking,

'Then why the hell am I wasting my time scouring the archives for scraps to feed Six?'

Laing wouldn't normally question his standing orders out loud to a department head, but it wasn't as if anyone else was in earshot, and White looked frustrated enough to afford him a little discretion.

'The same reason I'm shut up in here trying to remember not to suffocate myself,' he replied. 'Operational security.'

'By keeping us in the dark and making up absurd stories?'

'The first part is up to Holland,' White said as he leaned back over the coils, reminding Laing that his discretion had limits. 'But if you're so offended by my narrative creations feel free to make up some of your own. All that myth-hunting you've been doing should make you the perfect man for the job.'

Laing was about to protest until he realised that White was actually right. He was the ideal person to run a disinformation campaign out of Leconfield House. The only problem was that he couldn't do it without the director general's approval.

As if he could sense Laing's realisation, White added, 'I'll speak to Holland about it.'

CHAPTER 21

The diner was having some kind of late afternoon rush – full of people making a quick stop before they pushed on to wherever they needed to get before nightfall. It was on the outskirts of Delta, a town twenty miles from Hotchkiss, and thirty from Paonia.

Valera couldn't tell if the roadside restaurant was called Eddie's or Emma's, though she wasn't sure if that was because the script on the giant red-and-white sign bolted precipitously over the entrance was too stylised, or if her eyes just weren't able to read what was in front of her after ten hours of walking without food or water.

She reached her hand out slowly, just in case the chrome-edged glass front door was actually a mirage, along with the rest of the building and the car park full of cars and trucks. Then, when she felt the warm metal of the handle resist her tired grip, she pulled the door open and stepped through.

No one acknowledged her arrival, or even seemed to register it. Inside was more red, and metal, both dulled after at least twenty years of daily use and exposure to the Coloradan sun, which still streamed through the wide windows. Every stool at the long counter that ran the length of the diner's back wall was occupied, and so was each booth beneath the wall of waist-to-ceiling glass – except for the furthest one, next to the two toilet doors.

Valera had put her shirt back on as she'd crossed the car park, wanting to make herself look as respectable and anonymous as possible by covering up her sweat-crusted and sunburnt skin, but as she passed person after person who looked equally beaten down by their own long journeys, she realised she needn't have bothered and, instead of dipping into the ladies' to splash her face with water, she dropped into the empty booth, her back against the wall and facing the entrance.

A minute later, a waitress in a red-and-white-striped uniform, with a high beehive and pencil-thin eyebrows, arrived at her side. She filled, without asking, a pair of the table's four cups and glasses from jugs of black coffee and water she carried one in each hand, and dropped a narrow piece of folded card that had been pinned under one of her elbows so that it landed squarely in front of Valera.

Valera opened the menu as the waitress, whom she guessed was neither Eddie nor Emma, continued on her circuit of the diner, providing unrequested refills and taking mumbled orders in silence. Then she checked that the couple of five-dollar bills and several more singles were still in her shirt pocket. Confident she could pay her way and still have enough left over for an overnight bus ticket, she started to drink. The water first, then the coffee. She finished them both in a short succession of long gulps.

When the waitress came back round to her, Valera ordered a steak sandwich. And when it was delivered five minutes later, she was shocked to find it almost completely smothered in unappetising bright orange, oily melted cheese. However, by that point she was far too hungry to turn it down or send it back so she got on with devouring it. She was almost done when she noticed the woman three booths down staring at her.

Valera didn't know if she'd just arrived, or if she'd been in the diner the whole time. But she couldn't believe she wouldn't have spotted her if she had been. Not a single strand of her long, dark hair was out of place. Her skin was radiant, and, unlike everyone else in the diner, she gave off an aura of being exactly where she wanted to be. When they made eye contact, the woman offered up a wide, warm smile that unnerved Valera.

The woman left her booth and walked towards Valera's. Her steps were so even and smooth it was as if she was gliding, like an angel. An angel, Valera suddenly thought, of death.

She slid into Valera's booth and, still without looking at anything but Valera, pulled a wad of napkins out of the little dispenser nestled under the windowsill and passed them over.

'What's going on?' Valera asked, as she slowly took the stack of paper.

'I was about to ask you the same thing,' the woman replied. Her accent was impossible to place, a jumble of American and European inflections, but her tone was measured, relaxed, disarming.

Valera wiped her hands, balled up the napkins on the plate with the rest of her sandwich and asked, 'Are you here to kill me?'

'No,' the woman said. Then she nodded towards the window and added, 'but I think he might be.'

Valera couldn't tell if it was a trick to distract her and make her drop her guard, but she also couldn't resist looking out through the glass.

There was a man crossing the car park. A tall man. His pace was as measured and even as the woman's had been, but rather than drifting through the world almost carefree and untouched by it, as she had, he seemed driven by cool, determined purpose. He was a predator stalking his prey.

Her fight-or-flight response tried to kick in, but what little energy she had was too busy trying to keep her awake, digest her sandwich, and process what was happening to have much spare to help her actually deal with it.

She kept her attention fixed on the tall man as he got closer and closer to the entrance. His clothes were nondescript, his hair was cut short to his head, and most of his features were forgettable – except for his eyes. Either his irises were entirely black, or his pupils were completely dilated. And they were staring straight back at Valera.

The woman slid a set of keys across the table to her. 'The Studebaker.'

Valera pulled her gaze away from the window and looked down. She frowned. There were a few English words she still didn't know. She had no idea what a Studebaker was.

'The red car in the far corner,' the woman said, answering Valera's question before she could ask it. 'Don't look for it. Wait until he gets to the door, then go to the ladies' room. There's an open window in the second stall. Start the engine running while I deal with him.'

'Why?'

'Because I still want to know what's going on.'

Valera looked back at the man. He was almost at the entrance

'Or,' the woman added, 'I could ask him when he's done with you.'

Valera still had no clue who this woman was, or what she really wanted from her, but she was convinced the man was here to kill her and the stranger opposite her had given her a way to escape. Maybe she was a guardian angel after all.

She waited for him to briefly look away as he swung open the diner's door, then bolted for the bathroom. There were two cubicles inside and she took a chance on which one was supposed to be the second. She guessed right, and clambered up onto the toilet bowl lid and vaulted through the small square window.

Valera hadn't paused to check what she was leaping out into, and she didn't stop to check the ankle that rolled underneath her as she landed on a pile of uneven rubble. The joint still took her weight, so she kept going.

She kept low as she dashed round the side of the diner and along the furthest row of cars and trucks. For a split second she thought she'd been tricked, and there was no red car waiting for her, but then it appeared, nestled and gleaming between two battered pickup trucks.

She shuffled down its left-hand side, opened the driver's door, got in and started the engine. Then she edged forward enough to be able to see what was happening inside the diner.

The man was passing her booth, but showed no signs of slowing down. In fact, he was turning towards the bathrooms. Valera silently chastised herself for not shutting the window behind her, or the cubicle door, and wondered if she should pull the rest of the way out of her space and just keep driving.

But then the woman got up and pounced with sudden, ferocious abandon at the man. They crashed into a large trucker at the end of the counter, who, after pulling himself up out of his dinner, looked like he was ready to join the fight himself until he turned round, saw what he'd be up against and clearly thought better of it.

The woman and man were fast, and vicious. Fists jabbed at sides and necks. Occasional bits of crockery and cutlery flew into the air or at faces. Yet it looked to Valera almost as if they were sparring, playing with each other, testing each other. At least, until the woman threw a steak knife and it lodged in the man's right shoulder.

The drawing of blood changed the tone of the fight.

They got closer to each other, determined to do damage. They wrestled, rolling first along the counter and almost back over the trucker, who, like the rest of the diner's staff and customers, was watching what was happening in stunned silence, then across the table of Valera's booth, and, finally, with both of them seemingly choking each other, crashing through the bathroom door.

After a long, pregnant moment, the door opened again and the woman stepped through. The man didn't follow her.

Everyone in the diner stayed rooted where they were as she walked, almost gliding again, past them. The trucker didn't demand that she buy him a new dinner, the waitress didn't tell her she needed to pay for the mess she'd caused.

As the woman reached the entrance, Valera pushed down on the accelerator and turned out of her space. Again, she thought about just keeping on going, but that would mean having to get past her guardian angel now, and she suddenly thought having her coming after her would be even worse than the man she'd just either knocked out or killed.

Valera stopped at the car park exit and shuffled over to the passenger seat as the woman strolled round to the driver's side and slid behind the wheel. Somehow, in the walk from the bathroom, her hair had fallen back perfectly in place, and nothing about the rest of her appearance suggested that she had just been part of a two-person brawl.

'How many times did you think about driving off?' the woman asked as she revved the engine.

Valera paused for a second, then said, 'Twice.'

The woman threw her head back, let out a loud laugh, then swung the Studebaker out of the car park.

CHAPTER 22

The woman drove them south, keeping the Studebaker a few miles an hour under the speed limit and a safe distance from the other vehicles in front of and behind them.

They didn't look like they'd just fled a violent attack. They looked like two sisters or friends who had reached that point on a long journey when the conversation had dried up, their bodies had relaxed into comfortable slouches, and their eyes were lazily focused on the road ahead.

After almost half an hour of quiet, Valera broke the silence and asked her driver-rescuer her name.

'Call me Anna.'

It was more of an instruction than an answer, and Valera was going to press her on it until the woman turned off the road that Valera thought was going to take them out of Colorado and towards Albuquerque and they started to head east instead.

'Where are we going?' she asked.

'Denver,' Anna replied.

'Why?'

'Because that's where my hotel is.'

'Shouldn't we get out of the state?'

'I'm betting that's what our friend will think.'

'He's not dead?'

Anna smiled. 'I settled for knocking him slightly unconscious. He's probably awake already, and hopefully on his way to Utah or New Mexico with one hell of a headache. But even if he's smart and he's guessed where we're really heading, I'd still rather have just him on my tail than the police and the FBI too.'

Valera didn't know if she should be more relieved that the woman next to her wasn't a killer – or at least hadn't killed anyone in the last hour – or worried that the man who now probably wanted both of them dead was still alive. But she could see the logic in Anna's evasive manoeuvres.

Part of Valera wanted to ask more questions, be more certain about where they were headed and what would happen when they got there. But another part told her she was safe enough for the moment, and reminded her she'd only eaten most of a sandwich all day and had already burned through the energy it had given her.

As if sensing the tiredness starting to sweep over her passenger, Anna reached behind her, retrieved a jacket from the back seat and dropped it in Valera's lap.

'Before you pass out and headbutt the dashboard,' she said.

Valera rolled up the coat, put it between her head and the window, and promptly fell asleep.

She dreamed of fire.

When she woke up, the sun had set and she could see the twinkling lights of a city rising up ahead through the windscreen. She felt even more stale and crusty than she had when she'd reached the diner, and the woman next to her looked just as composed and relaxed.

'How long have I been sleeping?' she asked as she tried to stretch out the stiff crick she could feel in her neck.

'About four and a half hours,' Anna replied.

The Studebaker crawled through Denver's outskirts, and then its heart. It was the biggest place Valera had been in over a year, and even late in the evening there was more life and activity than she was used to – cars, buses, taxis, people strolling down pavements in pairs and falling out of bars and restaurants in loud, rowdy groups. Like everything else that had happened to her today, it was jarring.

They reached a triangular city block that appeared to be entirely taken up by a single red-stone building and Anna pulled up to the kerb. A moment later a man in an almost military-looking coat and cap was at her door, and another in a rather more normal suit appeared at Valera's.

They'd arrived at Anna's hotel: the Brown Palace.

While the valet parked the car, the two women were ushered inside and across the wide floor of the hotel's towering atrium by the man in the suit. The space was enormous, yet luxurious and intimate. Couples drank cocktails at its widely spaced tables, a piano played somewhere quietly out of sight.

Valera looked around her and up at the wrought-iron galleries and high stained-glass roof, and felt both extremely out of place and not at all anonymous. Anna, however, yet again seemed to glide effortlessly through this new environment.

'Would you like drinks, or dinner?' the man asked her as he summoned an elevator next to the hotel's wide cedar concierge desk.

'I think we could both use a martini,' Anna replied. 'With twists. And anything you have left over from afternoon tea would be greatly appreciated. We'll have them in my room.'

The man nodded, then disappeared as another member of staff escorted Anna and Valera up to the eighth floor.

Anna's room, it turned out, was a very large and very pastel suite.

It had an expansive living area with three couches arranged in front of a fireplace that was stuffed with logs, and a six-person dining table, along with two bedrooms and bathrooms, which, Valera decided, explained both the overly attentive service they'd received downstairs and the lack of surprise that Anna had arrived with a guest in tow.

However, as she finally washed away the grime of the day in the shower that belonged to the slightly smaller of the bedrooms, it also made her question just how many of the events of the last almost-twenty-four hours had been orchestrated by her guardian angel. So, she dried herself off, changed into a pair of trousers and a cable-knit jumper she found in the walnut wardrobe next to her bed, and went to find out.

Anna was sitting on one of the two couches that faced each other. She'd changed into a thick cotton bathrobe and held a thin-stemmed martini glass in one hand and a miniature eclair in the other. On the low coffee table in front of the fireplace there was another glass and two multi-tiered china stands containing an array of tiny sandwiches and pastries.

Valera sat down opposite Anna in what felt like the complete inverse of their first meeting in the diner. She knew she should be suspicious, and still couldn't completely trust her surroundings or the woman who had devoured her cream-filled choux and was now considering a small tart topped with raspberries. But she also couldn't resist her curiosity – or her need for sustenance.

She picked up a triangular sandwich filled with mayonnaise-slathered prawns, ate it in two bites, and asked Anna for the second time that day what was going on.

'Like I already said,' Anna replied, 'that's what I want to ask you.'

'And I told you I have no idea what's happening,' Valera said.

Anna took another sip of her cocktail and put it down. 'People are being killed. I'm curious about why. And I know who you are, Irina. Who you really are.'

Anna's last four words shot fear through Valera and she had to stop herself from hurling the contents of the table at the other woman and tumbling over the back of the couch. Was this whole thing an elaborate ploy to lure her off her mountain after all? Was she about to be tortured in these elegant surroundings? Toyed with by a GRU or KGB killer before her body was dumped in a hidden bunker or a shallow grave?

'Are you an assassin?' she asked, doing her best to keep her voice somewhere near even.

Anna smiled. 'Among a few other things.'

'Do you work for Russia?'

'I have done,' Anna replied, picking her martini up again and taking another sip. 'But not at the moment. Hence my interest.'

Then she let out a short sigh. It seemed to Valera somewhere between wistful and frustrated, and it had the unexpected effect of almost completely defusing her fear – at least her fear of the woman who called herself Anna.

She reached out for her glass and tasted the strong bitter-sweet alcohol in it.

'You think they're cleaning house?' she asked.

'It certainly looks that way,' Anna replied.

'And you want to be ready if they come after you.'

'Don't you?'

For a split second Valera thought about stepping back into that world she'd done so much to get away from. The science, the secrets, the schemes. She shook the idea from her head.

'No.'

Another smile. 'I thought you'd be a better liar. Most Russians are.'

'I'll just disappear again,' Valera said.

'You might not be as good at that as you think either.'

'I did it for years.'

'And got sloppy. You gave it a good go, but running isn't your calling. You're the type of person who needs to answer questions, not hide from them.'

Valera wanted to defend herself, but she had to concede that the other woman was right, at least on one point. She hadn't even known she was in danger until her world had been destroyed. It was, really, a simple calculation – keeping close to Anna gave her a better chance of staying alive.

'So, what do you suggest?' she said. 'We go to the CIA?'

'I'd rather they had no idea I'd been in the country. We need to get out of America. Tomorrow.'

Valera took another sip of her martini. 'And go where?'

'London.'

Valera's hand shook at the thought of the British capital, sending a single drop of liquid into her lap. She'd been to London before, six years ago. She didn't have good memories of the city.

'Why?'

'Because I've never killed anyone in MI5.'

'Do they know that?' Valera asked, which earned her the second booming laugh of the day from Anna.

'I'll find something white to wave at them from the plane,' Anna said, finally reaching out for the raspberry tart.

'One issue,' Valera said, the memory of the fire that had consumed her cabin and all her worldly possessions erupting in her mind. 'I don't have a passport.'

'Oh, don't worry,' Anna replied after swallowing a bite of the tart. 'That won't be a problem.'

CHAPTER 23

The following morning, Knox was waiting for Zhou in the lobby of his hotel bright and early. It was his unspoken acknowledgement that with Lady Reeve's death there had been a subtle shift in the nature of their partnership – murder, suicide, or even accidental death; all fell clearly under the aegis of the police.

After his late-afternoon excitement on Peel Street the previous day, he'd returned to the Waylian for another perfectly fine dinner in its restaurant, accompanied by a promise to himself to try somewhere more adventurous now that he was staying in Hong Kong longer. Then he'd ended up back in his bedroom, gazing out at the city once more.

Looking down again on all the sinuous streets and tentacle junctions as they flickered into orange and pink light, drawing taxis, strolling couples, and opportunistic hawkers to them, it had been hard not to let connections form between all the things in his head.

Lady Reeve's unexplained move to Stanley so soon after he'd arrived. Her sudden demise before he'd had a chance to have a coherent conversation with her. The other deaths and disappearances that had made Holland curious about China. It was tempting to draw twisting lines to link them. Maybe even to the mysterious penetration of Leconfield House too. It would be convenient if they were all part of one single, tangled web. But also convoluted – and jumping ahead, forcing evidence to fit a hypothesis before it had even been collected.

It could all be a grand conspiracy, but it could just as easily be a coincidence.

Zhou and Atwood had both mentioned Triads. Had a combination of revolutionary zeal and naivety put Lady Reeve in the wrong place at the wrong time to make the wrong friends? It wouldn't be the first time a wide-eyed Western traveller had said, done, or taken something they shouldn't have and realised too late how severe the consequences would be. Nothing more than Atwood's 'sorry misadventure'. The Occam's razor answer. Yet, while Knox had cautioned himself not to will invisible links into existence, he'd also reminded himself that in his line of work the simplest answer was rarely the right one.

Zhou's Mercedes pulled to an abrupt halt in front of the hotel and Knox strolled out to meet her, already thankful for the linen blend of the new suit he was wearing. The morning was hot and humid.

He got in the car, and Zhou looked him up and down. He wondered if she was going to mention the protest, somehow aware he'd ended up in the middle of it, but she just said, 'We're going to Kowloon. Lady Reeve's apartment.'

That made sense to Knox – he wanted to see where she'd lived and, if her death might end up becoming a full-blown police investigation, he was keen to take a look before too many people trampled through it.

Halfway between the Waylian and the car ferry pier, Knox started to hear music. Quietly at first, then quickly becoming louder. He looked down at the radio in the dashboard to see if it had come to life of its own accord. It hadn't. He wound down the window and recognised the song that had just started – John Lennon repeatedly begging for help. He peered through the windscreen, searching for the source, but there were no record stores with speakers piled in front of them, no surprise concert by the world's most famous four-piece in a blocked-off side street or on the roof of a nearby building.

The closer they got to the harbourfront, the more deafening the music became.

'It's the government,' Zhou said, as Knox turned to her to ask what was going on.

'Why?'

'You'll see in a moment.'

The car turned a corner and a large building appeared in front of them. It looked like a lazy architect had copied the Empire State but cut it off at its knees, and it was draped with ten-storey-long red banners, like blood gushing down its sides. Each one was scrawled with white Chinese script.

'Help!' finished, and before the next song started up Knox heard a set of short, repeating phrases in Mandarin. He could guess where the loudspeakers blasting them were.

'The Bank of China,' Zhou said.

'What are they saying?'

'Unkind things about the governor.'

Knox remembered the stark headlines from the briefing coda, and wondered how much of an understatement that was.

'Can't the police make them stop? Public nuisance or something.'

'We are busy with what's happening in the streets. This is just posturing. But sending officers in there would make things worse.'

'How?'

'There are two places in Hong Kong that most people consider de facto parts of China. That building is one of them. Marching into it would be considered an invasion.'

Knox processed the implication – and the slight irony – that the closest thing the Communist People's Republic had to an embassy in Hong Kong was a bank. Then he asked the inevitable follow-up question.

'What's the other one?'

'Kowloon Walled City,' Zhou replied, swinging the car through a turn away from the bank. 'An old military fort that technically remained Chinese after Britain took over the New Territories. It has been lawless ever since.'

They reached the harbour.

There were no clouds in the sky, but the water was choppier today. Knox couldn't see any dragon boats out practising in the swell, or any sailing yachts criss-crossing the strait. The junks were all at anchor, their fan-like sails fastened tight. Even HMS *Bulwark* seemed hunkered down, holding position near the Kowloon docks. In fact, Knox realised, it was only the Star Ferries that were actually moving across the water.

As they drove down the ramp to the bobbing, open rear of a car ferry they passed a sign that read: TYPHOON SIGNAL T1 IS HOISTED.

'I assume the scale goes up,' Knox said.

Zhou nodded.

Lady Reeve had rented an apartment on the fourth floor of a large block in the Mong Kok district of Kowloon. Knox was curious as to what it would tell him about the dead woman. Had she fully embraced her beliefs, eschewing the kind of luxury most titled people sought out or expected, or were her egalitarian leanings only for public display and didn't extend through her front door?

He didn't find an answer when he and Zhou first stepped inside, because her apartment was pitch black. No lights on, no curtains open. It immediately put Knox on his guard, even as he remembered that the protest Lady Reeve had been arrested at had happened at night, so it was entirely possible that she'd drawn the curtains before leaving and reasonable that the place was now shrouded in darkness. Still, he kept his body tense, ready to defend against an attack as he shuffled his way across what seemed to be a decent-sized living area, letting his eyes adjust to the gloom and avoiding amorphous shapes he guessed were chairs and a sofa, towards the opposite wall, where he assumed he'd find a window.

He managed the journey without injury, reached out his hand, felt fabric, pulled it open, and found himself face to face with another man.

He was standing in another living room, directly opposite Knox. The man was old, very old, wearing a stained vest and thick-lensed glasses. The alley between Lady Reeve's apartment and the next building was narrow, the distance between windows little more than five feet – close enough for Knox to count the liver spots that covered the man's cheeks and forehead.

The old man was staring straight at him, yet he had the feeling that he couldn't see him, or at least refused to register his existence, and that his real interest lay in the room behind him. Knox was about to raise his hand and wave to break his odd focus when Zhou finally found a light switch, pulling his attention back into the apartment, where he found ten more men looking at him. However, these men were all himself.

Reflections.

Every wall in the apartment was a floor-to-ceiling mirror.

Knox looked at Zhou as she stepped forward, multiplying herself, then back out across the alley. The old man had gone. He let his eyes drift over the windows of the countless other apartments in the opposite building he could see into – and which, therefore, could see into Lady Reeve's – and pulled the curtain shut again, wondering if it had always been kept drawn.

He took in the apartment's main room properly. It also repeated itself. There was a seating area, as Knox had guessed, a small kitchen and dining table, and two doors – both mirrored – that were open and led to a bedroom and bathroom.

Apart from the landlord's bizarre choice in wall covering, the place seemed entirely unremarkable. It looked lived in, not perfect like an immaculately staged set, but not ransacked by gangsters wanting to send a message either.

They checked each room in turn, searching for clues that might give something away. A head of wilted pak choi in the fridge, soil in a pot plant that was a few days away from drying out, bed sheets straightened, clean clothes in her wardrobe, dirty ones waiting to be laundered. All completely normal. There were no secret stashes of seditious pamphlets, or drug paraphernalia. No needles, spoons stained from repeated heating, pots with unidentified powders, or curiously coloured pills. There wasn't even any paracetamol in her bathroom cupboard.

'This doesn't look like the home of a revolutionary,' Knox said, back in the living room. 'Or an addict.'

'No,' Zhou said. 'But she may have been both, and if she was she would likely hide the evidence.'

Knox sighed and walked a circuit of the room, ignoring his reflection following him, and tapping each mirror panel, just in case one sounded more hollow than the rest. Then he went over to the curtain and opened it an inch to see if the old man had returned or if anyone else was loitering at another window across the alley, hoping to catch a glimpse of what was happening in Lady Reeve's living room.

'If Blue Peacock is a drug,' he said, letting the curtain fall back shut once more, 'how would it get into the city?'

'If it wasn't manufactured here, by land or sea,' Zhou replied. 'We have armed patrol and speedboats stationed in the Kowloon docks and island typhoon shelters to intercept smugglers.'

'And the border with China?'

'It's fenced.'

'Perhaps we should go take a look at it.'

'We are unlikely to stumble across a drug-running operation in the middle of the day.'

'Humour me,' Knox said. 'I'm probably never going to get to visit the People's Republic. It would be nice to at least take a peek at it.'

CHAPTER 24

Zhou was right. The sole land border between the present incarnations of two of history's greatest empires was a fence, running along the bank of a river.

It had only taken them half an hour to drive north from Mong Kok and through the New Territories to a bluff that gave them a clear view of the Chu River, the wide fields dotted with trees on either side of it, and the small Chinese town of Shenzhen in the distance.

The view was peaceful, the border itself easy to miss. The row of wire hardly looked like it divided two radically different ideologies. But then, Knox thought, it didn't. The tension in Hong Kong was testament to the fact that propaganda and philosophy couldn't be held back by chicken wire and checkpoints.

Knox turned through three hundred and sixty degrees. The road they'd travelled along was quiet. In fact, they hadn't seen any other cars since they'd passed a turn-off for the Hong Kong Golf Club fifteen minutes ago. To the west, he could just about make out an observation post on the crest of another hill, but it was too far to tell if anyone was actually stationed at it. To the east, more open land.

'It's not mined, is it?' he asked Zhou as he gestured towards the fence line.

'Not on our side,' she replied.

'And the Chinese?'

'I doubt it. They want to keep the ground good for building.'

Knox had a vision of Shenzhen growing into a city to rival Hong Kong, with its own precipitous edge – its high-rises kept in check by a river rather than the South China Sea.

'On both sides of the border,' Zhou added.

Knox sensed a change in her tone and cast her a look that requested further explanation.

'There are thirty years left on Britain's lease of the New Territories. Eventually everything you can see from here will be China again. And when it is, the People's Republic may demand the rest of the colony back as well.'

'How do you feel about that?'

'I'm a Hong Konger.'

It was an oblique answer, but Knox doubted he was going to get anything more explicit from her.

They fell into a brief silence as a lone cormorant glided across the sky in front of them, landed in the river, and started diving for fish.

'Why are we really here?' Zhou asked.

Knox smiled, and glanced at the road again. 'I wanted to see if we'd be followed.'

He explained that he hadn't been able to shake the possibility that Lady Reeve's transfer and death so soon after his arrival weren't a coincidence. He didn't go into the larger possibilities of conspiracy Holland had charged him with exploring.

'But you have no proof,' Zhou said.

'Still just suppositions.'

'Which leaves us with our original theory, that she took a drug she shouldn't have.'

Knox nodded and leaned on the bonnet of the car. It was warm. 'I guess distribution works the same here as everywhere else. Nightclubs, bars, dark corners, and exclusive parties.'

It was Zhou's turn to nod.

'But pulling a random dealer off the street wouldn't do us much good, even if we caught them red-handed and got them to talk.

They might not know how many more links in the chain there are, and the operation could go to ground. We need to know where the masterminds are running things from.'

'Unfortunately, there are many options for that. A tenement, a factory front, a disused dock warehouse. We make regular checks and raids on locations associated with the Triads.'

Knox squinted into the distance, watching the cormorant dive again, then take off and happily soar over the border fence.

'So if they wanted to make sure the police couldn't find them,' he said, 'they'd have to be somewhere you wouldn't go.'

CHAPTER 25

Knox recognised Kowloon Walled City as soon as they got near it. He'd seen it before, through the window of his BOAC Boeing 707 as it banked over the city on its approach to Kai Tak.

Up close it looked even more dense and fragile, as if a whole metropolis had been compressed into the size of a single city block, held together by its own gravitational force yet liable to collapse on all the lower roofs that surrounded it at any minute.

Some of its towers reached over ten storeys high and could only be one or two rooms wide; others were thick, squat, with more windows than Lady Reeve's apartment building and its close neighbour combined.

The whole thing seemed impenetrable. It was its own strange world. Small and large at the same time, every side of it a back turned away from the city it was a microcosm of.

They reached a junction at one of the walled city's corners and Zhou began to orbit it. Traffic slowed them down, and Knox felt her stiffen next to him. He wondered if it was just that there were too many vehicles on the road for her to dodge and swerve around, or because the lawlessness of the place he'd cajoled her into driving to was such anathema to her that just being near it put her on edge.

They completed two full loops, crawling along blank ground-level walls punctuated occasionally by narrow alleys and shopfronts that didn't look all that different from the ones that covered the rest of Kowloon.

Knox could sense Zhou getting more tense the longer they stayed, and he could tell she was about to suggest they head back to the ferry. He gestured at an empty space by the kerb on the opposite side of the road to one the alleys before she could. She pulled in, but didn't turn off the engine.

'Quite the thing,' he said.

'Its name in Cantonese means City of Darkness.'

'That makes it sound like demons live there.'

'They do.'

Knox looked at the people who emerged from or disappeared into the alley. They were all generations. Some were furtive, possibly embarrassed by their home. Others were relaxed, or oblivious. Children chased each other in and out of sunlight. It reminded Knox of growing up in Bethnal Green in east London with his grandmother. Normal people, getting by. However, he stopped himself telling Zhou he didn't think her judgement seemed fair. He had no reason not to believe her assertions that the neighbourhood was also home to gangsters and drug dealers – the East End was.

Yet, no one Knox could see looked like they belonged to a Triad, or lived in constant fear of one. There were no obvious thugs guarding the alley or standing lookout, no telltale bulges on people's hips or under their jackets. In fact, the only person who looked out of place was the man Knox could see through the windscreen striding down the pavement towards the alley. He had European features, close-cropped sandy hair and a short beard, and was wearing a neat black suit. He looked serious, like he was on his way to an important meeting.

Knox nodded to Zhou and they both watched the man as he got closer to the alley, then turned in to it without slowing down or breaking stride.

'Maybe you're right,' Knox said as he reached to open his door. 'They say the devil dresses well.'

'What are you doing?' Zhou asked.

'Seeing where he's going. Want to come?'

'I can't. This is a police car. It will have been noticed. I've already been here too long. And I won't be able to protect you if you go in there after him.'

It was the reply Knox had expected. He was surprised Zhou had let them linger as long as she had. But something about the man who was rapidly disappearing felt like a thread Knox wanted to pull on.

'I'll be careful,' he said, climbing out of the car. 'Meet me back here in twenty minutes.'

Zhou looked like she wanted to say something else. But she didn't, she just nodded, and pulled out into a gap between two overloaded trucks as soon as Knox had shut his door.

Knox waited for his own opening before jogging across the road.

They'd parked too close to the alley for him to try to clean himself of a tail before he headed into it. Plus the man in black had a head start and Knox was already concerned about losing him in the city of darkness.

He slowed to a casual but purposeful walk as he reached the opposite pavement, mimicking his mark, then turned in to the alley – and immediately appreciated how accurate the Cantonese name for the walled city actually was.

He was instantly plunged into deep shadow. The humidity of the street became a hot dampness, and his nostrils were assaulted by the smell of decaying meat, fish, and rubbish.

After a few moments of walking blind but keeping his pace even as if he knew exactly where he was going, his eyes adjusted and the insides of the City of Darkness began to emerge.

He saw glimmers of light poking through gaps high above him and emanating from lower holes and gashes, light that hinted at the lives that inhabited the place and gave him the briefest warning when his feet were about to hit a puddle of what he hoped was old rainwater. Then, after a few more yards the alley opened up a little, became brighter and wider. Electric lights were strung along its walls and down its middle. On both sides of him he could now see through doorways that revealed tiny kitchens, factories, laundries and even, judging from the two openings next to each other with rows of ivory-white false teeth displayed between them, dentists.

Knox was in a hidden high street. And it was busy.

Noisy too. The walled city might be lawless, he thought, but there was an order to it. The wires that stretched over his head were haphazard, but they were there and they worked. And while some of the faces he saw on the people he passed were hard and suspicious, most displayed the passive blankness of completely normal people doing completely normal things.

He couldn't imagine any of the doors he passed having an industrial-scale drug factory behind them, complete with long rows of vats, centrifuges, enormous pestles and ovens, or whatever else was used to create Blue Peacock. But then again, there was plenty of walled city for such an operation to be tucked away in.

Knox kept going, keeping his gait relaxed and casually avoiding any eyes that might land on him.

After another hundred yards he realised he could no longer see his target ahead of him, and began to worry that he'd missed the man ducking into one of the high street's less well-lit corners. But then he spotted him in the distance, his head briefly haloed as it passed under a lamp strung between junctions. Knox dared to pick up his pace, confident that the background cacophony of afternoon shopping would cover the quickening of his feet.

The man had turned left at the junction, which, Knox discovered, led to a bare concrete staircase.

Knox followed it up to the next level and found another junction – and no sign of his mark. The routes to his left and right looked identically dark. He flipped a coin in his head and went right. After a few paces he found himself on a metal grille walkway suspended over the alley. For a brief moment it reminded him of the end of his chase with Rabe through Euston. He put the image of the giant

Scotsman plummeting down onto the Tube platform out of his mind and continued on. To an abrupt dead end.

Almost immediately on the other side of the alley the way was blocked off, bricked up with old, uneven cinder blocks.

Knox doubled back, clattering across the grille and racing through the junction, inwardly scolding himself for his bad guess.

There were more doorways in this direction, and Knox could tell from the dark-red glows, heady aromas, and wafts of smoke that emanated from them that he'd entered a very different part of the walled city – a district that bore much closer relation to Zhou's descriptions of the place. Had he ended up pursuing someone who was simply intent on paying for sex or another brief high? He hoped his initial instinct was correct and the man was on his way to a different kind of appointment.

Knox continued on, shaking his head at a pair of eyes and a bare arm that drew back a heavy curtain as they heard him approaching, and reached another turn. The corridor narrowed, squeezing its way between two buildings that didn't quite reach each other. The light faded again. Knox had to turn to his side to fit through the tightest parts, and ducked and weaved his way through the tangle of boxes and pipes on the other side. It wasn't a route anyone would take in error, but he could tell from the smudged footprints in the sparse wells of light that several people had recently traversed it.

This, he thought, might be where someone would hide an illegal drug lab. He found himself thinking of Rabe again, and the clinical cleanness of his subterranean lair. He wondered if the filthy mess he was currently navigating was intended to deter curious wanderers or if he'd discover Blue Peacock being created in extremely less than sterile conditions beyond it.

Once he'd clambered through the maze, he was about to start sprinting again, then realised he might not need to. Twenty yards ahead of him was a single door, slightly ajar. He shuffled over to it, and paused to hear what was on the other side.

Voices.

He couldn't tell how many, or what they were saying. The only thing he could do was gently nudge the door, hoping he could open it wide enough to peer through without drawing attention. Thankfully, the constant damp hadn't rusted its hinges yet and it swung open easily and silently.

Inside was a large room. Not a factory but some kind of warehouse, three times the size of the cavernous space White had hollowed out of the middle of MI5 headquarters. Its edges were lined with piles of boxes and stacked barrels, but in the centre was a wide, clear area lit by a cluster of tube lights suspended from its double-height ceiling, and a circle of six well-dressed people, including Knox's man in black.

Knox couldn't resist creeping inside and ducking behind a pallet of barrels that smelled like they were full of oil.

The six people were all speaking in turn. They were an even split of men and women and a mix of ethnicities, but they all spoke Cantonese, which meant he had no idea what they were talking about. Until he heard his man, another who appeared Chinese, and a woman Knox would have pegged as Central American all say the one phrase he knew:

Lán kŏng què.

Blue Peacock.

Knox tried to imprint the faces of the four people he could see clearly in his mind as they continued with their apparent reports for another five minutes. Then, as if they were responding to a timer only they could hear, they all stopped speaking and waited in total silence as each one of them left the warehouse alone.

Knox remained crouched in his hiding place for another two minutes after the last of them had gone, giving them enough time to get through the assault course outside before he followed them.

However, as he finally got up to make his way to the door he realised there'd been a seventh stranger in the room with him the whole time, hiding directly across from him.

Except they weren't a stranger to Knox.

He watched, dumbfounded, as they stepped out into the light, a smirk on the lips below a pair of piercing blue eyes, and said, 'You're a long way from Leconfield House,' in an unmistakable Midwestern accent.

CHAPTER 26

'What on earth is Abey Bennett doing in Hong Kong?' Knox asked after another bamboo basket of steaming dough parcels had been slid onto the small mahogany table between them in the back of the quiet dim sum restaurant in Wan Chai.

It was three hours since they'd left Kowloon Walled City, Knox first and then Bennett, after they'd agreed to regroup on Hong Kong Island.

Knox had told Zhou most of what he'd found inside the walled city: the clandestine meeting, the mention of Blue Peacock; but not the appearance of a CIA field agent he had history with.

'The same thing as Richard Knox, from the looks of it,' Bennett replied, her familiar smirk on her face as she deftly picked up one of the parcels with a pair of chopsticks and blew steam off its top. 'Sticking my nose where people don't want it.'

Knox looked at the woman sitting opposite him. The woman who had helped him expose a mole in MI5 six years ago, and then brought Williams back to him. She seemed more relaxed, confident, comfortable in herself and her surroundings than when he'd last seen her a year ago. Her jet-black hair had grown out a little from its defiant pixie cut – it was a little less provocative, a little more anonymous. But her blue eyes still retained that intense, searching quality they'd always had – the eternal determination of someone forever outside the centre to prove that they were able, they were better, they belonged.

'You dropped off the radar after the Kosygin incident,' Knox said, clumsily trying to balance a large dim sum between his chopsticks before giving up and stabbing it through the middle.

'I could say the same about you,' she replied.

'I've been taking care of Jack. It ended up being a longer assignment than any of us expected.'

'I heard that. Sounded like a cover.'

He smiled, wondering if she was bluffing or if the CIA had really kept such close tabs on him and, by extension, Williams. 'I assure you it wasn't.'

She took a swig of her near-empty bottle of beer and signalled the old man who was both chef and waiter for two more. 'How is Jack?'

'Good, thank you. He'd have sent his best if he'd known I'd be seeing you. But, again, why am I seeing you?'

'Langley finally got sick of station chiefs complaining that I wasn't following their rules, so they sent me somewhere there weren't so many to get in my way. The Wild East.'

'Vietnam?'

'I skipped that one, thank God. I was in the Philippines for a while, then Taipei, Seoul, and Hong Kong the last couple of months.'

Her tone was almost boastful, but that didn't sound like the career trajectory of a rising star to Knox. It felt more like the CV of someone the agency couldn't fire but wanted out of the way. Of course, Knox knew Bennett's whole career in the CIA had been built on her superiors trying to sideline her and her proving their prejudices wrong. It was how she'd become such an important ally to him. It also made him more curious about why she'd been in the walled city. Was she there on orders, or following a hunch against them?

'Your turn,' she said.

'Just a simple chaperone job,' he replied.

'Which was why I found you crouching behind a barrel.'

'In a roundabout way.'

The right-hand side of Bennett's mouth crept up, a sign that she knew Knox wasn't being completely honest with her, but that she wasn't going to push him too hard over it. 'Tell me about your new partner.'

Knox wasn't surprised Bennett had watched him leave the walled city and be picked up a few moments later by Zhou, who had barely pulled alongside the kerb long enough for him to climb into the Mercedes before speeding off again.

'My local liaison.'

'Special Branch?'

He nodded.

'The chaperone's chaperone.'

Their new beers arrived, along with another bamboo basket. Knox wondered if dim sum would keep coming until they started sending it back. Bennett thanked the man in Cantonese.

'Technically this is breakfast food, but I like a place that doesn't stand on tradition,' she said to Knox as she lifted the lid to reveal their next course.

'You've picked up the language quickly,' he replied.

'Just a few phrases. Hello. Thank you. I'm not a communist. What about you?'

Knox looked around the restaurant. No one had come in after them, and the few other customers were far enough away not to hear their conversation. There had been no lingering glances in their direction, no twitching eyebrows or ears, no excuses to move tables or repeated trips to the bathroom. It was time, he decided, to tip another hand.

'Only one. *Lán kǒng què.*'

Bennett's eyes widened, and managed to turn an even more intense shade.

'Blue Peacock,' she said, her voice almost a whisper.

'You're familiar?'

'There's talk it's some new Maoist cult that wants to turn the whole world Red.'

Knox thought about the meeting they'd both spied on. They didn't strike him as a bunch of zealots with global ambitions. They were an international group, but they looked more like division heads of a corporate conglomerate than cultists.

'The people in the walled city? Didn't seem the type.'

'Communists come in all shapes and sizes, and they don't always have a red star pinned on their cap.'

Knox conceded the point, remembering the very similar exchange he'd had with Zhou in Lady Reeve's apartment, and that he himself hadn't looked any different from the protestors in Peel Street.

'Do you know who they are?'

Bennett shook her head. 'I've seen a couple of them before in different combinations, but not all together at once. How do you know about Blue Peacock?'

He told her about Lady Reeve. 'I was supposed to escort her back to London, but when I went to see her in Victoria Prison she was incoherent, babbling "Blue Peacock" over and over. The next time I saw her she was dead. Zhou, my liaison, is convinced it's a new drug. One that can easily kill, or that someone will kill to keep secret.'

Bennett's eyes narrowed. 'If their plan is to use a drug to destabilise the West then Hong Kong is the perfect place to flood it from.'

'It would be hard to claim the moral and political high ground on top of a pile of addicts and corpses,' Knox said.

'Or put up a fight if you're out of your mind,' Bennett added.

They stared at the basket of rapidly cooling dim sum. It seemed they had both suddenly lost their appetites.

'Of course,' Knox said eventually, attempting to lighten the mood a touch, 'we don't know for certain that's what's happening.'

'No,' Bennett replied. 'But we need to work out whatever is going on quickly.'

'Why?'

'Because I've also learned the days of the week in Cantonese, and the people in the walled city kept talking about something that's supposed to happen on Monday.'

'Today's Friday.'

'Yes,' Bennett said, signalling the old man for the bill, 'it is.'

CHAPTER 27

Bennett hadn't technically lied, but she also hadn't told Knox the whole truth – not about what had happened to her in the past year, how she'd ended up in Hong Kong, or why she was really interested in Blue Peacock. She didn't feel too bad about it, though. Because she knew Knox hadn't been completely honest with her either. MI5 didn't send its most senior agents across the world simply to collect private citizens, even if their father was a political figure. He was here for another reason.

And she could tell what he thought about the potted career history she'd given him. She was fine with that, too. She preferred to be underestimated – including by people she hoped she could still consider her friends.

The question she needed to answer was, was Knox's presence in Hong Kong directly related to Blue Peacock, or was it something completely different and their agendas were now overlapping purely by chance?

She'd planned to spend her evening in her small apartment several twisting alleys away from the dim sum restaurant, mulling over which possibility would be better – and safer – for her and Knox. But, after walking through the warren of turns that led to her home enough times to be sure there was no one else in it with her, she stopped fifty feet short of her building's entrance.

The street Bennett had lived on for the last two months was one of Hong Kong's standard contradictions – old faded pink and blue blocks with exposed balconies wrapping round them, newer, taller buildings plated in smooth concrete and glass, tiny shops butting up against even smaller temples. And on the kerbstone in front of one of the gaudier places of worship and reflection, whose front was festooned with ornate carvings and intricate bamboo latticework, almost invisible in the pool of phosphorescent yellow beneath a street lamp, was a thin white chalk dash.

An hour later she was sitting at the back of a low-ceilinged bar on D'Aguilar Street on Lan Kwai Fong.

By day, Lan Kwai Fong was street-hawker territory, covered with stalls selling food, homewares, and pretty much anything else. By night, the vendors were replaced by men and women in various states of undress tempting passers-by into basement bars and nightclubs.

Bennett didn't like it.

She understood the need to blow off steam and escape the humidity that lingered outside long into the evening in summer, the appeal of an ice-cold beer or strong martini to soothe a mind and loosen a body. But something about Lan Kwai Fong's claustrophobic topography of tight spaces and music so booming it became physical meant it was not a relaxing place. It was frantic, manic, pressured. People competed to be the funnest, dumbest, loudest.

And so did the venues. There were Irish-themed pubs, clichéd oriental fantasias, bare rooms lined with speakers that blasted atonal noise. The bar she was in, mercifully, favoured Motown and was decorated almost entirely in deep orange velvet.

The tension between workers and the police that had swept across the city in waves for the last couple of months was nothing compared to a regular Friday night in Lan Kwai Fong. It felt like the whole district was always one spilled drink away from exploding and turning revellers into rioters.

Which, Bennett was forced to acknowledge, made it the perfect cover.

The chalk mark was old-school, a coded language invented by drifters and the homeless to tell each other where was safe to sleep or where a good, free meal could be had, and co-opted by spies to signal when a dead drop had happened or an extraction or meeting was needed.

The mark Bennett had seen, and casually smudged with the side of her shoe as she passed the temple and her apartment building without slowing or looking at it, was requesting the latter. Though, it wasn't really a request. It was an instruction.

She'd ordered two beers when she'd arrived – draught this time – and found the small table at the back of the bar, where she'd been nursing one of them for almost half an hour.

The bar was busy with the kind of people Bennett spent most of her time avoiding. The type who swamped Asian cities in falsely friendly groups and got to call themselves *expats* by virtue of their ethnicity or social standing, rather than *migrant* or *itinerant*.

So far, no one had bothered her, joked that her date had abandoned her or that she shouldn't drink alone. However, as she glanced at her watch, she wondered if she had in fact been stood up. The protocol for these meetings was simple – a drink at seven o'clock on D'Aguilar Street. This was her fourth summons, and she was in the fourth bar on the street's south side, so, unless another one had somehow squeezed itself between the three she'd already visited, she was in the right place.

After another ten minutes the crowd in front of her began to shuffle and part, making way for a tall, swaying figure in the white uniform of a US Navy seaman. He looked drunk, just another sailor making the most of his shore leave. But Bennett knew he was neither of those things. He was her boss.

Ray Mason was an oddity, like Bennett herself. She was, as far as she knew, the CIA's only part-Native American female field agent. And, again as far as her subtle yet extensive digging had revealed, Mason was its only six-foot-five black operative from South Carolina with a passion for fancy dress.

She realised he'd always been in sort of costume whenever they met.

'They don't see me, they see the outfit,' had been his reply when she'd asked him at the end of their very first meeting a day after she'd arrived in Hong Kong why he was dressed as a tram conductor.

After a childhood spent standing out – too dark-skinned for the white children of Lakin, Kansas, too light-skinned to be embraced by her mother's ancestral Kiowa tribe – Bennett worked hard to blend in wherever she went, to fade into the fabric of a situation. Mason, however, took the opposite approach. And, Bennett had to admit, it appeared to work. She doubted any of the morass of people he was wading through to reach her would actually remember a single detail about him beyond the uniform.

When he got to her, he grabbed the still-full pint glass and took a long, large gulp before dramatically collapsing onto the stool opposite her, as if he was exhausted from some epic trek rather than about to quiz her about her visit to Kowloon Walled City.

For all Bennett's waiting and Mason's performance, the debriefing lasted barely five minutes.

'Fun trip?' he asked, leaning into her as if he was offering a heartfelt, slurred apology for his tardiness.

'A bit of a dud,' she replied, a coded response, and an incomplete one. 'Just the usual gang.'

She took a sip of her beer, ignoring how warm and flat it had become.

'When's the next outing?'

'A few of us are thinking about getting together tomorrow.'

'So soon?'

She shrugged. 'To make up for today.'

Mason raised his glass in a mock toast. 'Here's hoping.'

She offered hers up too, then said, 'I did bump into an old friend today out of the blue.'

'Old friend or old flame?' Mason asked, grinning. 'Should I be scared?'

She forced a blush. 'Nothing like that, and nothing you need to worry about.'

Mason's smile widened, and his southern accent deepened. 'Well, you just let me know if I need to get all gentleman-like and defend your honour.'

'I can handle him,' she said.

'I bet you can,' he replied.

Then he drained the rest of his glass, stood up, saluted her, and lumbered his way back into the crowd.

As the bodies briefly parted and swallowed Mason up, Bennett rolled the bottom edge of her glass in circles across the top of the table and considered him. The spy who loved to put on a show. Who had a fetish for analogue tradecraft. Who made himself obvious to become invisible. Who claimed to have personally requested her transfer. Who was so eager to encourage her investigation into Blue Peacock. Who she'd withheld information from. And she thought, as she did after every one of their evening meetings, about just how little she trusted him.

CHAPTER 28

Bennett didn't know it, but Knox was only a few hundred yards away from her, nursing his own drink and musing about the limits of trust.

After he and Bennett had left their late-lunch-cum-early-dinner, he'd headed to Sheung Wan to check if anything had come from Lady Reeve's relatives about the post-mortem and send a fresh request to Leconfield House on the off-chance Pipistrelle might have picked up some chatter about Blue Peacock somewhere.

When he reached Bonham Strand and buzzed Avalon Logistics there was no answer. He tried three times, as well as the dummy office on the next floor, before he resorted to pressing buttons at random and was eventually let in by someone.

Hong Kong Station was deserted, its lights off and door off its latch.

Knox stilled himself, pressing his body against the corridor wall and slowing his breathing. He ran his fingers up and down the door frame, feeling for any signs of forced entry, then nudged it open and stepped into the office, tensing his body in case he needed to duck a fist or dodge a bullet. But there was no one there. No balaclava-clad invaders. And no staff.

The early-evening light cast vague, ominous shadows on the walls and bookshelves, but they all refused to move no matter how much Knox stared at them.

The main office was ramshackle, but not quite ransacked. Its disordered stacks were still teetering at the same perilous angles they had been last time Knox had visited. He decided, as he made his way over to Charlie's desk, that the Service's Hong Kong outpost had not been broken into.

Knox checked the time – still business hours, just. He wondered if Atwood and Charlie were actually off working somewhere, collecting information, meeting informants, or doing something so urgent they'd forgotten to lock the door on their way out. Or if they'd knocked off early and it was just rank incompetence and laziness that had made basic security slip their minds.

He flicked on a lamp balanced on a pile of old ledgers and shuffled through the papers it lit up, hoping to spot a communiqué from London and an answer to at least one of the questions rattling around his brain. Then he froze again as he heard a low, long groan behind Atwood's door.

A few moments later it opened and the SLO stumbled out. He wasn't clutching his stomach, trying to stem blood gushing from a knife wound, or nursing a bruise that had turned a temple bright purple. He was confused, dishevelled, his jacket – lilac today – askew, and tie loose round his neck. He looked like he'd just woken up.

Atwood appraised Knox with glassy eyes, as if he was trying to place him, remember where he recognised him from. Then his brow furrowed.

'I was wondering when we might see you again,' he said, lumbering over to a light switch and obliterating the shadows.

'Thought I'd check in,' Knox replied. 'In case there'd been an update from HQ.' When Atwood's forehead creased even further, he added, 'about Lady Reeve.'

'Oh, yes.' Atwood patted his jacket pockets, but didn't pull anything out of them. 'Too late, I'm afraid. She's already on her way home.'

'When did you find that out?'

More patting. 'Heard earlier this afternoon, I believe.'

'When were you planning on letting me know?' This time Knox didn't hide the irritation in his voice.

Atwood looked affronted and stopped searching for whatever he'd been hunting for. 'When you appeared. Don't know where you're staying, do we?'

Now Knox was annoyed at himself. The other man was right. He hadn't told them which hotel he'd moved to. But even his omission was still an indictment of Hong Kong Station's competency – if they'd been any good at their jobs they'd have found out.

In that instant he decided he wasn't going to tell Atwood about his trip to Kowloon Walled City, or Blue Peacock and the different theories that had been posited by representatives of Special Branch and the CIA about what it could be. He'd send his next message to London himself.

Knox watched the SLO's face brighten at the half-point he'd scored.

'Anyway,' Atwood said, 'how's the investigation going?'

'Stalled,' Knox replied, doing his best to make it sound like all the wind had been taken out of his sails and that this was the true source of his irritation.

'Ah, shame. I'm sure Zhou is feeling sore too. That one doesn't like letting things go.'

'Me neither, but I think on this occasion we'll have to.'

Atwood affected a sage nod, then started towards his office door. 'Heading home then?'

'I thought I may as well take the weekend, maybe see what the Dragon Boat Festival is all about, then I'll be out of your hair.'

'Then it was a pleasure, if a short one,' Atwood said. 'Enjoy London when you get back,' he added, a wistful look spreading across his face. 'Summer's the only time I really miss the city.'

'I will,' Knox replied, offering his own nod and a smile in return for Atwood's sudden moment of sincerity.

Knox left Sheung Wan and walked to the Waylian, checking he'd placed the city's landmarks in the right place in his head. He made it back without any wrong turns, and by the time he strolled into the foyer he'd composed the message he was going to send to Leconfield House via one of the lobby phones.

Once he had, he felt the urge for a drink, but not in his room or the hotel bar. He asked the concierge for a recommendation for somewhere quiet with a good view and, after showering and picking out a fresh outfit, he walked down into Central to the corner of Pedder Street and Des Voeux Road and a cocktail bar eight storeys up that looked down over a bright, wide junction busy with evening shoppers.

The bar was elegant, restrained. Straight edges, polished surfaces, a perfectly pitched rumble of jazz-muffling conversations. And peopled by clientele and staff who all seemed preternaturally attractive and serene, as if they belonged to a better world than the one they hovered above. The petty concerns of wage levels, workers' rights and political philosophy were nothing to do with them. They were the type Williams used to call 'beautiful ones' whenever he and Knox saw them float out of a black cab and into a hideously overpriced restaurant somewhere in Mayfair, their expensive shoes seemingly hovering above the London pavement. He was glad he'd changed clothes.

After being shown to a vacant table in the corner of the bar's balcony and considering its comprehensive drinks list, Knox had opted for a gin and tonic. The first one he drank quickly, its coolness helping his body adapt to the slight drop in temperature with the setting sun. The second one he savoured.

Knox had expected to be irritated by Atwood. He hadn't antici-pated pitying him. However, the short glimpse of the sad man too long separated from his homeland hiding under the SLO's cavalier bravado wasn't enough for Knox to want to bring him into Blue Peacock and give him the chance to prove that he might actually be of some value to Queen and country. He'd proved himself too incompetent and too slack to be worth the risk. It was better for everyone that he didn't know what Knox was up to.

Of course, Knox was still guessing what the risks associated with Blue Peacock might actually be, because he still couldn't be one hundred per cent certain what it was. Bennett seemed to agree with Zhou's theory that it was a drug, but the evidence was less than circumstantial, the only possible lead currently interred in the cargo hold of a commercial jet somewhere on its way back to Britain. And yet, even though Knox didn't have an alternative to proffer, as he finished his drink and ordered a third from a hovering waiter in a sharply cut suit he found himself willing one to materialise out of thin air.

He saw again Lady Reeve lying in front of him, delirious, writhing, no idea of who or where she was, mind gone then life too. Then he pictured the same fate befalling even one or two of the other patrons in the bar, or members of the crowd milling in the streets beneath him. People at dragon boat parties collapsing in chaotic agony. The drug appearing in London, Paris, New York, San Francisco. A pandemic that could spread round the globe before people even realised it was happening.

Knox wasn't a stranger to death, he'd seen it enough in gruesome configurations throughout his life, but the idea of losing your control, your identity, yourself in slow, painful, irreversible terror disturbed him deeply. So, as much as he trusted Bennett, he also hoped she was wrong.

His next drink arrived with a wide, professional smile from the waiter.

There was nothing he could do right now. He'd signalled Leconfield House for help, and arranged to meet Bennett in the morning and take a more thorough look at the walled city. He could hardly go table to table telling people to stay away from something that might kill them but also might not exist without looking like the one who'd lost his grip on reality. He had to wait, investigate, find something to back up the current hypothesis or point towards a new one.

All he could really do for the moment was shake the image of the waiter's grin turning rictus and his eyes rolling back into his head and try to enjoy the view.

CHAPTER 29

The MS *Tasman* arrived in Hong Kong almost a week late. Bad weather and high waves in the Bay of Bengal had kept the boat anchored off Chennai on the eastern side of India for three days. Then, after making a break across to the Andaman Sea and the Malacca Strait, they'd been delayed another three by a backlog of ships ahead of them at Port Swettenham on the Malaysian coast.

Six days added onto a trip that had taken almost two months was not that unusual, but until the distant lights of the Kowloon docks started to appear out of the night over the *Tasman*'s prow, every extra hour the boat was at sea made the chief mate more anxious. Because Friday was the last day the two crates that had been loaded into the hold at Piraeus could reach Hong Kong if he was going to get the second half of the payment he'd been promised for arranging their transport to the other side of the planet.

The chief mate had no idea what was inside the two large wooden boxes. But that wasn't so unusual either – he also didn't know what the rest of the *Tasman*'s hold was filled with beyond the vague descriptions and codes that filled the ship's manifest, and didn't really care. He used to. He used to make it his business to know exactly what he was risking his life to ferry across the planet, out of both pride and caution. But he was tired of the sea. Tired of the endless complaints from below him and orders from above. Tired of the rewards of his position never matching the responsibilities. He'd planned for this to be his last run. He wanted it over, and the longer it wasn't the more it grated on him.

He'd taken out his growing irritation on the crew. They had assumed it was the combined result of being behind schedule and a man down. No one had noticed Visser's disappearance until after the *Tasman* had left Port Tewfik at the southern end of the Suez Canal, but when they did the rumour quickly spread that he'd got homesick and snuck off the ship. The chief mate didn't correct it.

He felt bad for killing Visser. He'd actually liked the young man. His eagerness to impress reminded him of the determination that had driven him out onto the high seas and quickly up the ranks of the Dutch merchant navy twenty years ago. Though perhaps that was also why he'd reacted the way he had to discovering him snooping through the hold – he was an echo of a version of the chief mate that wasn't jaded and didn't hate what his life had become.

Attacking Visser had been impulsive. He could have spun him another lie, assigned him to duties that would have kept him far away from the hold for the rest of the trip, maybe even brought him in on his secret, an extra pair of eyes and ears to keep watch over whatever it was that was about to pay for his retirement. But there was no point dwelling on the what-ifs. It was done and there was no way to undo it. And, by the time the man's family realised he was never coming back to them and started asking questions, the chief mate would be long gone.

He stood at the captain's side on the *Tasman*'s bridge as it manoeuvred its way through Kowloon's vast dockyards to its berth, relaying the orders everyone around him knew to follow without prompting one last time.

Once the ship was secured, and the captain had congratulated him and the rest of the bridge crew for getting the ship all the way to Hong Kong in one piece, he went down to oversee the unloading.

The hold was now full to capacity and it needed to be completely emptied. The crew worked fast to get it done, so they could disappear before the night got too late and scratch whatever personal itches they hadn't been able to for the last two months. The dock workers were keen to finish quickly as well – the *Tasman* was the last arrival of the night, and the sooner it was unloaded the sooner they could go home.

After a few hours of hard work, the ship was sitting considerably higher in the water and the floodlights that had lit it up along with the dockside next to it started to shut off.

The chief mate watched most of the crew wander off towards the city, joking and goading each other in small groups. Then, checking that the few poor souls who had ended up on watch duty for the first night in Hong Kong weren't paying attention to the dock, he headed to the warehouse beyond the one where all but two crates from the *Tasman* had been taken. No one but him had noticed the forklift carrying the large boxes from the very back of the hold to a different storage area. And even if they had, they wouldn't have thought anything of it – the rhymes and reasons of port logistics weren't their concern.

This was the last part of his job. The handover that would end with him leaving the docks richer than the whole crew of the *Tasman* combined and multiplied several times.

After half an hour of silently leaning against the crates in the dark of the warehouse the chief mate's nerves started to return. His contact should have known when to meet him. Once they'd finally been ready to leave Port Swettenham, the ship's radio officer had sent a message to Hong Kong with an updated arrival time. And, given how close he'd ended up to the end of the delivery window – through no fault of his own, he would argue if someone were to mention it – he'd imagined he'd find someone waiting for him, as eager to complete their transaction as the *Tasman*'s crew and the dock workers had been.

Another ten minutes went by without anyone else appearing, and the chief mate started to wonder if he was going to have to spend the whole night guarding the crates to make sure whoever eventually did turn up to collect them would give him what he was due.

He felt his body whispering to him that it would need sleep soon, and began pacing up and down in front of the crates to keep himself awake. He started off marching just a few feet before turning round and retracing his steps, but soon enough was covering lengths of the whole warehouse.

He passed the crates over and over, keeping his mind awake by fantasising about the plane ticket he would buy for wherever he wanted to go once he was done enjoying the delights of Asia. Then, on perhaps the tenth time, he noticed something had appeared next to them. A rough block of concrete about the size of a small boulder. It was in shadow, tucked up against the side of one of the crates, but he was sure it hadn't been there before.

He leaned down over it to take a closer look, and had just noticed the length of chain that had been wrapped round its jagged bulk when a silenced bullet sliced through the nape of his neck and severed his spinal cord.

CHAPTER 30

The pageantry was farcical. But, as far as Knox understood it, that was the point.

The Jardine Noonday Gun was fired at midday, every day. It was a tradition and a punishment. In the 1860s Jardine Matheson's private militia had taken to firing it whenever one of their executives sailed up to their offices on the Hong Kong Island harbourfront. The navy took exception to the company's co-option of a practice usually reserved for military officers and high-ranking government officials. So, as a bizarre penalty, it was ordered to fire the gun daily at 12 p.m. forever. When land reclamation had shifted the northern edge of the island, the gun was moved to its current location next to the Causeway Bay typhoon shelter. The Japanese had disassembled it during their occupation of the colony, but it had been replaced once they'd surrendered.

'So very British,' Bennett had said at the end of her explanation of its curious history.

The gun was also a tourist attraction and, being close to the Star Ferry terminal, it usually drew a crowd. Which was why Bennett had chosen it for their rendezvous.

Knox had expected her to want to return to Kowloon Walled City first thing – like he did after his short morning shower had been filled with more visions of frozen grimaces and cloudy eyes – but he saw the logic in her suggestion that they wait until the middle of the day. It was Saturday now, a day when a couple of

Westerners snooping round the walled city early in the morning would draw attention. By waiting a few hours, they were less likely to be noticed.

The atmosphere of the city seemed lighter to Knox today. Maybe it was just that it was the weekend, or maybe people were already starting to embrace a more celebratory, relaxed spirit ahead of the Dragon Boat Festival. Knox hadn't heard any Mandarin slogans or top ten singles blaring over the rooftops on the way down to the harbour, and the rows of high-speed police interceptors he could see next to the sampans and smaller junks that called the typhoon shelter seemed overly aggressive, serious, and out of place.

The water in the bay was calmer too. No typhoon signal had been hoisted, and the only waves sloshing against the reclaimed promenade were caused by the wakes of criss-crossing boats. At least the meteorological threat to the city had evaporated for the time being.

Knox and Bennett mingled among the tourists who had come out to watch the Jardine guard pull the lanyard that fired the light blue Hotchkiss three-pounder. Then, once a few of them had given a muted round of applause and the guard had marched off, they strolled over to the Star Ferry terminal. Where they found Zhou waiting for them, next to her Mercedes.

Knox had assumed she wasn't the type of police officer who would take the weekend off in the middle of an investigation, but she didn't know about his and Bennett's conversation the previous night. He'd intended to fill her in if and when they found anything in the walled city. Instead, he found himself introducing her to another ally of his a little earlier than planned.

'Captain Madeleine Zhou, meet Abey Bennett,' Knox said once he was back in the Mercedes' passenger seat, Zhou was behind the wheel, and Bennett was perched in the middle of the rear seats.

'I'm aware of Miss Bennett's identity,' Zhou replied.

'I'm honoured,' Bennett said, with a smirk. 'And for the record, I know who you are too.'

Zhou didn't return Bennett's smile. She hadn't exactly warmed up over the last couple of days, but Knox had liked to think he'd got the police officer's guard down a little. Now it seemed firmly in place again. He wasn't sure if it was because she sensed – or knew – he hadn't got round to sharing all his information, or the presence of a CIA agent, or both.

With a cautious nod from Bennett, he filled Zhou in on what they were about to do.

'You wanted to go there without telling anyone and without backup?' she said once he was done.

'I wanted to know if there was anything to add to our theory before I brought it to you,' Knox replied, answering the question he knew was lurking under Zhou's rhetorical one.

'I've been to the walled city a couple of times and never had much of a problem,' Bennett added.

'Then you've been lucky,' Zhou replied.

Bennett opened her mouth a fraction, but then apparently thought better of whatever she was about to say.

'How long do you need?' Zhou asked Knox.

'Half an hour at most. We know where we'll be looking.'

Zhou was silent for a long moment, then she turned over the Mercedes' engine.

'Very well,' she said, as she lurched the car away from the pedestrian ferry and drove to the car pier further along the harbour.

Twenty minutes later, during which time Bennett had added a few more details to the physical descriptions of the people she and Knox had observed after he'd followed the sandy-haired man, they reached the walled city. Zhou parked in almost exactly the same spot she'd dropped Knox at across from the alley entrance the day before.

'I'll return here for you,' she said, confirming her lack of intention to join them on their escapade. 'Please do not talk to anyone you don't have to. If Blue Peacock is being manufactured or distributed there, asking questions could put you in more danger.'

'We'll be careful,' Knox said, 'and we'll see you back here shortly.'

He and Bennett got out of the car and were halfway across the lanes of early-afternoon traffic when a truck with a battered and rusted container bolted to its flatbed suddenly stopped directly in front of them, blocking their path.

Knox instinctively looked beyond the truck's cab, checking to see what had prompted the driver to brake, but there was nothing in the road ahead.

The vehicles behind started to blast their horns, but this only lasted a few seconds until the rear of the truck opened and what Knox suspected was about to happen did.

Six men leapt out of the container.

Some of them were wearing shirts, some vests. Half of them had close-cropped hair, half of them had ponytails. All of them were carrying long clubs and short knives.

They went straight for Knox and Bennett.

Knox reacted first, moving between Bennett and the men, and yelling at her to run back to the car, but there were too many of them, and they were too close to get away from.

No one on the road or the pavement came to their aid, raised the alarm or called for help. No one seemed willing to even acknowledge what was happening lest they be attacked too.

Knox took three hard swings to his side, and managed to connect one of his fists with a face before he felt two pairs of hands pin his arms and a thick length of wood pull across his throat. He kept fighting and struggling to free himself until the club was joined by a blade.

He heard Bennett's nearby grunts and shouts abruptly stop and glanced over to where they'd been coming from to see that she also had a knife digging into her neck. Then they were both dragged over to the truck and hauled up into its dark, empty container.

The last thing Knox saw before a thick hood was pulled down over his face was Zhou, unarmed and framed in daylight, squaring up to two of the club-wielding men.

CHAPTER 31

Laing's new career inventing mysteries just preposterous enough to be believed was cut short by the arrival of a real one. Almost as soon as word had reached him that Holland had agreed to the suggestion that he take over the production of the chicken-feed the Service was spooning out to its own agents, both he and White were summoned to the director general's house to discuss Knox's latest report from Hong Kong, and, specifically, its reference to something called Blue Peacock.

It was another first for Laing.

It wasn't unusual for Holland to work from Wytchen House, his imposing home in Highgate that was jokingly referred to as *the cottage*, but normally only senior officers were hosted at the property that had been in Holland's wife Sarah's family of politicians, business leaders and social figureheads for over a hundred years. Laing assumed his invitation must have had something to do with the bug in White's glass box.

'As I seem to be saying rather too frequently at the moment,' Holland said once they'd all read through the decrypted transcription of Knox's message around his kitchen table, 'I don't know what this means. It could be as simple as a new strain of drug or a cult leader with a flair for the dramatic, or something else entirely.'

'Nothing technological comes to mind,' White said. 'But I'll look into it.'

'Likewise,' Laing added, 'I haven't seen anything about any blue peacocks in the archives, but I'll go through them again.'

'Do so,' Holland said to both of them. 'Discreetly.'

Laing had driven a black Ford Consul from the Service pool up to Highgate from Leconfield House. White had strolled to it over the Heath from his own home in Hampstead.

'I'll start on the records once I'm back from seeing Williams,' Laing said as they both walked down *the cottage*'s short front path.

'I'll come up to Hertfordshire with you,' White replied, drawing a quizzical look from his younger colleague. 'Williams might have some idea about this thing, and I could use the country air.'

The drive was quick – what traffic there was on the roads was still making its way into the city rather than out of it – and when they reached Rabley Heath they found its large iron gates open in anticipation of their arrival.

Laing and White had both visited the manor since Williams's return from the dead, but not for several months. The home, and Williams – who was waiting for them on the gravel front drive – looked better than when either of them had last driven up from London to pick his brains about an old thread they'd been trying to pull on or rumour they'd wanted to put to bed.

Laing was glad this trip now had more of a purpose than a few hours ago, but it felt slightly grafted on, and he wasn't sure it would take. At no point in Williams's extensive debriefing sessions had he ever mentioned anything called Blue Peacock, so Laing couldn't imagine the man would now have the answer to the question they were suddenly seeking. But then he reminded himself that he hadn't found anything in the archives that made sense of the two words either, and he was prepared to delve back into them, so he could afford to give Williams a chance, just in case.

'You've been keeping busy,' White said once they'd parked and Williams was leading them round to the rear of the house.

'Still can't get the front door to open properly,' he replied. 'But at least the place isn't quite on the verge of falling apart any more.' Then he gave his visitors a wide but thin grin and added, 'Like its owner.'

The trio stopped in the kitchen briefly as Williams poured a kettle of just-boiled water into a cafetière, then they proceeded into the drawing room. This morning there was no opera blasting from the fireplace, and the curtains and windows had all been flung open.

'Sorry there isn't more of a spread,' Williams said, gesturing to the three cups on the low table in front of the wide sofa as he filled them with coffee. 'I don't have many guests these days.'

Laing recognised the dark emotions skulking under Williams's jovial surface – frustration mixed with resentment.

'So,' Williams continued, sitting in a high-backed chair placed at a right angle to the sofa, 'how is Richard getting on?'

White and Laing moved to either end of the sofa with their coffees.

'Fine,' White said.

'But he's why we're both here,' Laing said. 'He's looking into something we want to ask you about.'

'I guess I'm still useful after all,' Williams replied, offering a slightly less wide smile. 'Just not enough to warrant a trip to headquarters.'

'Actually it's the opposite,' White replied. 'At least for the moment.'

Laing wondered if White was going to spell out the problems at Leconfield House, but the heavy frown that replaced the hollow grin on Williams's face made it clear he'd already extrapolated something close to the reality of the situation.

'Anything I can do to help with that?'

This time the question seemed to Laing to be free of sarcasm, genuine with that deep sense of duty that still burned away at the core of every MI5 officer, himself included, even when they felt overlooked, useless, or abandoned.

However, before either White or Laing could answer, Williams's head tilted, as if he'd heard a noise on a frequency the others couldn't detect, got up from his chair and stepped over to one of the open windows, through which he could see two women walking up the driveway to the house.

'Friends of yours?' he asked as White and Laing left the sofa and stood next to him.

They both shook their heads.

CHAPTER 32

Williams led White and Laing back through the kitchen and to the front of the house to meet the new arrivals.

From a distance the women looked fairly similar, as if they were friends out for a midsummer country wander. But as they got closer Laing could see differences between them. The one on the left seemed calm, relaxed, like she knew where she was going. The one on the right looked like her composure was an act. Her eyes darted between the men and her surroundings, as if she was constantly assessing potential threats and escape routes, while her companion's focus was squarely directed at the owner of Rabley Heath.

'Can I help you?' Williams asked her as the two women and three men lined up ten feet apart.

She answered his question with her own.

'What have they done to you?' Anna said, looking him up and down.

'Do I know you?'

'No,' she replied. 'But I know you.'

Laing sensed Williams tense. Whoever this woman was, it had taken her less than ten seconds to get under his skin.

'And who am I?' Williams asked.

'Someone who shouldn't let themselves be locked up in a cage. Even one as gilded as this.'

'I assume you haven't come for a tour,' Laing said, before the woman could push the man next to him even further. He knew

Williams hadn't lost control of the demons that simmered inside him since he'd been at Rabley Heath, but he also remembered the damage he could do when he did. Laing also wasn't interested in letting this odd interruption to his and White's mission go on longer than it had to. 'So, why are you here?'

His question earned him a smile, and a look that felt like it was simultaneously staring deep into him and right through him.

'I come bearing gifts,' Anna said, gesturing at Valera next to her.

'What?' Valera replied, in a voice that made it clear she hadn't expected to be casually offered up to three strange men.

'Darling, you'll be as safe with these gentlemen as with anyone else, and this is your best chance for putting that brilliant mind of yours to good use again.'

She gave Valera's arm a squeeze, then turned back to the men.

'May I present Irina Valera, the world's greatest living radio physicist.'

White's face, which up until this point had been a mask of confusion, transformed into one of astonishment.

'Welcome to Britain, Miss Valera,' he said, unconsciously taking a step forward. 'My name's Malcolm White.'

'MI5's chief scientist,' Valera replied, recognition now registering on her face.

'Indeed. It's an honour to meet you.'

Laing interjected again, irritated that White had so freely given up his identity to a stranger.

'A gift in exchange for what?' he asked the woman whose name he still didn't know.

Another smile.

'Information,' Anna replied. 'On who's vanishing people.'

'I don't know what you're talking about.'

'Come now, Mr Laing, there's no reason to be obtuse. We're all friends here.'

'Are we?' he replied, covering his surprise at her knowing his name. 'I don't know who you are.'

'Really? You've been at this for a year. How many more clues do you need?'

'She's Line Z,' Williams said, before Laing had a chance to reach the realisation Anna had been leading him to.

'Was,' she corrected Williams.

Laing was torn. He had a new potential source in his quest to learn more about Line Z standing right in front of him. But he didn't have clearance to share sensitive information about ongoing Service operations with a possible foreign agent. And even though White was technically his superior, he wasn't the kind who could give that type of approval.

'I'll have to speak to headquarters,' he said.

'In that case, I guess I'm done here.'

Anna turned to leave, then, a few yards back down the wide gravel path, she called over her shoulder, 'Let me know when you're allowed to talk.'

'How?' Laing instinctively shouted back, then inwardly kicked himself for how desperate he sounded.

'I'll figure that part out,' Anna said, throwing one last smirk his way.

The three men and Valera watched Anna stroll through the gates at the end of the drive, then listened to the sound of an unseen car's door open, engine turn over, and wheels squeal away.

After a few more moments of silence, White took another step forward.

'Would you care to come to London, Miss Valera?' he asked. 'There's something I think I could use your help with.'

Valera looked at him, then again at her surroundings, then shrugged.

'I don't think I have any other choice.'

Williams's attention, which had stayed focused beyond the gates, suddenly snapped back to the people next to him.

'Another coffee before you leave?'

The men all looked at Valera. She gave a cautious nod.

Inside the house, Williams made a fresh cafetière for him, Laing and Valera while White called in to Leconfield House.

'You're Russian,' he said to Valera as he handed her a mug.

'Yes.'

'West. Leningrad?'

'Originally.'

'But then a little further north. There's a trace of something almost Finnish buried deep in your accent. Have you ever spent any time in Karelia?'

Valera's eyes widened. 'How do you know Karelia?'

'Forgive me,' Williams replied. 'I've just had more than a little experience with your mother tongue. I guess it's become a bit of an unconscious skill.'

White came back into the kitchen, looking as close to ecstatic as Laing had ever seen him, and suggested it was time to get on the road.

'I'll follow you out,' Laing said, tacitly reminding him of the still-unaddressed reason for them coming to Rabley Heath in the first place.

When Valera and White were gone – and out of earshot – Williams began clearing up everyone's cups. Laing watched him, struck by how domesticated this trained, damaged killer had become. He wondered how much willpower it had taken for him to not react more explosively to the barbs the woman who had arrived with Valera had levelled at him – or stop himself from leaving with her.

'Well,' Williams said eventually, shaking Laing from his pondering.

'Knox has come up against something called Blue Peacock,' Laing said. 'Don't suppose it means anything to you?'

Williams stared blankly out through the window above the sink for a few long seconds, then he started to laugh.

'Oh God, are they trying to bring that stupid thing back to life?'

Laing raised an eyebrow. 'What stupid thing?'

'Blue Peacock. It was an experimental bomb the army dreamed up in the early fifties. They wanted to bury a load of them across Germany, in case the Soviets decided they wanted to advance a little bit further west after all.'

'How do you know about it?'

'A drunk captain told me about it over a dinner. I'd been training with his regiment. Somehow we'd ended up talking about the biggest crackpot wastes of money we could think of. He thought he was onto a winner. They'd just mothballed the project because they realised the ground got too cold in winter to keep the bomb's mechanism working. Guess what someone suggested as a fix.'

Laing shrugged.

'Chickens,' Williams said. 'They were going to turn each bomb into a coop. Chuck in some birds and feed and use the body heat to make sure the bomb stayed warm enough to keep ticking for a few days.'

It was Laing's turn to let out a short laugh. But it wasn't a mirthful one, because he was already trying to work out the implications of a communist sympathiser in Hong Kong knowing about a long-forgotten and probably highly classified prototype bomb.

'Chickens,' he repeated half to himself. 'I guess White's exploding stoats weren't so stupid after all.'

CHAPTER 33

Anna didn't feel bad about handing Valera over to MI5. She never felt bad about anything she did, which was one of the traits that made her so successful in her chosen profession.

Their short alliance had been mutually beneficial, but it had reached its end. Valera had got Anna closer to whoever was making people disappear than she'd managed by herself, but she didn't actually know anything about them, and now that she was as safe as she could practically be, the chances of them coming after her again were relatively slim. She couldn't be of any further use to Anna, so it was time to move on and continue the hunt.

Anna drove into London.

She had told Valera the truth. She'd never killed anyone from MI5. But she had ended more than one life in Britain, including the most recent time she'd visited the country's capital, just over a year ago. That trip, her last mission for Line Z, had involved two deaths. One planned, one a surprise – a brief, brutal encounter that had resulted in her assailant crumpled over, lifeless, in an alleyway and Anna deciding to lie low and tap into her reserves of international currencies and aliases for a while.

The timing and tactics of that attack had made her think her superiors were trying to clean up after themselves – that they believed Anna, after decades of diligent service and flawless results, had reached the end of her usefulness and was due a permanent retirement. She hadn't complied, but she had taken the hint.

For a full twelve months, she'd avoided doing anything that might have provoked any other interest in her, travelling the world as a woman of sometimes modest and sometimes rather more comfortable means, trying on personae she'd left dormant for years, enjoying seeing if they still fitted or what subtle adjustments were required. Until a conversation in a down-at-heel and near-empty *osteria* in the Spanish Quarter of Naples aroused her curiosity.

Three young men, barely in their twenties and wearing the razor-sharp black suits of recent Camorra indoctrinates, were drunkenly boasting to each other in the booth next to hers about the jobs they'd just been given by their bosses – jobs that, to Anna's mind, would require far more expertise in the arts of intimidation and death than any of them were likely to have at their age. She wanted to know what was going on. So, once she'd finished her dessert baba, which had been doused in sweet wine rather than the traditional rum and topped with wild strawberries, she left her booth, joined theirs, and seduced one of the men.

She took her target, the oldest and also quietest of the three, back to her hotel on Riviera di Chiaia, and her room that looked out over the bay towards Capri and the tip of the Amalfi peninsula. And, after half an hour of sex that made her further question his levels of life experience, she flattered him into revealing that the Camorra was suffering a sudden manpower shortage, because several of its mid-level members had been either killed or vanished in the last two weeks without warning or trace.

It was obvious to Anna that underneath the man's earlier bravado was an acute fear that following his promotion something similar might happen to him. She wondered if he hoped she might comfort him, beyond the orgasm she'd already provided, to quiet the dread inside him a little longer. She didn't. But the next day she did embark on another global tour.

She reactivated her network of feelers and informants, re-engaged with the versions of the world she'd spent her life moving through, and found them all notably reduced.

People who had once been more than willing to talk to her suddenly wouldn't, or couldn't. A whole slew of experts in assassination, wet work and torture had been removed from the face of the planet, and no one appeared to be taking credit for it. While she had no issue with the thinning out of her potential competition from the freelance murder market, she wanted to know who she should thank, or be on her guard against.

She rekindled her suspicions about Line Z – destabilisation had always been one of its preferred modi operandi – however, the more places she went, the more conversations she overheard in dark corners, the more vague newspaper obituaries she read between the lines of, the stronger her belief became that she was tracking the wake of an organisation that had greater resources and reach than even a clandestine autonomous division of the KGB.

Before Colorado, Anna had never seen anyone from this mysterious group in action. The nearest she'd come was in Havana, three weeks ago, when she'd visited a crumbling but brightly painted bungalow in La Vibora and found its tenant, one of the planet's best snipers for hire, lying in the middle of its living-room floor, his throat slit and the blood pooling around him still warm.

She'd wanted to ask the man with the staring eyes in the diner on the outskirts of Delta if Havana had been his handiwork, but he wasn't the talkative type, and had fallen unconscious after fewer slams of his head against the bathroom sink than Anna had expected.

Britain had been the next destination on Anna's itinerary after America. She knew how seriously MI5 had been taking the disappearances from the West's scientific community and wanted to find out if they'd realised operatives as well as assets had been going missing or dying inexplicable deaths. She was also confident no one in British intelligence had any idea who she was, or the full extent of what she'd done on their home turf a year ago. Taking Valera as a peace offering was a bonus.

Superficially, it might have looked like a wasted trip. A dead end. But she could see enough going on beneath the surface to have made it worthwhile.

First, MI5 had managed to capture and tame someone who had clearly once also been a Line Z operative. This told Anna that she may have underestimated the Service's competence after all.

And second, the man called Laing both plainly knew more than he was willing to let on but was also frustrated with the gaps in his own knowledge. He struck her as the driven, determined type, but not so much so that she couldn't manipulate him. This appealed to her.

Anna needed a new lead and, as she weaved through Mayfair and pulled into a parking space a hundred yards along Curzon Street from Leconfield House, she decided that Simon Laing would be it.

CHAPTER 34

Valera had no intention of letting MI5 take care of her. She was, however, content to let its agents drive her back to London.

She sat in the back of the car that had been parked in front of the grand house she'd briefly stepped foot inside, as White, next to her, alternately told her that she didn't have anything to worry about and praised her for various pieces of work British intelligence had apparently credited her with over the years.

Valera refused his reassurance and neither confirmed nor denied any of his assumptions. Because she remembered another very similar conversation she'd had with a British spy six years ago. A conversation that had ended up being yet another set of lies and a knot in the string of betrayals that had seen her passed between the GRU, MI5, and the CIA.

Anna had claimed she'd never killed a member of MI5, but Valera almost had, and she couldn't believe that its operatives wouldn't eventually let their overly civil masks slip and attempt to exact some form of vengeance on her.

She also had no interest in letting the cycle of exchanges she'd already been through once repeat itself again, with her ending up back in Washington or some less pleasant location, explaining her own disappearance to the Americans. However, she was still keenly aware that someone, somewhere, wanted her dead. So, she would do what she'd always done – always, until she'd got sloppy, as Anna had now both pointed out and proved – use the people who wanted to use her, and keep moving.

They passed through the countryside that seemed so flat and unremarkable after Colorado, and along the same quiet lanes and well-tarmacked roads Anna had steered them down barely an hour earlier, at no point letting slip that she intended abandoning her passenger.

She hadn't imagined her and Anna sticking side by side forever. She knew their partnership was one of convenience, and only a few days old. Still, the speed with which it had dissolved stung.

Eventually, they reached the city and Valera and White were dropped off at the rear of a low-rise office block partway down a shopping parade in what felt very much like the outskirts of London.

Valera knew that not every intelligence organisation made its presence as obvious and felt in its capital as the KGB did with the looming Lubyanka in the heart of Moscow, but she found it hard to believe this three-storey building shoved between green-grocers and butchers could be the home of MI5, or even just its scientific division. She'd noticed White's mood becoming more serious the closer they'd got to the city, and she was on her guard as he led her into the building, down a corridor of flickering strip-lights, up a flight of bare concrete stairs, and past a row of doors that each had a different company name on identical signs next to them. However, she knew she couldn't make a break for it just yet. She had no money, little clue about where exactly she was, and none yet about the problem MI5's chief scientist apparently needed her help with – and she wanted at least that leverage first.

She could sense activity behind each door – a quiet shuffle of feet or occasional low cough – but the only person she saw other than White was a short, wide man standing outside the last door in the row, which was opened and marked Avalon Logistics. He was wearing a beige mackintosh despite the warm day, and held a folder in his right hand. His face looked like it had been carved from granite.

White accelerated towards him. Valera didn't. But she needn't have been worried – up close he looked more bored than ominous. He handed White the folder without saying a word, and shuffled past Valera without acknowledging her existence.

The room White led her into was stale and empty – not so much gutted as never really occupied. There were a couple of trestle tables in the middle, lined up under another strip-light, and a small tower of chairs in one of the windowless corners. White dropped the folder on one of the tables and pulled two chairs off the top of the stack.

Valera, now more confused than fearful, shut the door behind them herself, then took the seat offered to her while White opened the folder, flicked through its contents, nodded to himself, and spread out a set of close-up, high-resolution photographs in front of her.

'What do these look like to you?'

She recognised what she was being shown immediately. Or, at least, the elements of it. Limiters, amplifiers, oscillators – the basic components needed for a radio transceiver, all blown up.

Her interest was piqued.

Every intelligence agency on the planet used some sort of eavesdropping device to clandestinely gather information, and Valera had seen schematics or recovered examples of several in her time on both sides of the Iron Curtain. But she was sure White would be more familiar with any recent models and innovations than she was. She wanted to know why this one had stumped him. She also wanted to know how it worked.

Valera wondered if the images also explained why she was where she was right now, which she guessed was some long-dormant and hastily reactivated safe house far away from MI5 headquarters.

'Is this a test?' Valera asked.

'Of my sanity,' White replied.

She noticed that he'd transformed again. He seemed tired, his burst of determined energy gone.

'Do you want to understand them, or stop them?' she asked.

'Whichever means I don't have to worry about how loudly I say goodnight to my wife.'

Valera looked again at the photographs, wondering just how enlarged they were. 'How small are they?'

'Very.'

'Undetectable?'

'Extremely.'

'In that case I need to look at this in person. And in an actual laboratory.'

White nodded again. 'I'll see what I can do.'

CHAPTER 35

Laing went straight back to the School Hall to quietly check the archives for any mention of Blue Peacock before he relayed what Williams had told him to Holland. It was a short trip – there was nothing.

He made his report to the director general in writing, handed it silently to Miss Albury, Holland's secretary, then he retreated to his office to rack his brain about the identity of the woman who had delivered Valera. He knew he didn't stand much chance. Williams was the only person that MI5 had managed to establish with absolute certainty had been a Line Z asset. Even the department's precise position within the KGB's chain of command was still a mystery. Yet, there was a quality to her that he thought he might be able to detect in the archive he'd built up in his own head – a flippancy and flair that might make her stand out if he looked hard enough.

After an hour of rumination, there was a knock at the door. It was Holland.

'We have two problems,' he said, as Laing awkwardly hovered out of his seat for a moment, wondering if he should give up his desk, before the director general sat down in the small leather-backed chair pressed into the corner of the room behind the door. 'Blue Peacock wasn't just a tactical bomb. It was a nuclear one.'

Laing just managed to stop himself from swearing and said, 'That's not good.'

'No, it isn't.'

'Why would someone in Hong Kong want a nuclear bomb?'

'I can't think of a good reason.'

'Might it just be a coincidence? Two completely unrelated things with the same name?'

'It's a possibility,' Holland replied. 'But not a chance we can afford to take. Army intelligence can't confirm yet if one of their prototypes has gone missing, but if it has they've assured me it wouldn't still have a warhead inside.'

'So, we're looking at a hostile government,' Laing said.

Holland removed his glasses and retrieved a small chamois from his trouser pocket.

'Unfortunately, nuclear powers aren't the only ones with access to nuclear weapons,' he said, giving his lenses a quick polish. 'It took the Americans two months and twenty-seven boats to find the warhead they lost over the Mediterranean last year, and that's if they really did, and if they were honest about the number that went missing in the first place.'

Laing remembered the story of the B52 that had collided with a tanker plane while refuelling above Palomares on the southern coast of Spain, sending nuclear bombs tumbling into the sea. The press had dubbed the warhead, finally located by a specially equipped submarine, the *Costa Bomba.*

'What was the Blue Peacock's yield?' he asked.

'Small, thankfully,' Holland replied, putting his glasses back on. 'We can only hope that if someone's got one they haven't been able to work out how to fit a bigger core inside.'

Laing thought about the potential devastation setting off even the most diminutive nuclear bomb could wreak on one of the most densely populated and politically precarious places on the planet. The fallout of such a catastrophe wouldn't be restricted to the few hundred square miles of the colony – it would be a shockwave that wrapped round the world.

Then it occurred to him how open the director general was being. There'd been no talking in code, no hushed request to accompany Holland outside or into White's soundproof box. Was

Laing's little domain so unimportant there was no risk of them being overheard? Or did Holland want whoever might be listening in to know that MI5 was taking Blue Peacock seriously, in case they were somehow connected? Either way, it reminded him that he was just a supporting player.

'Has Knox been told?' he asked.

'That's the second problem,' Holland said, fishing a small folded piece of card from another pocket and tossing it onto Laing's desk.

Laing opened it up and read the transcribed message inside:

Last meeting with European sales representative yesterday afternoon. All business concluded satisfactorily. Assumed en route to London. Avalon Logistics HK.

'He's on his way back?'

'Not as far as I'm aware,' Holland said. 'Or BOAC. But it's also too long since he last checked in, and it's not like Richard to go missing.'

'Does Atwood have people looking for him, and Blue Peacock?'

Holland gave the smallest shake of his head, and let the slightest degree of irritation creep into his voice. 'He's already doing poorly enough with his normal responsibilities. I need you on the next plane out there.'

Laing barely had enough time to process the latest abrupt change in his duties before he was despatched to London Airport with a cover passport, a wallet full of Hong Kong dollars and no other luggage apart from the same report on recent events in the colony Knox had been given, typed up as if it was an academic paper and folded inside his jacket pocket.

He was going to have to keep on the suit he'd already had on for most of a day for at least another full one. But he wasn't about to complain. Firstly, because while he'd be wearing it to travel halfway across the planet he'd be doing it in first class. And secondly, because he'd been given exactly what he'd wanted for so long – a chance to get out of London and prove himself.

Feeling a pang of responsibility, he'd asked Holland about his Line Z work, and the possible lead they now had.

'Six can manage being thoroughly unhelpful by themselves for a few days,' the director general had replied. 'And either Malcolm can question Miss Valera about her friend, or you can on your return.'

Laing hadn't argued with either suggestion.

Once he'd reached the airport and picked up his ticket, he had just enough time for a sandwich in the lounge before he was called to board the first leg of his flight.

His itinerary was not as direct as it could have been – Air France to Paris, Cairo and Bombay, then Air Ceylon to Colombo and Singapore, and finally Cathay Pacific to Hong Kong – but it would still get him to his destination earlier than waiting for the next BOAC through-flight.

He found his seat on the right-hand side of the first-class cabin, settled into the wide, soft leather and fabric, hoping that no one had booked the one next to him, and began to read through the report. It was identical to Knox's except for a small box of statistics buried in some footnotes that outlined what Leconfield House had managed to cobble together about the size and potential yield of Blue Peacock.

Laing liked to think he kept himself well abreast about what was happening across the Commonwealth – his interest driven by his hope that he would eventually get to work in one of its outposts again – but he was still surprised about how rapidly the situation in Hong Kong seemed to be deteriorating.

He'd already gone through the report once by the time the plane pushed back and started to taxi. In fact, he'd become so engrossed in it so quickly he didn't even realise the plane was taking off until he felt the G-force of its acceleration down the runway. He'd missed all the pre-flight announcements, and hadn't paid attention to the appearance of another man in the seat next to him, or the arrival on the opposite side of the cabin of the mystery woman from Rabley Heath.

CHAPTER 36

Knox was in his flat at the top of Kemp House, on Berwick Street in London. And so were a lot of other people. He was at a party. His party. A celebration – for an achievement or victory he couldn't quite remember. Whatever it was didn't really matter. What was important was how happy everyone seemed. How nice it was to have his home filled with people. How beautiful London looked through the living room's wraparound windows.

Holland and his wife, Sarah, were lounging on his Mies van der Rohe Barcelona sofa, deep in conversation with White. Williams was holding forth by the drinks trolley, making Laing and Charlie almost keel over in amusement. Bennett and Zhou were leaning close over the kitchen island, whispering secrets to each other. And Atwood was standing alone in the corner, gazing out at Soho with a beaming smile and bright eyes.

Between all of them other, faceless bodies moved, talked, and danced to the low, percussive music that was playing from invisible speakers.

Knox drifted between the groups, letting the nonsensical sounds and non-words that came out of everyone's mouths wash over him.

He felt good. Happy. Right.

Even when the strangers who filled the spaces between his friends and colleagues kept turning their backs to him so he never saw them from the front, it seemed completely normal. Like they actually didn't have eyes or noses or mouths and their hair, necks, and shoulders were all he was supposed to see – were all they really were.

Bennett began to float. And that felt entirely reasonable too.

Knox watched her gently lift off the floor, giggling as she drifted upwards an inch, then another and another, and Zhou, also sniggering, reached out for her hand and became weightless too.

Their quiet laughter got louder and soon it was joined by more voices. Holland, Sarah, and White were all pointing at the two airborne women, guffawing and lifting their own feet off the floor to see if they would stay in the air. Williams, Laing, and Charlie started pogo-ing up and down, trying to see who could leap as high as Bennett and Zhou and not come back down.

Even Atwood at last turned away from the skyline, which Knox could see was also now bouncing and undulating as buildings swelled, rose and shrank in time with the music, and joined in, hooting with a voice that sounded halfway between a car horn and a cartoon roadrunner.

Then the SLO started jumping too, flapping his arms as if they would keep him aloft, and honking faster and faster. Soon everyone else was doing the same, but it was only Bennett and Zhou who were actually flying, now dancing through the air near the ceiling and squawking down at the crowd beneath them.

Knox willed himself to join in, but suddenly found himself stuck in place. His legs refused to obey him, his hands were stuck firmly by his side, and his lips wouldn't open. And then he realised it wasn't just his limbs and mouth that wouldn't move. No part of him would.

His eyes were fixed upwards, watching Bennett and Zhou glide in and out of view as their yells got more and more deafening. He could no longer feel his chest rising and falling, or air moving in and out of his nostrils. Even his pulse was gone, his heart no longer pumping his blood around his body.

He was static, still, every single atom of his being totally at rest.

It was, he found, extremely peaceful.

CHAPTER 37

Valera expected an excuse, a delay, to be dragged at last to some dungeon somewhere to have the help she'd tentatively offered up forcibly extracted from her.

She didn't expect to be taken out for dinner.

White had left her alone in the empty room with the photos – door open and unguarded – for a few minutes, then, when he'd returned, confirmed that arrangements had been made for her to visit MI5 headquarters. But not until the morning.

'When did you land in London?' he'd asked.

Valera hadn't admitted how she'd appeared in Britain. She wondered if her fake passport had actually been noticed and logged at the airport. Or if British intelligence had been tracking her ever since she'd last been in their capital. Or if he was just guessing.

'This morning,' she replied.

'Then perhaps you might like a nap.'

Valera hadn't realised how drained she was until just then. There had been a time when she'd survived on nothing but adrenaline and spite for days on end before feasting on whatever meagre scraps she could find. Now, an overnight flight and a few missed meals and she could feel her edges fraying. She reminded herself that wasn't all she'd been through recently.

White collected up the photos, and gestured towards the door. Valera waited in the corridor as he re-stacked the chairs and turned the light out. Then she followed him downstairs, out onto the high street, and waited next to him as he hailed a passing cab. The action looked natural, but Valera recognised the broad figure behind the snub-nosed black taxi's steering wheel – it was the man who had been waiting for them when they'd arrived, his coat swapped for a light-blue shirt and flat cap.

They drove across the city. Valera looked for landmarks she might remember from six years ago, but saw none. They ended up in another area that definitely wasn't the centre of town, but was much quieter and leafier than the neighbourhood they'd left.

The taxi pulled up in front of a set-back semi-detached house with a sage-green door and an almost purple Japanese maple in front of its bay window. White pantomimed leaning forward to pay the cabbie, then got out, holding the door open for Valera, and led her up the short path to his house.

'Watch out for Stella,' he said, as he slid a key into the bevelled lock halfway up the front door.

'Your wife?'

'My dog.' White pushed the door open and was greeted by an almost-elderly Irish setter nuzzling his thigh and licking the back of his hand before doing the same to Valera. 'My wife is visiting her parents this week.'

Valera imagined taking assets home with them wasn't usual behaviour for British intelligence agents.

'How will she feel about having another woman in your house?' she asked, following White down a herringbone parquet-floored hallway hung with paintings of flower-filled fields to a large kitchen.

'Highly amused, I'd imagine,' he replied, as he refilled the water bowl Stella had lumbered over to. 'The guest room is at the top of the stairs, second left. Bathroom is first. I'll be down here standing guard if you need anything.'

Valera nodded, turned, and walked back along the hallway. Again, she could have kept going and walked straight out through the front door and vanished, assuming the courier-cum-chauffer wasn't lying in wait in the street. Yet, the twin allures of rest and solving the mystery that had been laid at her feet stopped her.

She went upstairs and found the guest room.

The small, neat space was decorated with more flowers, in patterns on the wall, dried in vases, and on every piece of upholstery. It was cosy. It reminded her of her cabin. Not exactly to look at, but she sensed an echo of the comfortable privacy she'd borrowed in her mountain retreat – a place that wasn't hers, but was, until it wasn't again. She felt a wave of longing for the Colorado wilds, but let it wash over her without carrying her away.

Valera closed the door behind her, and moved a wooden chair with a poppy-covered seat from next to the bed to under the brass door handle.

Now memories of her last time in London flooded her mind. She remembered the MI5 safe house she'd been taken to by someone claiming to be her saviour. The man who called himself Devereux but whose real name was Peterson. The mask of polite concern that had quickly slipped to reveal hard, mercenary motives. The fragile, uneven partnership she'd brokered to guarantee her survival, and that had ended in death.

She told herself that the situation she was currently in was different in several crucial ways.

She was being asked for her help this time, by a man who wasn't pretending to be someone else, and she wasn't being threatened with a bullet to her head if she refused to give it.

There were no thick, bulletproof doors trapping her. The frame of the narrow window that faced its identical twin next door moved when she touched it. And when she lay down on the bed, the duvet smelled recently laundered in a fragrance that matched its floral pattern. This house was a home.

Valera didn't know how long she slept, only that she hadn't moved a single inch for the duration, and that her dreams had been a jumble of mountains, tundra, and deserts that she eternally traversed, with a tall, spectral shadow forever following her.

The room was the same, only a little darker, the light coming through the window a touch faded. It was early evening.

Valera's limbs were stiff, slow to prop her up off the blanket she'd fallen asleep on top of. But they didn't ache. Her stomach, however, did. She went to the bathroom, splashed some water on her face, and went downstairs. White and Stella were where she'd left them, only this time the dog was devouring a bowl of food.

'I thought we'd go out to eat,' White said. 'Mainly because feeding a foreign national my cooking would probably constitute a war crime.'

'Then what?'

'Then we throw you in shackles. Actually, I was imagining an early night. We've got our work cut out for us in the morning.'

Despite the suspicion hardwired into her, Valera found herself warming to White. He was droll, sarcastic. She knew people tended to think of scientists as dull, serious automatons, but the best had a dark humour deep within them. It was a kindred bond among those who were egotistical enough to challenge the constants of the universe and dared to make theoretical absolutes bend to their will.

The restaurant was a ten-minute stroll through the warm evening from White's house. They were early, the only customers aside from the cab driver who arrived thirty seconds behind Valera and White and quietly insisted on taking the table immediately next to the door.

It was extremely French. Bright red candles stuck up out of wine bottles in the centre of each table, the walls were a riot of mismatched patterned tiles and miniature etched mirrors, and the windows were trailed with faded blue, white, and red nets.

'Come here often?' Valera asked as their menus were delivered.

'First time,' White replied.

Valera wondered if this was typical – the constant changing of routines to avoid slipping into patterns that bred familiarity or drew recognition. She also tried to imagine what Ledjo would say about her going out for dinner with a man, and allowed herself a small inward smile at her guess that he'd be more interested in the food on offer than her dining companion.

White ordered steak, while Valera opted for coq au vin. By the time their meals arrived so had other diners. The noise of conversation started to rise over the warbling female voice that floated up from speakers hidden behind the narrow bar at the rear of the space, next to the kitchen door.

Valera had thought their ruse was more than a little ridiculous when they'd first arrived, their chaperone obvious and their performance as a local couple transparent. But the busier the restaurant became, the more unnoticed and unremarkable she felt.

The evening was rapidly becoming the closest she'd been to normal life in a very long time. Still, she couldn't stop herself from glancing at the door every time someone walked in, just in case whoever arrived stared at her with black, unblinking eyes.

'Expecting someone?' White asked, watching her watch an arriving middle-aged couple.

She stopped herself from saying yes. She wanted to believe that even if Anna had abandoned her, she had at least got her far enough away from the man in Colorado that he couldn't find her again.

'Force of habit,' she replied, eventually, turning her gaze to her dining companion.

'Entirely understandable from what I've heard. But I think you're as safe as you can be at the moment.'

Valera smiled thinly as she stabbed a piece of chicken with her fork. 'You know, I was told that the first time I came to London.'

White nodded. 'I'm sure you were.'

'And that ended badly for several people.'

'Well, knowing them they all probably did something to deserve it.'

Valera laughed at that. It was a loud, full laugh. The kind she hadn't heard come out of her mouth in years. And she didn't care if it drew a few odd looks from the restaurant's other patrons.

CHAPTER 38

Knox came to. His eyes focused slowly on a faint strip of light that felt far away from him. After a few seconds of disorientation he realised he was lying on his back and staring up at a very high, round ceiling.

He slid a hand out from his side, running his fingers and palm across the surface he was on. Metal. He could hear faint, muffled thrums and screeches coming from somewhere, but couldn't tell what any of them might be.

He rolled his head slightly from side to side and watched the line of light above him dance. Suddenly he had a vision of Bennett hanging in the void above him, turning, diving, and cooing. He screwed his eyes shut until it disappeared.

There was an odd, acrid taste in his mouth. He'd been drugged.

Knox remembered the gang that had set on him and Bennett outside the walled city and forced them into the back of the truck. The memory was accompanied by jolts running up both sides of his torso. He felt bruising, possibly a couple of cracked ribs.

He pulled himself up, wincing at both the pain across his abdomen and his spinning brain.

There was no other light apart from the thin shaft above him, but even in the gloom he could tell that the walls of the space he was in matched its ceiling. He was in a large, cylindrical tube standing on its end. For a split second he thought he'd been spirited across the border to some disused underground missile store hiding beneath a field in the People's Republic.

He got to his feet, with a little more wincing, and took in his strange prison properly.

The floor was also curved, concave, with a square seam in the very centre of it that suggested some kind of door to a chute beyond. Knox stamped on it, but it didn't give. Then he walked a loop, banging the wall and running his hand across it to see if there were any other hidden ways in or out. There weren't. But he did find a lump of old welding with a twin a foot apart from it. He looked up and saw more marks leading up to ten feet of ladder halfway up the wall. He wondered if it was a relic of some long-gone function, part rusted, part collapsed, or if its lower rungs had been removed more recently and purposefully, maybe even in preparation for his arrival.

He hammered on the giant tube's sides a few more times and shouted to be let out, but no one came to his rescue and after a couple more loops he picked a spot opposite the suspended ladder and slid down the wall until he was sitting with his legs sticking out in front of him.

His mission to Hong Kong wasn't shaping up to be the triumphant return to the field he'd wanted it to be.

He thought about Rabe again, how lucky he'd been that the scientist had actually been up to no good. But it had been total luck. MI5 had been completely unaware that he was passing highly sensitive work on to a third party, or who these people were that had made the man run for his life, and almost end it. An enemy the Service didn't even know they were fighting, with an agenda and ends that were completely invisible. He could sense his brain forming parallels again.

Knox gazed up at the shaft of light, which now ran at ninety degrees to him, and let himself get irritated. That he didn't know where he was or how long he'd been here. That he had no clue about what had happened to Zhou or Bennett. That he also had no idea what was going to happen to him next. Was he being held while someone decided what information they wanted to extract from him or how they wanted to kill him? Or was he going to be left to starve if he couldn't find some way to raise an alarm?

He couldn't even say for certain who had kidnapped him. Had the group he and Bennett been spying on noticed them and arranged to have them dealt with if they ever returned to the walled city? Or had the appearance of Zhou's car on the edge of the walled city two days in a row just angered a local Triad or group of leftists?

Mostly, though, he was angry with himself. He'd got swept up, ignored warnings, and jumped to act without thinking things through. He hadn't even observed basic operational safety – he'd let Atwood think he'd given up on his investigation and hadn't sent an update to Leconfield House. Not only did he not know where he was, it was entirely likely that no one who might possibly want to come to his rescue did either.

He wished he'd insisted on Williams coming to Hong Kong with him, or that he'd brought him along regardless of approval. And not just because he'd always been better in a street fight. Knox still felt constant echoes of the pain he'd lived with for so long after losing his best friend with no knowledge of what had really happened to him. He hated the possibility that his incompetence might end up putting Williams through the same uncertainty.

Knox registered the bad taste once more, and recalled having coarse fabric shoved in his mouth as well as over his head when he'd been hauled into the rear of the truck. At the time he'd thought it was just a way to stop him from screaming out, but now he wondered if it was how he'd been drugged.

He checked himself over again. His nostrils didn't feel raw. He took off his jacket and rolled up his shirtsleeves but couldn't feel or see any injection marks. Maybe the gag had been doused in something. Or a pill slipped into his mouth in the melee, and the wad of material used to make sure he swallowed it.

Had he been given Blue Peacock? Was he now part of some experiment, like Zhou and the doctor at Stanley had described, to test its effects and see how it made him lose control – to see how much would make him fantasise about flying and how much would make him try to throw himself off something? Should he be grateful the ladder didn't reach all the way to the floor?

He clenched a fist and smacked it against the metal behind him again, sending a dull, low echo reverberating round his odd cell. Then he balled up his jacket and put it behind his head.

As he stared up at the ceiling again he noticed the strip of light was a little brighter, and not quite perpendicular to him any more.

'Morning, then,' he said to no one.

He counted up how many hours he'd lost. It was at least sixteen.

Knox didn't know how long he'd been asleep for the second time, and he couldn't use the line of light to narrow it down, because it was obscured by the thing that had woken him up – a gushing torrent of tiny beige and white shapes pouring from a chute that had appeared or opened near the top of the cylinder.

They'd already obscured most of the floor up to Knox's feet and, as they started to pile around him and he picked up a handful, he finally worked out where he was. Inside a grain silo.

After a few more seconds his legs were covered and he had to stand up. Within a minute the grain had passed his knees. Another two and it was up to his waist. He banged on the wall frantically and cried out, but his strikes and shouts were lost in the noise of the cascade.

He started jumping and splaying out his arms, not to try to take flight, but in an attempt to get on top of the rising tide of grain.

After two attempts that resulted in him diving and crashing down onto the floor, he jumped backwards, his body rigid and his arms and legs spread as wide as possible. He felt himself sinking, but slower this time, and, after a few strained breaths as the grain nearly swallowed him, it took his weight.

Knox held himself in the same position, every muscle in his body straining to stay firm as the silo filled and its contents carried him upwards. It took almost ten minutes for the grain to rise up to the section of ladder that was still attached to the wall. Luckily, he had ended up on the right side of the giant cylinder to grab at it. And, equally fortunately, the torrent abruptly stopped halfway up it.

The sudden silence was almost as disorienting and bizarre as what had just happened.

Knox was exhausted from the effort of holding his body tense. He was also not out of danger. He needed more rest, but he knew that if he lost consciousness and let go of the rung he was gripping on to then he'd plunge back into the grain and very probably suffocate.

He pulled himself up the ladder, letting his legs fall beneath him so his feet could find a rung to rest on. Then he reached down, undid his belt, removed it from its loops, threaded it round his shoulders and through one of the ladder's stiles, and tightened it until his chest was pressed up against it.

CHAPTER 39

Bennett didn't trust Ray Mason because he was the only person other than Knox and Zhou who had known she was going back to the walled city, and now she was trapped in a grain silo, nursing a shoulder that she hoped wasn't dislocated.

She remembered her and Knox being attacked in the middle of the road, the club that had slammed into the top of her arm and the knife that had dug into her throat, and being dragged into the back of a truck.

Then everything had gone black and silent before it erupted into a mesmeric kaleidoscope of shapes and colours that transcended dimensions and obliterated her senses and limits of understanding for what felt like an eternity of absolute and total ecstasy.

Then she'd woken up, head spinning, shoulder throbbing, mouth feeling like it had been scrubbed with dirt and bleach, and feeling generally terrible.

Bennett recognised the silo from her childhood in Kansas. She'd lost hours in the ones that belonged to the depressed farms that bordered Lakin, alternatingly hunting her brothers, trying to get them to do their fair share of chores, or hiding in them herself, stealing moments of peace to read whatever book she'd persuaded the library in Garden City, the next big town over, to let her borrow.

She didn't know precisely how this one worked, but she figured it couldn't be that different from Kansas – a chute somewhere unreachably high up where the grain would pour in

186

from, another at its base it would stream back out of. She could make out a seam on the floor, and she guessed its partner was above the long ladder that climbed two thirds of the way up from the enormous cylinder's base – the ladder she was currently perched on the top of.

She was exhausted. She didn't know how long her trip had lasted and how long she'd been asleep for, but she did know it was a long time since she'd eaten and her energy levels were low. The climb had made her shoulder burn – though not give out, which she took as a positive sign – and the narrow rung dug into the backs of her thighs. But the tiredness and lack of comfort were preferable to being smothered to death if someone turned up to make a delivery while she was curled up, unconscious, on the floor.

Bennett had tracked the single beam of light that illuminated the silo since she'd woken up. She couldn't say how long she'd been trapped in it, but she'd worked out that she'd been awake for three hours, give or take, and that, as the light had got steadily brighter, it was Sunday morning.

Almost a whole day out of action. The attack had been sudden, violent, planned. But then nothing had followed it. No torture, no interrogation, no demands. Why?

She'd convinced herself it had something to do with Mason.

The CIA had trained her – albeit reluctantly – to be a field agent. But long before that she'd taught herself to be suspicious, and never take anything or anyone at face value.

She knew that her fundamental conviction that more often than not there was a hidden agenda operating under the one you could see – including when you were already multiple levels of secrecy and deception deep – made her look paranoid even to spies who had spent entire careers lying and living under cover. But she also knew she'd been proved right too many times to ignore her instincts.

And something had never smelled right to her about Mason, or his reasons for wanting her in Hong Kong.

She'd looked him up in the Seoul CIA archives as soon she'd been told about her transfer, and found vanishingly little. The records weren't as comprehensive as the ones held in Langley or the basement of the US Embassy on Grosvenor Square in London. Mission reports were more piecemeal and the gaps between them longer, both a result of the agency's less structured and more reactive approach to operating in Asia. But even given that, for someone who had supposedly spent the last five years rising through the ranks in this part of the world, Mason was a ghost. His name scarcely appeared, and she found very few coded references to top-secret operations that could theoretically be attributed to someone like him.

Then she'd arrived in Hong Kong to a barrage of flattery and zero formal remit. Mason had wanted her to 'get a feel for the place', and 'see what she came up with' – the kind of thing she'd do wherever she found herself, but not an order she'd ever expected to be given by a superior.

They'd met sporadically before Mason had instituted their D'Aguilar Street protocol, seemingly on a whim. After their first couple of meetings in Lan Kwai Fong, to which he'd turned up as a tourist with a battered Canon Cine 8T strung round his neck and then as a Catholic priest, dressed all in black bar a few white inches of dog collar, Bennett had tried to tail him and see where he spent most of his time given the CIA didn't have an official, permanent station in the city's American consulate. But each time he'd disappeared almost as soon as they'd finished. And it wasn't as if he'd pulled some clever move to evade her, it was like he'd just evaporated – standing out in his costume one moment, vanished the next.

Things had changed a month ago, when she'd caught her first sniff of Blue Peacock. It was just one of a list of phrases that had lodged in her head as she'd spent long hours traversing Hong Kong Island and Kowloon's seedier backstreets and more liminal corners, getting to grips with the city and the Cantonese language.

But it was the only one Mason had encouraged her to look into further. And now, just when she'd got close to working out what it was and who was behind it, she'd been taken out of action. And so had everyone else who knew what she was doing, apart from Mason.

Had this been his plan all along? To let her get this far and then get her out of the way? And if it was, did that mean he was after any glory that might have rightfully come her way, or was he working for someone other than the agency? Maybe even the very people Bennett had been investigating? Had her real job not been to uncover what Blue Peacock really was but to test its security and report back to someone who was already inside it?

It was Sunday. She was sure something was going to happen on Monday. Was she trapped in an empty silo because whatever that something was was already in motion?

She was about to tell herself that she was letting her suspicions and exhaustion get the better of her. That even her paranoia should have limits. That just because she didn't know exactly what her boss's agenda was didn't mean it had to be working against hers. That even though she was trapped with no obvious means of escape she wasn't in any immediate danger. But, before she could, a deluge of grain began tumbling through the air in front of her.

CHAPTER 40

Williams's mood had spent the day darkening. Because the impromptu conference had proved there was a lot going on in the outside world beyond the walls of Rabley Heath, including things that were going to keep Knox away from home for longer than he'd promised. And because of the woman who he'd never met before but somehow knew him. He recognised her too. Not who she was, but what she was – a predator who hadn't let herself be trapped.

He moped through the afternoon, energy and irritation bubbling up inside him. He hadn't gone for his morning exercise in order to be sure he'd be in when his captors came for their latest favour, and had been the consummate host when they'd arrived. Now, he wondered why he hadn't done the former, and why he'd bothered doing the latter. Why was he so determined to be a version of Jack Williams that could only ever be an imperfect reproduction of the man he'd been? Why was he expending so much effort trying to contain the man he'd become? Why was he wasting his days trying to stop a hidden, forgotten house from crumbling into the dirt?

At seven o'clock his body finally got the better of his mind and forced him into activity. He went for a run, and kept running for three hours.

He went out through the gates he hadn't bothered to close after White and Laing had left with their new asset, and headed north, down the middle of lanes, then along the sides of roads. He passed open fields, hedged-off farms and thick wooded areas. He never broke stride or flinched as a car or lorry sped past him. His concentration was entirely inward, the only sound he could hear the rhythmic pumping of his legs, heart, and lungs. He was in deep meditation, his mind completely focused on putting one foot in front of the other.

It took him an hour to reach Hitchin, a market town that could date its history all the way back to the seventh century, which he skirted, heading west towards the Pegsdon Hills on the edge of the Chilterns. Slowly, the ground began rising up, meeting his heel earlier with each stride until he found himself atop the highest point for miles, surrounded by only bright-blue evening sky.

Williams finally stopped running and took in the view. It felt like the whole country stretched out beneath him and that now, having crested one hill far from Rabley Heath, there was nothing to stop him from summitting another, and another; from keeping running forever.

But he didn't.

He didn't race down into the valley ahead of him either, heading for the Midlands or the Cotswolds, bedding down in a field or barn overnight, stealing provisions from an unattended farmhouse table or understaffed village grocers, and seeing how far he could get before MI5 or someone else tracked him down and he could face them on his own terms.

He turned back.

The hue of the sky was deepening as Williams closed the gates to Rabley Heath. It had taken him another hour and a half of solid running to return. And with each metronomic step he'd told himself he wasn't a coward. That he'd made a promise he had to honour. That he still owed his best friend an unpayable debt. And that he was being sensible. Because if he was going to leave, then he needed to plot his escape properly so only people he wanted might stand any chance of finding him.

He walked up the driveway, wondering if his muscles were going to seize up after what he'd put them through, lingered briefly at the back door in case Stinky was hiding nearby in hopes of a saucer of milk, went inside and upstairs, and had a long, hot shower.

Twenty minutes later exhaustion finally hit and, after just managing to dry himself off, Williams fell asleep, naked, on top of his bed.

Four hours later his eyes burst open as his sixth sense told him something wasn't right in the house. And this time, in the second it took him to roll off his mattress and land in a silent crouch on the floor, he knew it wasn't because he'd accidentally locked a cat in the kitchen.

He moved quickly, still naked and completely silent, along the landing to the grand main staircase, guided by the sensation that felt like a sub-audible vibration in his chest. Downstairs, it led him along more pitch-black corridors and into the ballroom, with its vast, sprung floor, scattered dustsheet-covered furniture, and long row of curtainless, moonlit windows.

Williams ignored the strange, deep shadows thrown by draped chaises longues and wingbacks as he crouched again and shuffled lightly along the outer edge of the long, wide room to the very middle window. Then he raised one hand up to it, feeling the faintest draught seep through the gap between the pane and its frame, and stretched the other one out in front of him, sweeping the floor until he found the tiny piece of cut-through dowel that had been wedged in that gap for the last twelve months.

Someone had broken into Rabley Heath. And, thanks to the minutest mistake, they'd given themselves away.

He replaced the short length of semicircular wood, silencing the hum no one else could ever have felt, so he could listen for any other slightest sound or movement in the house.

It took a few moments, but eventually Williams registered a faint, faraway creak, which he recognised instantly – the floor-board immediately inside the doorway to the drawing room.

He leapt like a sprinter out of his crouch, racing out of the ballroom and deeper into the house just in time to glimpse a dark shape duck into the kitchen and, a few seconds later, hear the muffled double pop of two bullets being put through the lock of the back door.

Williams accelerated, not caring that whoever had invaded his home was clearly armed and he was completely naked. He flew through the kitchen and out into the night, where he saw the black-clad silhouette of a man sprinting into the tangle of bushes on the far side of the lawn.

He chased after him, adrenaline overriding any stiffness his limbs might have dared feel. He quickly made up ground, but the figure ahead of him was in good shape as well, and had too much of a head start. By the time Williams reached the high wall hidden beyond the bushes, the other man had already vaulted it. And, when Williams had scaled it barely a few seconds later, he could hear the sound of a car engine revving and tyres spinning.

Accepting defeat – or victory, for he'd driven his invader away – he walked back to the house. As the adrenaline started to fade, he began to feel all the small slices the burrs and thorns he'd run through had cut into his skin.

He looked for the two bullets outside the back door, but they were lost in the gravel. Then he went into the drawing room. He trod carefully, in case the intruder had set any booby traps. But everything looked exactly as it should. Everything except the light switch. As he flicked it on, Williams noticed that one of the two screws that held its metal cover in place was a couple of degrees off vertical.

He retrieved a knife from the kitchen and used it to unscrew the cover. Inside, balanced in the hole in the wall the switch's wires passed through, he found a tiny black box, half the size of a fingernail.

CHAPTER 41

Valera fled. It was an inevitable, if delayed, response to the latest strange turn her life had taken and the kindness that had been shown to her.

The meal and the evening stroll back to White's house had been nice. Too nice. A tantalising, seductive glimpse into the pleasant world that Valera had been denied her entire life. And she'd spent so long convincing herself that such a life could never be hers, that her rejection of it was only a matter of time.

As she lay again on the bed in the spare room and suddenly began to find its softness utterly, hideously unbearable, she decided she had to escape.

She got up and sat on the floor next to the slim window for half an hour, knees tucked up against her chest, hating even the presence of something so indulgent as carpet under her as she heard White shutting up the house and putting Stella to bed in the kitchen. And for another hour after he came upstairs, waiting to make sure he was asleep.

Then she crept out of her room, pausing on every step of the staircase to make sure she didn't rouse Stella or her master, before gliding along the hallway to the front door, where she slowly twisted the handle of its Yale lock and silently clicked the notch that would hold the mechanism open so the door wouldn't make a noise when she pulled it shut behind her.

Valera headed out into the night. But she didn't go very far.

She counted her turns and lingered round corners in case she was being followed, by the stocky man who had been her near-constant shadow since she'd reached London or by anyone else.

After ten minutes of zigzagging past more houses that all looked like they had well-stocked larders, stayed warm through winter, and were unlikely to spontaneously combust, she reached a well-lit main road. Instead of following it left or right, she crossed straight over it and continued weaving her way through quieter, darker side streets for another five minutes, until the one she was on abruptly turned into some kind of forest that had somehow escaped being swallowed up by the city.

She could make out the black, silhouetted outlines of huge, ancient trees, and the slow glimmer of moonlight on water. The amorphous shapes and shadows were alluring, familiar. She could have been on the banks of Lake Onega outside the high wire fence of Povenets B, or in the woods at the bottom of her nameless mountain in Colorado.

It was as if her old life had intruded on this new one, trying to tempt her back into the wilderness to survive alone on just her wits and her own scant resources. A reminder of where she really belonged, and a call to return to an existence defined by absence and loss.

Yet, to her intense surprise, she stopped at the very edge of the pavement, where it gave way to dirt and grass.

She peered into the gloom, waiting for Ledjo to materialise and beckon her into it. But he didn't. Then she looked for any real dangers her mind might have sensed ahead of her. But no figures, human or animal, emerged from the shadows to attack her.

She remained fixed to the spot as she tried to work out why she wasn't racing into the darkness.

Was it that she hadn't really wanted to escape at all, she just needed to know that she could? That White hadn't deceived her and she might have found someone she could truly trust? And that Anna had been right all along: that she'd been running for more than long enough and it was time for her to put her mind to use again, thinking and theorising instead of just worrying and reacting, pushing the boundaries of science and reason rather than the limits of her stamina and resilience?

Valera wasn't sure if it was all of these things, some of them, or something else entirely, that had brought her this far but now refused to take her further. But, after a few more minutes of staring at the trees and the water, she turned round and made her way back to the house.

CHAPTER 42

Knox had fallen asleep again. He woke up to discover the light above him had moved and faded, and the grain he'd been propped up to his stomach in was now five feet beneath the bottom rung of the ladder and falling fast.

The silo was being emptied.

He twisted himself out of the belt that had kept him pinned in place. His muscles were slow and his sides still sore, but he moved quickly because the longer he took, the further away the top of the grain would be and the faster he'd hit it.

When he was free, he pushed himself backwards and let himself fall, all limbs splayed again.

Once more, the grain held him and he started to sink down the silo with it. After a minute he realised his mistake.

It was possible that whoever had imprisoned him in the giant metal tube had decided that he was probably dead by now, his lungs and throat full of seed and husk, and this was his chance to surprise them. However, it was equally likely that whoever was draining the grain had absolutely no idea he was in here with them and wasn't planning on removing the entire contents of the silo.

At any moment the trapdoor could be closed and Knox would find himself stranded between the ladder and the floor, waiting to see how long his muscles held up before they gave in and he was swallowed up.

The only way out was through the grain.

He let his legs relax first, letting them fall under his hips again, then brought his hands up to his face, cupping them over his mouth and nose.

He started to slide downwards, slow then faster before the concentrated pressure of his vertical body started to compress the grains directly below him quicker than they were escaping the silo and he reached terminal velocity. He kept his eyes closed, fought the claustrophobia he felt as he was pressed at from every angle, and resisted the urge to reach out or struggle.

Then he hit the bottom of the silo and felt his knees buckle under him. He instinctively struck his arms forward, and tilted over, but only slightly; the grains pressing up against him kept him near vertical – and quickly found their way into every exposed crevice of his unprotected face.

He didn't dare open his mouth for fear of choking instantly, and he could already feel his nose blocking, which meant he only had a few seconds to find his way out.

Knox stilled himself, ignored the heartbeat that was now pounding louder and louder in his ears, and tried to sense the current of the grain as it flowed past his skin. But he couldn't feel anything.

His heart began to pulse faster, and his lungs cried out to release the air they were filled with. He swung his arms through ninety degrees, then forced himself to pause again.

It took five long seconds, but eventually he detected movement to his left, and frantically half-swam, half-dragged himself over towards it. And then he was tumbling, being sucked downwards. Knox let his body go limp as he crashed through the trapdoor and banged into the edges and corners of the chute. Then, suddenly, he was back out in the world.

He landed with a cushioned thud onto another solid metal surface and opened his eyes to find a very confused man wearing a grey shirt and small white cap staring down at him and saying something in Cantonese.

Knox propped himself up on his elbows and realised he was lying in the middle of a large, square-edged tub, which, along with the surprised man's cap and shirt, was branded with a logo and name: Kowloon Flour Mill.

He sat up, looked to his right, and saw another silo being drained, another bewildered mill worker, and Bennett sitting in her own tub staring back at him.

CHAPTER 43

'Where the hell are we?' Knox asked Bennett as they walked away from the flour mill, shaking seeds and dust from their pockets and trouser legs.

'No idea,' she replied.

Then they heard the booming roar of a jet and saw the fuselage of a green-striped Boeing 707 fly across the gap in the buildings ahead of them just a few feet off the ground.

'By the airport, I guess,' she added.

They continued on until they reached a waterfront that looked out at the Kai Tak runway and, beyond that, Kowloon Bay, the stubby curve of the Tsim Sha Tsui peninsula, and Victoria Harbour.

They were in Kwun Tong, one of Kowloon's industrial districts.

Knox watched a plane coming in to land, and saw several small boats at the very end of the reclaimed spit scuttle for cover from the sudden waves caused by engine wake. They huddled against the concrete edge of the runway and alongside the hull of a much larger boat that sat low in the water with mounded peaks of what looked like gravel, cement, and sand sticking up out of it.

As soon as the water settled again, the boats struck out once more, darting between the barge and the spit, like ants that had successfully avoided a dive-bombing bird and were eager to get back to their work.

Knox remembered Atwood talking about the runway's planned extension and was equally impressed and shocked that whoever was in charge of the project seemed to be trying to get it done between landings and take-offs.

Bennett hailed a cab that took them north-west past the airport terminal and then south to the Star Ferry. They didn't say a lot in the back of the taxi, or as they crossed over to Hong Kong Island.

'I should check in,' Knox finally said as they walked up the ramp near the Noonday Gun, whose crowds had already departed for the day. 'And maybe checked over,' he added, running a hand up his sides.

'You shouldn't go back to your hotel yet,' she replied. 'We don't know if it's safe. I can patch you up at my place.'

Knox didn't disagree. He was eager to find out if his request to Leconfield House had resulted in there being some information waiting for him back at the Waylian, but didn't know if something or someone else would be too. They still weren't sure who had been behind their kidnapping or the exact motives for it, but whoever they were, if they knew who Knox was then he had to assume they also knew where he was staying.

They walked to Bennett's apartment, taking a route so circuitous Knox was sure he'd never be able to find it again, until they reached her actual street and he made a mental note of the row of temples and the names hung outside them on carved wooden boards in English and Chinese script.

Bennett's home was on the corner of the ninth floor of her building, with a balcony on two of its sides, facing the street and the strait.

Once they were inside and Bennett had checked that no one had visited in her absence, she found some long bandages in a kitchen cupboard and they debriefed each other on the rattan-and-green-cord sofa that sat in the middle of her living room.

'Were you drugged too?' Knox asked.

Bennett nodded. 'Probably the best bit of the whole thing.'

'How was it?'

Bennett's face clouded. 'Good. Too good. Like anyone could have done whatever they wanted to me and I wouldn't have cared. Which I guess is exactly what happened.'

Knox removed his shirt and started wrapping long lengths of gauzy cotton round his midriff. 'Did anyone question you?'

She shook her head. 'Nothing. Didn't see a single soul until the poor guy whose tub I tumbled into.'

'They certainly looked like they didn't expect us to be there.'

'It feels like we were being kept out of the way.'

Knox nodded. 'Like whatever is being planned for Monday couldn't be disturbed.'

'Like we might already be too late, and now those six from the walled city have done what they needed to, they're not worried about us any more.'

Knox twisted left and right, testing the bandages. 'If it was them.'

He finally told her about the other reason for his trip to Hong Kong. The disappearing scientists, the suspicion that China's political or military intelligence apparatus might be behind it.

When he was done, for the first time in their history together Bennett was completely lost for words. Knox knew how much she both enjoyed and needed knowing more about what was really going on in the world than anything else, but his revelations seemed to have completely blindsided her.

'We haven't seen any reports of it in Asia,' Knox said. 'Hence in part the theory that this might be where it's being orchestrated from. Maybe there's no local agency chat about it because it just isn't happening here.'

'Or it's being buried. Or kept from me.'

Bennett got up and went into the kitchen. When she came back she was carrying two glasses of neat whisky and had a determined, calculating look on her face.

'Did you see what happened to Zhou?' she asked, handing Knox one of the glasses and taking a long drink from the other.

'I saw her coming after us, but she didn't get very close.'

'Any fighting?'

'Just squaring up. Why?'

'Because I didn't see her take a hit either, or end up in a silo, or come to our rescue.'

Knox cradled his whisky in his lap. 'Let's not leap to make more unsubstantiated accusations. We've got more than enough of them on our plate already.'

Bennett was about to say something else – something, Knox guessed, about him being too quick to trust someone who was, really, still a complete stranger – but before she could there were three short, sharp knocks at her door.

She gestured towards the kitchen as she dipped into her bedroom and reappeared carrying a Beretta. Once Knox was out of the line of sight from the front door, Bennett slipped the gun behind her into the waist of her trousers, and opened it.

Zhou was on the other side.

'Where have you been?' she asked, stepping past Bennett into the apartment.

'A flour mill,' Knox replied, walking back out of the kitchen and putting his shirt back on.

The oddness of his response did not appear to faze the police captain.

'And what have you been doing for the last twenty-four hours?' Bennett asked her.

'Looking for Knox,' Zhou replied, her voice even but loaded with the implication that while the safety of an MI5 officer was her concern, that of a CIA field agent was not. 'Checking police stations for reports of murders or bodies, and trying to track down the truck you were abducted in.'

'Any luck with that?' Knox asked.

Zhou shook her head.

'What about tracking down the walled city gang?'

'That is ongoing, but there is hardly a lot to work with.'

'How did you know to come here?' Bennett said, her tone still accusatory.

'Because Special Branch makes a note of where all foreign agents operating within our territory are based.'

'Including allies?'

'Yes.'

Zhou reached into her pocket and Knox saw Bennett's hand drift behind her back. He gave her a look to hold fire.

Zhou pulled out a small card with the Waylian's logo debossed along its top edge and handed it to Knox.

He read the coded message, then folded the card in half and slipped it into his own pocket.

'Interesting,' he said. 'I asked Leconfield House for any information they might have come across about Blue Peacock.'

'What did they send?' Bennett asked.

'Backup.'

'How much?'

'One man.'

'That's it?'

'For the moment. I imagine we'll find out more from him in the morning.'

Bennett shook her head. 'More waiting.'

'Afraid so.'

'Not good enough.'

She walked back into her bedroom. When she returned a moment later, she was shrugging on a dark-grey silk bomber jacket.

'Where are you going?' Zhou asked.

'To see if I can get us some answers tonight,' Bennett replied. 'There's more whisky in the kitchen. I'll be back in a couple of hours.'

CHAPTER 44

Man Mo Temple on Hollywood Road in Sheung Wan was dedicated to two deities. The god of words and the god of war. A reference to the fundamental nature of the intelligence game that Mason had seemed extremely proud of and amused by when he'd explained to Bennett how to make emergency contact with him.

She stepped over the thick stone threshold, letting the heady miasma created by twenty enormous burning incense spirals envelop her. They were supposed to inspire calm and contemplation, but they did nothing to dampen the fury churning inside her at the possibility that she hadn't only been played by a traitor but that she'd actively helped him too.

Then she walked, purposefully but without rushing, to the joint shrine at the rear of the dark wood and maroon-lacquered main hall, which was festooned in bright silk tapestry, flowers, and food offerings.

She placed a single red apple she'd bought from a hawker on her way from her apartment in the dead centre of the plinth between the two gods.

After that, she went into the adjoining smaller hall, where she exchanged a few dollars for a bamboo box of painted sticks. But instead of shaking them until one fell out to tell her fortune, she removed one herself, handed it and the pot straight back to the old woman she'd just paid, and left.

Sixty minutes later, she was sitting on a bench in the botanical gardens in Central, waiting for Mason to appear.

And then she kept waiting.

The protocol for emergency contact was clear. After Man Mo, Bennett would have an hour to shake herself clean of any tail and make her way to the botanical gardens. When she arrived, Mason should have been there, ready to give her whatever she needed, whether that was medical attention, a larger gun, or an extraction plan. Except he clearly hadn't dropped whatever he'd been doing to rush to her aid.

For the first half-hour she was on the bench she gave him the benefit of the doubt – he might have been on the far side of Kowloon or over in Aberdeen or Chai Wan when the message she'd sent from the temple had reached him. Her generosity faded over the next one. And for the whole second hour she waited she wondered if he was coming at all, or if he'd used the time she'd been trapped in the silo to completely disappear, once and for all.

When Mason finally materialised, he was dressed in the overalls of a park custodian, his tall frame folded over a cart full of long-handled brushes. And he was, from Bennett's perspective, irritatingly calm.

'What's up?' he asked, once he'd made a show of sweeping around the bench and sat down at the end opposite Bennett.

They both kept their eyes facing forward, their mouths moving little and slowly. Bennett was glad of the pretence that they were strangers with nothing to do with each other – it stopped her from screaming at him.

'I've just spent twenty-four hours sat on the top of a ladder in a giant pit of wheat.'

'Why would you do that?'

'I didn't have a choice. I was grabbed and drugged when I went back to the walled city.'

Bennett should have kept up their usual code, but they were outside, the gardens were quiet, and she was angry.

'Huh,' Mason replied. No confession. No evasion. Just a coolness that bordered on utter disinterest about what his operative had gone through. 'Did they do any damage?'

'I'm alright,' Bennett replied, dangling the opportunity for him to make a slip and ask about Knox.

He didn't take it.

'Good. Sounds like you spooked them. It'll be interesting to see what they do next.'

'We need to move. I've got first-hand experience of what Blue Peacock can do now. We have to get it under control.'

'Did you get a solid ID on your kidnappers?'

'No.'

'Any names for your walled city gang?'

'No.'

'Then it's going to be a pretty hard sell.'

They were sensible questions, and a reasonable conclusion, but Bennett couldn't stop herself thinking Mason was now fishing himself, checking she was still in the dark about what he was really up to.

'Look,' Mason continued, 'they're probably going to lie low for a while now, and you seem stressed. Take a couple of days for some R and R and we can pick up the hunt when there's another trail to find. Maybe head down to Shek O and rent a hut on the beach.'

'And miss the festival?'

Mason let out a quiet chuckle. 'It ain't all it's cracked up to be. The races get real boring once someone takes a clear lead.'

For a brief moment, Bennett entertained the possibility that he was right. That she and Knox hadn't been shut up out of the way but had scared their unknown enemies into going to ground and stopped – or at least delayed – whatever they had been planning for the next day. But then he said something that made her want to get up, pull her gun on him, and demand that he stop lying to her.

'I'll be skipping town for the duration, anyway,' he said. 'Catching the late flight to Seoul tonight. Actually, why don't you take more than a few days? Hop a plane somewhere for a proper break while you have the chance.'

Now she was absolutely convinced that Mason was involved with Blue Peacock. That he was making sure he was going to be well clear of whatever was planned for Monday. And that he'd used her.

But she didn't leap to her feet, reach behind her back for her Beretta and force him to admit it all. She just nodded slowly and said, 'Maybe.'

Mason got up, leaned back over his cart and started to stroll away.

'I'll be seeing you,' he called over his shoulder after a few paces.

'Definitely,' Bennett replied once he was gone, as she silently promised herself that even if she was going to let him go this evening, she wasn't going to let him get away.

When she got back to her apartment, the lights were off and Knox was lying unconscious on her sofa. She briefly let her rage at Mason transfer onto his prone form – how could he sleep when there was so much to be furious about? – then she realised how tired she was herself.

She showered, finally ridding herself of the faint aroma of agriculture mixed with industry that had lingered on her all day, and stretched out the knots and kinks in her body, testing her shoulder, which thankfully now twisted and moved to her will without too much complaint.

Then she lay in bed, contemplating over and over in increasingly catastrophic circles the knowledge that after years of struggling to prove her ability and loyalty, she'd ended up working for the bad guys.

CHAPTER 45

Laing had continued to read the report about the current situation in Hong Kong over and over, first as he flew to Paris and then on the leg to Cairo, until he'd committed it to memory. It seemed clear to him that however legitimate or inflated the worries and demands of the leftists were, they were being stoked and taken advantage of for larger political ends. Ends, he couldn't help but feel, that wouldn't ultimately benefit them.

Then, as his plane began climbing over the Arabian peninsula he took his suit jacket off, folded it on the seat next to him, which hadn't acquired a new occupant since the French capital, wedged the report between his thigh and armrest, and turned his attention to Knox.

What had happened to the man? Was he simply off on a jolly? Had a year cooped up in Rabley Heath made him sloppy on protocol and desperate to blow off some steam? Or was it something worse?

Knox's last message to Leconfield House had implied he had no idea just how serious Blue Peacock might be. He could easily have stumbled on something he wasn't prepared for, or attracted dangerous attention. Had he been attacked? Was he in hospital? Being held captive? Dead and floating face-down out of Victoria Harbour and into the South China Sea?

And if he was any of those things, who would be behind it? Who would want a nuclear bomb? That question had even more possible answers.

The world was full of governments, armies, and madmen who wanted to join the nuclear club, and it contained plenty of political and religious zealots who were prepared not only to die for their own peculiar cause but also to take an awful lot of innocent people with them.

The world had lived with the threat of nuclear-tipped ICBMs raining down on it for over a decade. But somehow, the more Laing thought about it, the worse Blue Peacock seemed. A missile gave you a warning. It could be tracked, maybe even shot out of the sky; it at least offered the possibility of a few moments to make peace with your triumphs and failures before it annihilated you. But a bomb that could be strapped to the back of a lorry and detonated anywhere, anytime – that wasn't a weapon. It was an instrument of terror.

But the question remained. Who wanted a Blue Peacock?

Laing's right leg shifted, rustling the papers wedged between it and the side of his seat and reminding him of where he was going. Hong Kong wasn't just one of the world's major ports and trading hubs, somewhere a small bomb could easily travel through without anyone noticing. It was also a powder keg, being primed to explode. Was someone simply using the turmoil in the colony as cover for moving their destructive merchandise? Or had the Chinese become so desperate to drive the British out that they were prepared to irradiate it if the leftists didn't do the job fast enough?

An air stewardess shook him from his increasingly perturbing chain of thoughts. It was time for yet another meal he would have struggled to afford on the ground. This one was large and heavy, designed, Laing guessed, to put as many passengers to sleep as possible for the long haul to Bombay.

Once he'd finished eating, he dutifully tilted his seat back and tried to push his dark musings from his mind. He needed to get what sleep he could between meals and stopovers so he'd be ready for action – whatever shape that might take – when he landed in Hong Kong.

However, as he cast his eyes around before closing them, he caught a glimpse of something he hadn't noticed before that made him sit almost bolt upright. His new angle gave him a fresh line of sight diagonally across the cabin, and he could now see through the narrow gap between the two seats at the very front of the plane, on the other side to his.

It was only a single long, loose curl of deep-brown hair, but he was sure he recognised it. And then, as if sensing his gaze, the head the hair belonged to turned, and he saw a sliver of the face of the Line Z woman from Rabley Heath smiling back at him.

There was no way he'd be able to sleep now. But he also couldn't just go over and demand she explain why she was on his flight. The cabin was too open, and it would be too easy for her to blow his cover if she wanted. All he could do was stew, and bide his time until the plane was back on the ground refuelling and he had the chance to get her somewhere out of the way where they couldn't be overheard.

In Bombay, Laing got off first, and lingered in the stiflingly hot gate, waiting for her. But she didn't appear behind him, and eventually he was politely shepherded on to make way for the economy passengers. After another ten minutes in an even hotter glass-walled corridor, he began to wonder if he'd actually been seeing things after all, or if she'd somehow managed to sneak ahead of him and was already making her way through the arrivals hall.

A few false starts and wrong turns down busy corridors, which were corrected by airport staff with extreme politeness at high volume, took Laing to the transfer desk where he checked that his next departure was still on time.

It was, which meant he had an hour to kill. He wondered about finding a lounge or a bar, but he wasn't sure how much more indulgence his stomach could take. So he kept walking, re-treading a safe route that orbited the next gate he would eventually board through.

The beige-and-green Air Ceylon Vickers VC10 was a little larger than the bright white-and-blue Air France Boeing 707, and its interior a little less plush, but it was still more than comfortable enough for Laing's two and half hours to Colombo and four more to Singapore.

He was one of only three passengers he could see in first class, and he slept for almost all of both flights, his body finally giving in to the exhaustion of crossing time zones.

He woke up on the approach to Singapore. It was the middle of the night, but he wasn't sure which one.

As the plane circled and descended, and he stretched out his stiff limbs, he gazed down at the ex-British colony twinkling in the darkness and thought about the minor geographical differences and stark historical similarities between it and his final destination.

Singapore was closer to the equator, hotter, flatter, and a few square miles smaller than Hong Kong. But it had also suffered Japanese occupation in the war, and communist sedition after it. And it had already rejected a return to old imperial rule and opted to become entwined with the politics and economics of its nearest neighbour, the recently established Federation of Malaya. He wondered if Hong Kong was destined for the same fate with China. And if, also like Singapore, it would find itself ejected from its new union in surprisingly short order.

Glancing one last time at the two other occupants of the cabin as they all disembarked, he reassured himself that his mind really had been playing a trick on him when he thought he saw the Line Z woman, and that it was time to start concentrating on what exactly he was going to do about finding Knox when he reached Hong Kong.

His focus lasted until he saw her two places ahead of him in the queue at the Cathay Pacific transfer desk.

He was dumbstruck, livid – and impressed. He wanted to storm past the people between them and demand that she explain how she'd appeared out of thin air, and why she was in Singapore. But he couldn't.

Instead, he let her leave the desk with a ticket to somewhere and a smile for the young, blushing man who had served her, and kept his eyes on her as she sauntered slowly away and he willed the queue to move quickly.

Luckily, it did. The two people in front of him were both just lost and asking the desk's tired-looking occupant for directions.

When it was his turn, he snatched his ticket with an apologetic grimace and took off after the woman.

He saw the long, loose curls of her hair disappear through a door – an accessible restroom. She'd let herself get trapped. There was no way for her to escape without him seeing, and all he had to do was wait. Yet after ten minutes she hadn't tried to leave the toilet, and after another five he decided to walk over and try the door. At which point he found it unlocked, and realised she'd been waiting for him all along.

'Following ladies into restrooms isn't very gentlemanly,' Anna said.

She was leaning against the side of the sink, her body and voice giving off a sense of relaxed boredom.

Laing locked the door behind him. 'What are you doing here?'

'Well, I was about to powder my nose.'

'What are you doing in Singapore?'

Anna pushed herself off the sink edge and casually adjusted her hair in the mirror. 'Going to Hong Kong, if I don't miss my connection because someone keeps asking me redundant questions.'

The barb stung, but Laing refused to let her get under his skin as quickly as she had with Williams. When he replied, he kept his voice calm. 'You're following me.'

A grin. 'Yes.'

'Why?'

'Because I like you. You cut to the chase, even if you don't know where you're racing to.' She turned to Laing, letting her smile fade and become a touch more sombre. 'And I think we have shared interests.'

'I don't think we do.'

'Or perhaps you just haven't realised yet. We could work together.'

'Why would I work with an enemy agent?'

'I'm not your enemy, Mr Laing. I could be your friend. I'm Anna.'

She thrust out a hand. Laing didn't take it. She smiled again.

'We don't have to be strange bedfellows quite yet,' she said, crossing the small distance between them. 'But my original offer's still open. You scratch my back and I'll scratch yours.'

Laing stiffened as she leaned in close to him and her hand drifted to the lock. He could smell her perfume, a mixture of lavender, lemon, and rosemary that was simultaneously light and earthy, sweet and acidic.

'You mean give you classified information,' he said, his voice instinctively lowering to a whisper at the sudden, unexpected intimacy.

'Or something else I might enjoy.' She stepped back, giving Laing space to move out of her way. 'It's up to you. And it really is. You're a long way from home and you might need an ally.'

She opened the door and strolled out of the restroom just as their plane's boarding announcement started.

CHAPTER 46

White had been right about rising early. And Anna, as much as Valera still didn't fully want to admit it, had also been right about delivering her to where she needed to be. Because she'd spent her morning feeling like she was reverting, like she was becoming an earlier, original, essential version of herself – the her before she was a political pawn, a grieving asset, and a lonely recluse. The her that was simply a scientist.

White had knocked on her door at the crack of dawn to deliver a cup of milky tea before he took Stella 'for a quick once round the block' while she was to help herself to whatever she wanted from the kitchen for breakfast. If he'd noticed her brief absence in the middle of the night, he didn't mention it.

Then he'd driven her to a building called Leconfield House, which he assured her was the real headquarters of MI5. She believed him. It didn't have the grandiosity of the Lubyanka or the scale of the campuses and compounds she'd worked on in America, but it did have several features within it that suggested it was home to an intelligence agency, including the glass box she'd been sitting inside with White for the last two hours.

They'd quickly fallen into a rhythm once White had explained the point of the construction, and the listening device, copper spiral and hourglass resting on a table in the centre of it.

They would discuss a hypothesis, test it by studying either the miniature bug, which had had its casing removed, or more enlarged photographs of its tiny nooks and crannies for twenty minutes, then take a silent break while the air in the box was recirculated.

Both their internal clocks were now in sync, and without signalling each other, Valera got up from the photograph she'd been looking at and went to open the two sets of glass doors, while White moved the listening device from beneath the magnifying glass he'd set up in front of him to back inside the precautionary copper coil magnet. They waited a few minutes, then Valera shut the doors again and turned over the hourglass.

'You could just use them, you know,' she said, eliciting a quizzical look from White. 'Work out what frequency activates them, then point your own transceiver where you think they might be hiding and listen in.'

'I doubt piggybacking on someone else's technology would satisfy the director general in the long term,' White replied.

'Then find them, retrieve them, and adjust the activation frequency. That way you could still benefit from their hard work while also taking their advantage from them.'

'True. However, that would let whoever had gone to all this trouble know we were on to them.'

Valera remembered an analogy she'd used years ago to explain the potential of radio-wave frequency bands to open thousands of invisible doors all over the planet through which people could talk to each other, or eavesdrop on each other, or lie to each other.

'And remove the opportunity to feed them whatever lies you wanted,' she said, nodding as she completed the tacit chain of logic White had started.

Valera picked up the photograph she'd been studying and handed it to White. It showed the curve of a miniaturised cavity microphone with two smaller square units soldered next to it.

'Amplifiers,' she said.

'Both?' White said. 'A redundancy?'

'I think they're set to run in tandem.'

He frowned. 'That's not how I'd do it.'

Valera stifled a smirk. As much as White had been subtly guiding her, she'd been doing the same to him, to test his real motive for building this box of his, and for inviting her into it. And he'd just confirmed it. He might work for spies, but his true master was still science. He wasn't a scavenger. He wanted to know who his competition was.

'It's a shortcut Soviet engineers sometimes use,' she said. 'Assume you'll need your backup, so have it working already.'

'So, it's the Russians,' White said, staring at the image.

'Possibly. But the only way to know for sure is to completely take it apart and inspect every element and connection.'

White looked again at the photo and then the bug itself. Then he let out a short sigh and said, 'At least then we can stop worrying if this one's still working.'

Valera took the listening device off its copper-wrapped plinth and placed it back under the magnifying glass. Then she picked up one of the scalpel-thin blades White had so far only used to nudge and scratch at bits of the bug, and began jimmying off the individual amplifier covers.

The first one came away easily, confirming Valera's guess about what was inside. The second one, however, put up more of a fight, and she ended up having to cut through the top of the casing to see what was inside. There was an answer, and a mystery. The compartment did house another amplifier, and it had been double-soldered, with thin lines of metal beading running along its outside edges and spot welds inside. Valera checked the first cover and saw the signs of spot welds inside it too, which must have been caught by the very tip of her scalpel.

It took her a few seconds to process the implication of this almost invisible detail.

'I've seen this technique before,' she said, pointing it out to White. 'At the NASA research centre in Langley.'

'The Americans?' White said, his voice suddenly a combination of surprise, concern, and confusion. 'Working with the Russians?'

'At least one American and one Russian.'

'It beggars belief.'

'I'm proof that it doesn't,' Valera replied. 'And I believe the man you have locked up in that country house is too.'

The groove above White's eyes deepened. 'You think Jack Williams is connected to this? He was a Soviet prisoner, not a collaborator.'

'I'm also proof that sometimes people cooperate willingly and sometimes they do it to survive. I don't know which he did, or if he has any idea about this. But considering what I've discovered, if you haven't already asked him about it I think it would be wise to.'

White's report to Holland on what Valera had discovered about the bug that had been extracted from the Bank of England took less than five minutes.

After they'd left the box, he'd summoned a lab technician, who was instructed to take Valera down to the car park. Then White had taken the lift up to the fifth floor.

The look he gave Miss Albury outside the director general's door made it clear that he didn't have time to take Holland out to the rose garden, or anywhere else.

'You look positively ebullient,' the director general said to White, who of course did not, as he stepped into his office. 'What can I do for you?'

'I've just heard some good news,' White said, continuing the charade. 'Uncle and Mother seem to have patched things up at last. Apparently they're in town celebrating as we speak.'

It wasn't a complex code, but that was the point – anything too obscure or convoluted would draw the attention of whoever might be listening in.

Holland's face was grim, but his voice was bright. 'That's wonderful. If they're going to be here for a day or two we should find out where they're staying and send flowers.'

'I'm about to do just that,' White replied, his eyes instinctively drifting over to the wall behind Holland's desk where he knew a bug was buried. 'Quietly. Don't want to ruin the surprise, after all.'

'Excellent, but be quick, and don't worry about the cost. It'll be worth it to see the looks on their faces.'

White left.

As he rode the lift down the building, he found himself unable to decide if he should be more excited about the potential of finally having made a breakthrough in his quest to uncover who was behind the silent invasion of Leconfield House, or terrified by the possibility that somehow members of Britain's greatest Cold War ally and enemy were working together against MI5.

CHAPTER 47

Williams was waiting for White and Valera when they returned to Rabley Heath.

White had driven them in another Service pool car, and he'd been much quieter than when they'd both been chauffeured into London by Laing the day before. Valera sensed that this wasn't just because he'd had to concentrate on the roads this time.

Williams too seemed to be in a stormier mood. Valera had suspected that yesterday's performance as a gracious host had been just that – an attempt to cover the obvious effect Anna had had on him – but now there was no mask. In fact, he almost glared at Valera and White from the front of the house as they drove up to it, then after a curt, silent nod as they both got out of the car, he strode round to the back door, clearly expecting them both to follow.

And they did, through the kitchen and into a large room with tall windows, an enormous fireplace that had a record player in the middle of it, and a wide leather sofa, high-backed chair and a low table, in the centre of which was a small pile of the miniature listening devices Valera and White had spent the morning taking apart.

'What the hell is this?' Williams demanded, standing next to the table, his body and voice both rigid.

Instead of answering, Valera watched as White went back into the kitchen and returned a few moments later with a copper pan. He scooped all the bugs into it, took it to the fireplace, put it on the floor in front of one of the speakers, and turned the record player on without loading an LP so a low white noise filled the room. Then he left the room again, beckoning the others with a staccato flick of his arm.

A few moments later they were in the middle of the rear lawn.

'Do you really think I'm wandering around here talking to myself, letting slip secrets I haven't told the Service?' Williams asked, his posture still stiff with anger.

This time White answered. 'No.'

'So how do you explain them, then?'

'We hoped you could,' Valera said, pulling Williams's attention from White.

'I've never seen them before, but I can guess what they are,' he replied. 'And my home is bloody covered in them.'

'When did you find them?' White asked, his eyes scanning the building.

'Last night. Someone broke in. A very professional job. And they got away before I could have a chat with them.'

'Well, it wasn't us. You're not the only one who's had his privacy invaded.'

Williams gave White a look that made it clear he wasn't ready to believe him, and turned to Valera. 'Why do you think I'd know anything about them?'

'I examined one earlier this morning,' she replied, her voice calm, even, and rational. 'It showed signs of having been worked on by people from more than one country, and I believe you used to work for an organisation that employed people from more than one country.'

'I'd hardly say employed,' Williams replied, his shoulders finally starting to soften. 'You really aren't spying on your own?' he asked White.

The other man shook his head.

'Then Miss Valera's deduction is a reasonable one.'

'And a worrying one,' White said. 'Because we don't think any other intelligence agency is close to producing something like them. And if Line Z aren't either, then that means we're dealing with a player we didn't even know was in the game.'

White's point was punctuated by an explosion thirty feet away.

The lawn erupted, sending grass and mud into the air.

All three looked at the crater and then, in perfect unison, at what had created it. A man, emerging from the bushes at the far end of the lawn, carrying an M79 Springfield Armory grenade launcher. A man Valera had last seen being dragged through a bathroom door in a roadside diner in Colorado.

'Get inside,' Williams shouted, grabbing at Valera's arm and dragging her when she didn't immediately start sprinting for cover.

The three of them raced back into the house and the room they'd been in only a few minutes ago. They reached it just in time to see the man raise the grenade launcher to his shoulder and fire again.

The first shot had clearly been intended to announce his presence rather than kill anyone, because his second one sailed in a perfect arc straight through the middle pane of one of the tall windows and landed in the centre of the room, between Williams, Valera, and White.

Williams was the first to react, kicking the 40mm olive-green round-tipped shell into the fireplace, then diving behind the sofa. He was followed a split second later by Valera.

White, however, went for the door. He was halfway through and round the frame when the grenade exploded.

This projectile had been designed to disorient and damage. It ejected bursts of intense light and sound along with sixteen 24-gram metal pellets at high speed. Ten of the pellets lodged themselves into the fireplace sides, passing through Williams's record player and the pan of bugs as if they were paper. Three slammed into the floor and ceiling, and two sailed back through windows and out across the rear lawn. But one found White's trailing upper arm, forcing him off his feet mid-stride and sending his body falling too fast for him to brace himself. His head bounced as the corridor floorboards knocked him out.

Williams and Valera, ears ringing, peered over the back of the sofa, checking themselves for injuries and the floor for more grenades. Once they were sure only one had been hurled into the drawing room, they got up and looked through the now-glassless window.

The man was still walking towards the house. Valera froze again, desperately trying to work out how he'd managed to track her down, as Williams dashed over to check White's prone body.

The upper half of the scientist's arm was a mess of flesh, blood, and shirtsleeve, and his forehead was already beginning to swell where it had hit the floor. He didn't respond to Williams's nudging, and his breathing was shallow.

'We need to get him help,' Williams called out, his voice loud enough for Valera to hear over the high-pitched whine that was still reverberating around her skull.

'We have to get away from here,' she replied, moving to the doorway, but keeping her eyes fixed on the man who was getting closer and closer to the house.

'Who is that?' Williams asked.

'He wants to kill me,' Valera replied.

'How do you know it's you he's after?'

'Because he's already tried. He destroyed my house.'

'And now he's doing a pretty good job of obliterating mine.'

Williams pointed to White's feet as he reached down to slide his hands under his armpits.

'Probably best you're out of it for this,' he said to White's expressionless face, then added, 'On three,' to Valera.

He'd reached two when another grenade exploded, this time in the kitchen, sending shrapnel fragments of cupboard doors and ceiling plaster out into the corridor ahead of them.

'Which way is the front door?' Valera asked as they picked up White's body.

'We aren't leaving,' Williams answered, which almost made Valera drop White's ankles.

'We must.'

'I'm not going out into open ground with a casualty. And I'm not letting someone get away with lobbing grenades through my windows.'

Williams started shuffling backwards, pulling White and Valera through another doorway and guiding them into a smaller room, then another, and finally into one that seemed like a dead end.

He nodded at Valera to let go of White, then at one of the wooden wall panels in the corner furthest from the door.

For a moment Valera couldn't tell what she was supposed to do, or be looking at. But then she saw the thin groove that ran parallel to the floor a few inches above her head, then turned downwards, cutting the thinnest slice through the skirting board. She pushed the panel and it moved slightly to her touch, trying to swing back on stiff, old hinges.

Williams laid White down and smacked the secret door with his palm, forcing it further open and revealing a hidden storeroom almost as big as the one they were in.

'Get him inside, and try to stop him from bleeding to death,' Williams said. 'I'll be back as quick as I can.'

CHAPTER 48

Williams felt cold rage ignite inside him. His home was being attacked, and so were his friends. Yes, Rabley Heath was more prison than sanctum, and true, over the last year White had played his own part as occasional interrogator, with little apology or sign of remorse. But still, however much he might want to escape it, Williams's world was under assault, and he had to fight back.

He darted across the room they'd carried White's body through, checking for telltale spots of blood on the floor that might give away Valera's hiding place. Miraculously there were none. Then he went to the kitchen to quickly assess the damage the third grenade had done.

This one was the same type as the second, and had gone off in the middle of the room, giving its pellets the chance to blast in all directions, slamming through cupboards, tiles, and lodge in the fronts of both the range cooker and fridge, while the explosive itself had caved in the counter it had landed on and brought down a hefty chunk of ceiling plaster.

Williams picked his way across the room, careful not to touch or step on anything that would make a sound and give away his location, and smelling the subtle mix of dust and gas that now filled the air.

His sixth sense – and the open back door – told him that the man was already inside the house, and once he'd reached the other side of the kitchen he took a split second to steady himself and work out where. A distinct, unique high-pitched creak, which

Williams had avoided making almost exactly twelve hours ago, told him he was in the ballroom.

The man had assumed, Williams thought, that he, Valera, and White had made it past the kitchen before the last grenade had detonated, so he was tracking their likely path to another escape route.

It was a smart guess, and pleasingly wrong. It also meant that he was on the other side of the house from White and Valera, and Williams knew how to make sure he stayed far away from them – by leading him on a cat and mouse chase through the rest of Rabley Heath.

He took the servants' stairs up to the first floor, then drifted along the landing, past the main staircase, to one of the guest suites at the far end that was still in a state of empty disrepair, and placed two heavy feet down in the middle of the space where its bed should be.

The effect was instant. The invader gave up on any semblance of guile and rapidly made his way up to the first floor. Williams, of course, changed rooms, light on the balls of his feet again.

He wanted to know what else the man might have in his arsenal alongside the grenade launcher, but he knew he wouldn't find that out until they confronted each other.

When Williams reckoned he was halfway up the servants' stairs he called out, 'Leave now and we'll forget this whole thing.'

He didn't expect a response and he didn't get one.

He made another guess, this time about when the man would be stepping into the empty guest suite and have his back to the door, giving Williams the first chance to strike. However, this time he was wrong. He swung out into the landing and straight into a right hook that sent shards of pain through his temple. He stumbled backwards, his palms grabbing at the wall to stop him as his eyes blinked back into focus.

The man had vanished.

Williams put his fingers up to his nostrils and they came away wet with blood. The bridge of his nose was tender, but not broken.

He tensed his body, coiled the springs of his muscles tighter, ready to defend and attack, and began stalking back along the landing.

He checked each doorway, and found every room empty. And none of them contained secret hiding places. He passed the grand, galleried staircase again, risking one single lean over the balustrade to see if his assailant had retreated downstairs, then he continued on.

Williams checked his bedroom, and Knox's, then approached the servants' stairs, his back pressed against the wall at the top so he couldn't easily be shoved down them. His sixth sense had momentarily deserted him. He couldn't tell where the man was, but the process of elimination had left him with only one more possible destination, and the thought of it brought a brief smirk to his face – the eastern turret. He'd tempted the stranger up into the house, and now he was trying to do the same to Williams.

He picked up his pace, letting the adrenaline he'd been keeping under tight control start to pulse through his body. It took over quickly, although not so much that his mind didn't warn him that there was actually one more place the man could be. And it made him duck as he reached the bottom of the turret stairs and a hammer flew out of the room next to them. Had he not crouched down, the metal head would have smashed his skull. Instead, it lodged in the wall, its handle sticking out, inviting Williams to retrieve it. He did.

Williams stepped into the room he'd set up his little workshop in. The man was waiting for him. He was no longer carrying his grenade launcher. Williams assumed he had at least one more firearm secreted about his person somewhere, but in his hands he cradled a sledgehammer roughly ten times the size and weight of his.

'You're trespassing,' Williams said, as he inwardly chastised himself for giving his attacker access to a veritable cornucopia of potential weapons. 'I'm afraid I have to ask you to leave.'

Then he lunged at the man before he had the chance to offer a riposte.

Williams had bet the other man would expect him to be cautious and not make the first move. He also hoped that the stranger would struggle to wield his weapon as nimbly as he himself would be able to. His luck held for a couple of blows to the man's arms and legs. However, neither of them were enough to bring him down, and the ultimate result was that the man simply dropped the sledge-hammer and came for Williams with his bare hands.

He was ferocious and precise, pummelling Williams with punches, finger jabs, and sharp elbows all over his body, forcing him to drop the hammer and never giving him a chance to get a hit in himself. His attack pushed Williams backwards, and he only stopped when Williams staggered into the door frame and he retreated into the middle of the room, claiming the centre ground once more.

They stared at each other, and for the first time Williams registered how dilated and penetrating the stranger's eyes were. He glanced at the saws and chisels that were out of his reach, and the rolled-up flag propped up in the corner of the room that he'd thankfully carried up here after he'd thought Stinky had invaded the kitchen.

The sight of it steeled him, but the smile that spread across the other man's face infuriated him. He knew he was being goaded, but he couldn't resist. He lunged again, and the man sidestepped him, dropping both of his elbows onto Williams's back as he passed him and sending him skidding into the opposite wall between the room's two sets of double-height windows.

The smile widened.

Williams pulled himself up onto his feet as he heard three bangs in quick succession coming from beneath them. They shook him out of his tunnel focus on the man. He also registered a slight sting in his eyes and tasted faint smoke on his breath. Part of the house was on fire, and he could guess which.

It was a concern, especially given Valera and White's proximity to the kitchen. But there was no way for Williams to deal with it while his way out of the workshop was being blocked and he was being so comprehensively beaten up.

His mind raced through all the combat training he'd voluntarily taken with MI5 and the armed forces, and the lessons in murder he'd been forced to learn by Line Z. In just a few seconds he came up with an impressively long list of tactics, but decided against all of them. Instead, just like the stranger had used Williams's own ploys against him, he was going to do the same.

Williams smiled back at the man who had invaded his home, broadly and openly, and did nothing.

They grinned at each other, both swaying and shifting their weight, but neither striking out. They danced in place for almost thirty seconds, eyes not blinking and mouths straining wider and wider, until the stranger finally gave in to his impatience.

He leapt at Williams. And Williams, spinning to his side, grabbed the man's shoulders and flung him out of one of the windows.

Valera dragged White through the secret door, eliciting an unconscious groan that proved he was still alive, and slumped him against a bare wall.

She pulled the door to behind them, then inspected him properly. His chest was still rising and falling evenly, but his left shirtsleeve was now sodden, and she could see muscle and sinew mixed in with the red of the blood, along with a sliver of bone that forced her to steady her stomach.

Valera knew she needed to stem the bleeding. Figuring that White's shirt was ruined, and that he wasn't really in a position to protest, she tore his right sleeve off and made a tourniquet from it, wrapping it round his left arm just below the shoulder, tightly enough to staunch the blood flow but not so much that it would cause irreparable damage to his circulation.

She thought about leaving. Let Williams distract – or hopefully finally deal with – the man who'd tried to kill her in Colorado and managed to trace her to a country house north of London. Take White's car, drive it as far as it had petrol, or to a backstreet in London where she could sell it with few questions for enough money to buy a plane ticket.

She'd done what she could for White. He wasn't her responsibility, and she didn't owe him anything... But didn't she? He'd been kind to her, trusted her, welcomed her into his home. Hadn't he earned a little more reciprocity?

Valera decided that he, in fact, had. She wanted to take care of him, as he'd looked after her. And she would trust Williams to protect both of them. She would stay where she was.

Except that she couldn't. Because she could smell smoke.

She didn't know if the man was trying to lure her out by burning down the house, or if the grenade in the kitchen had sparked an electrical or gas fire. But it didn't matter either way – the result was the same. She had to get White and herself out of their hiding place before they ended up being trapped, suffocated, or burned to death.

She yanked the old metal sliver of a handle on the door, suddenly terrified that it might come away in her hand. Thankfully it didn't. The door opened. Still stiff, but wide enough for her to carry White back through.

The next room looked the same as it had a few minutes ago, just with a few faint wisps of smoke drifting across its corniced ceiling. And the air was acrid.

There was no point trying to get to the back door – that was the direction of the fire. And Valera didn't think she had the strength to tip White out through one of the drawing room's windows. She knew the house had a grand entrance, and she guessed where she'd find it.

She hauled White down a corridor and through the large hallway, past a wide staircase to the towering vestibuled front doors. They were exposed, vulnerable to anyone who might be lurking beyond the slip of haze that hung halfway up the staircase. But there was no other way out of the house, and Valera reassured herself that it would only be for the few moments it would take her to prop White against the wall and open the door.

However, seconds rapidly turned into minutes as she discovered the door's lock was stuck. Any other time she might have tried to fix the problem, correct the mechanical failure. But right now she didn't have that luxury. So instead she simply kicked at the lock three times with all her strength, cracking and buckling the old, thick wood around it just enough for her to pull the doors apart.

She'd dragged White across the gravel almost to the MI5 pool Consul when she heard yet another window smash above her and the man who had crossed continents and oceans to kill her landed on the driveway, head-first, ten feet away.

CHAPTER 49

Williams waited, watching the man's body to see if had somehow survived its swan dive to Earth. When it didn't move after a minute, Williams did.

He went to his bedroom, pulled out a duffel bag from the bottom of his wardrobe, filled it with a few changes of clothes and a light jacket, then carried it downstairs through the thickening miasma of smoke that hung across the hallway void.

He didn't rush to the kitchen, struggle to put out the fire and stop all the restoration work he'd toiled over for months being destroyed. Or dash to Valera and White's hiding place, because he'd seen them on the driveway, Valera cradling White in her lap, motionless in shock at the abrupt arrival of another body a few feet away from them.

He only paused briefly to check the phone that was tucked away in a dark, hidden recess at the bottom of the stairs and confirm his suspicion that while he'd been tempting the stranger upstairs, the man had been pulling out its wires and cutting off Rabley Heath's connection to the outside world.

Then, for the first time in a long time, he stepped through Rabley Heath's front doors.

Williams had defended his home, protected those who had needed him, and proved he could outwit and out-fight a highly trained assassin. He had no interest in waiting around for whoever might want to test him next, whether that was Holland, a Service psychologist, or another enemy agent. He was also done with waiting for permission to do his part. He was a soldier, and he'd been sitting out the war long enough. It was time to head back onto the battlefield.

He found the dead man's body still splayed on the gravel, and Valera still holding White. Williams strode silently past all three, but he didn't leave. He headed to the gatehouse at the end of the drive, checked that its phone still worked, and made two calls. Then he went back to Valera.

'How is he?' he asked her, nodding at White.

'Alive,' she answered.

'Good. Five is on the way. So is the fire brigade. I'm not sure which will get here first.'

Williams turned to the body lying across from Valera and White. He could see the gravel around the thin man's head starting to stain reddy-brown. He nudged the man's side with his foot, then leaned down to pat his pockets and limbs.

There was no wallet, receipts or ticket stubs that might give away an identity, or any clues about who had sent him. But there was an MAB PA-15 semi-automatic pistol, still lodged in a holster in the small of his back, and a stiletto blade tied to his left ankle. Williams took both of them, wondering briefly why neither had been used against him.

'What are you going to do?' Valera asked, her eyes switching between Williams's duffel and his newly acquired weapons.

'Some good, I hope,' he replied. 'And you?'

Valera shifted her gaze to White. 'The same, I think.'

Williams nodded, picked up his bag, and started to walk down the drive again.

This time he went out through the gates.

CHAPTER 50

Laing didn't pay attention to the descent into Hong Kong. He missed the stunning views, the perilous geography, the feats of piloting that brought him back down to earth after his full day's travelling.

After checking every other seat in the Cathay Pacific Convair 880's front cabin for signs of Anna before his departure from Singapore and finding none, he'd managed a few more hours of sleep. Then, for the last two, he'd been going over the last thing she'd said to him in the airport toilet, his eyes staring blankly at the back of the seat in front of his.

With Knox missing and not much help to be expected from Hong Kong Station, he was going to be operating alone. And he had to succeed. He needed to find Knox. He needed to work out who had got their hands on a Blue Peacock bomb. And he needed to find it before they set it off. He found himself ever so slightly wishing that Leconfield House had sent a larger cavalry.

Once his plane had taxied to the terminal and he set foot on solid ground again, he became so focused on plotting out what his first moves would be when he reached the city proper that he didn't notice the brush-past as he made his way through baggage claim, which, even at this early hour, was full of people jostling and jockeying to retrieve their luggage. It was only when his nose detected the faintest echo of lavender, lemon, and rosemary that his hands went instinctively to his pockets and he found a note on a slip of Cathay Pacific-headed paper. It had the name of a hotel written on it in neat script: the Mandarin Oriental. And beneath that a person's: Gutierrez.

Laing assumed it was one of countless aliases that Anna had at her disposal. It wasn't a name he'd come across in any old mission reports, and it taunted him, which he was entirely sure was the point. It would be days before he could give some junior clerk in the Leconfield House records team the miserable task of combing through old London hotel registers to see if it had ever been used in any of them – which it probably hadn't. But it was also a kind of olive branch. A way for him to actually take up the offer of help she'd made in Singapore should he need to.

He memorised both names, tore the paper into several pieces and dropped them in a bin just in front of the wide doors to the entrance hall. Then he stepped through and immediately achieved one of his mission objectives.

Knox was there.

They didn't shake hands, speak, or even acknowledge each other. Instead, Knox just turned away from the arrivals board he was pretending to study and left the airport, and Laing, hoping he'd managed to mask his surprise well enough, casually followed him out past a rank of taxis to a black Mercedes.

'Good of you to come,' Knox said as they both got in. He started the engine and pulled out into the flow of vehicles heading into the centre of Kowloon.

Laing, still bemused that the man he'd come to rescue had been waiting to collect him from his flight, replied, 'Holland thought you could use some help.'

'How's Jack?'

'Fine,' Laing said, trying to ignore the inference that Knox would have rather been waiting for someone else.

Knox nodded. 'Bennett will be pleased to see you.'

Laing felt a twinge of phantom pain in his thigh at the mention of her name. He'd met Bennett before. A year ago. He'd ended up taking a bullet in the leg soon after the introduction.

'Abey Bennett's here?'

'Turns out she was looking into Blue Peacock too. We're working together, along with a member of Special Branch. And you're here in the nick of time. We think it's on the move today.'

'Really?' Laing replied, now not trying to hide his shock. 'Do you have any idea of the target?'

Knox shook his head. 'That's currently one of the larger pieces of the puzzle we're still missing. There's a festival today, but we don't know if it's going to be used as cover to ship it out, or an opportunity to distribute it through the city.'

Now Laing wasn't just surprised, he was also confused. 'Distribute it?'

'Well, that's our working theory. A new drug, a highly potent psychedelic that Lady Reeve, Bennett, and I have all had the misfortune to experience first-hand. Unless you know otherwise.'

'That's why I'm here,' Laing replied, his tone becoming more grave with every word. 'We couldn't get a message to you faster because we didn't know where you were. There wasn't anything in the archives or Pipistrelle feeds, but Williams recognised the name. Blue Peacock isn't a drug. It's a bomb.'

CHAPTER 51

Knox drove straight from the car ferry pier to Bennett's apartment. Suddenly time was a lot more important than stealth.

Even as it had seemed more and more certain that Blue Peacock was some form of narcotic, without irrefutable proof Knox had always maintained the possibility that it could be something else and that he, Bennett, and Zhou were all wrong. He'd actually hoped they might be. But he'd never imagined their theory would be so far from reality.

He and Laing had stayed in the Mercedes as they'd crossed Victoria Harbour, hemmed in on all sides by other cars whose drivers had gone up to the open deck to stretch their legs for a few minutes and snatch a quick look at the dragon boats being readied for the morning's races.

Laing had explained the truth of Blue Peacock. That it was an experimental bomb dreamed up by the army in the fifties. That it never got past the prototype phase. That MI5 was trying to work out how many had been built, where they'd been mothballed, and if any had gone missing recently. And that even without an active nuclear warhead the bomb shell could still be packed with a high enough yield of traditional explosives to do significant damage.

With each sentence, Knox's heart sank and his fear grew. He imagined an overloaded sampan being floated up against a Star Ferry or HMS *Bulwark* and blown up. Or the festival still being used as cover for a Blue Peacock to be shipped somewhere else and used in an attack that could, if the right remnants were recovered and questions asked, be blamed on Britain.

Knox had spent yesterday slowing himself down and chastising himself for acting too rashly. But now he had to move quickly again, because the stakes had abruptly become much higher.

When they reached Bennett's building, the introductions were short, just nods between Laing, Bennett, and Zhou before Knox brought the two women up to speed.

He expected Bennett to fire questions at him, ignore the temptation to navel-gaze and indulge in pointless wallowing about how they'd all got it wrong, and jump straight to coming up with a new plan. But she didn't. She stayed quiet, standing in the doorway to the kitchen, her face set in the same mix of irritation and calculation as it had been the previous night.

'So we can't be sure if it's atomic or not, or what its target is,' Zhou said.

Knox shook his head. 'We don't know if we're trying to stop a terrorist attack or a black-market trade.'

'If it's headed for the People's Republic by land it will be caught by the border guards. I've already requested more thorough checks at the port, but we don't have enough people to inspect every container in the hold of every cargo ship coming in and out of the city.'

'And it may have already passed through Hong Kong and be on its way to its final destination. That could have been what Saturday was all about, and today's the day the walled city gang celebrate either getting away with their deal or destroying one of the many viable targets within a couple of days' sail.'

'No,' Bennett said, finally breaking her silence. 'It's going to be here.'

Everyone turned towards her.

'How can you be sure?' Laing asked.

'I just can,' she replied, crossing over the living room towards her balcony and gesturing for Knox – and only Knox – to follow her.

He did, closing the glass door behind him and stepping round the narrow corner, where Bennett was waiting out of sight of Laing and Zhou.

'What's going on?' Knox asked, leaning against the window to the bedroom, next to Bennett, and alternating his glances between her and the harbour in the distance. He could see HMS *Bulwark* still afloat, holding position far off to the west, keeping well out of the way of the junks and dragon boats crowding the narrower part of the strait. 'How can you be so sure the attack is going to happen here?'

'Because,' she replied, refusing to make eye contact, 'I helped them set it up.'

Knox was stunned, confused, and glad he hadn't been leaning against the balcony edge. He couldn't imagine Bennett turning terrorist, or fathom how she could possibly be involved with Blue Peacock.

'What does that mean?'

'The walled city group. I don't think I was spying on them. I think I was working for them.'

'You think?'

Bennett took a step forward, and turned to face Knox. Her eyes, normally so bright and focused, were cloudy and dull. For a split second he wondered if she was going to tip backwards over the waist-high wall of concrete and let herself fall down to the street below them.

'I know what went through your head when I told you how I ended up in Hong Kong,' she said. 'I thought the exact same thing. I was being shuffled round, kept out of the way. Then a request was put in out of nowhere to send me here. Lots of praise, no details. I never trusted the transfer, or my new boss.'

'You think he's serving more than one master?'

She nodded. 'Which means I am too. He gave me free rein, was interested enough in whatever I brought to him, but seemed a little too curious about Blue Peacock when I noticed it cropping up around the city.'

'That's not enough to brand him a traitor, or you for that matter.'

'He was the only other person who knew we were going back to Kowloon on Saturday. While I was sitting on top of a ladder in my silo I got to wondering if my job was to work out what Blue Peacock was or if I was being used to make sure it stayed a secret.'

'I've learned not to second-guess your instincts,' Knox said. 'But that sounds like a bit of a leap, and still not much to go on.'

'I wasn't sure either until last night,' Bennett replied.

'That's who you went to see?'

She nodded again.

'What happened?'

'He told me he was leaving the city for a while, was practically on his way to the airport then. Suggested I should do the same. While I could.'

That, Knox thought, changed things. It was a clear message of intent, and a tacit admission of guilt. 'Why didn't you say anything sooner?'

Bennett sighed and crossed her arms. 'I was embarrassed. I hoped I was wrong. I thought we'd be able to contain Blue Peacock. There'd always be a backup if it was a drug. Stop a shipment, dump it in the sea, get the CIA to buy it all. But a nuclear bomb is a completely different level. I'm sorry, Richard.'

He looked at her, then at the harbour, which even with an aircraft carrier guarding its entrance suddenly felt dangerously undefended, and processed the implications of what Bennett had just said. He trusted her, so if she said an attack on the city was imminent, then it was.

'There's no need to apologise. We've been trying to put a jigsaw together without knowing what it looked like and only half the pieces. Now we've got a few more, and at least we know we're going to need help with the rest. And let's work on the optimistic assumption that it's not armed with a nuclear warhead.'

After another long sigh from Bennett, Knox led them back into the living room, where they found Laing and Zhou sitting silently at either end of the rattan sofa.

'How big is a Blue Peacock?' Knox asked Laing.

'About the size of a Mini,' he replied. 'Shaped like a big drum barrel on its side.'

'Small enough to move easily, but big enough that there's at least some limit on the number of places it could be hidden without drawing attention,' Bennett said.

Knox turned to Zhou. 'How angry would your people be if we pulled most of them from the port?'

'They'll do what they're told,' she replied.

'Good,' Knox said, crossing back over the room. 'Let's try to narrow down the list of possible targets while we go see Atwood.'

'Why?' Zhou and Laing asked in unison as they got up.

'I'm afraid we're going to need all the help we can get, including his.'

Zhou gave a resigned nod as Laing said, 'He'll be surprised to see you.'

Now it was Knox's turn to ask 'Why?' as he reached the front door.

'His last message to Leconfield House said you'd already left Hong Kong two days ago.'

Knox stopped in his tracks. The question he'd asked himself over and over about the SLO rushed back into his head. Was the man an idiot or a master of subterfuge? Had he simply forgotten the details of their last conversation, or had he deliberately misled the director general of MI5 about Knox's whereabouts, possibly to shift the Service's gaze away from Hong Kong at the very moment it should have been paying extremely close attention to the city?

'That is categorically not what I told him,' Knox said.

'What does that mean?' Bennett asked, repeating his earlier question back at him.

'That we might have found another piece of the puzzle,' Knox replied.

CHAPTER 52

The junk wasn't really a junk at all. It was a yacht, usually hired by the kind of rich executive or holidaymaker who fetishised authentic experiences but was unable to sacrifice the luxury they were used to.

Normally it spent its days leisurely sailing round the smaller islands south of Lantau and Lamma, its passengers filling themselves up on champagne and oysters. But its owners didn't mind it being used as a glorified sea taxi first thing in the morning – they'd been paid a hefty premium for the boat's services, and they'd still have plenty of time to ready it for the group of well-to-do Hong Kongers who had chartered it so they could enjoy the day's dragon boat races from the water.

The fake junk had spent the last hour speeding from Tsim Sha Tsui to Macau, care of several submerged rotors at its rear. And Anna had spent the whole time on deck, letting the wind blow the long flights out of her hair and clothes, smiling to herself at the dangle of her hotel name and alias she'd left in Laing's pocket in Kai Tak, and giving whoever might be watching her approach a good, clear look at her.

Macau was Hong Kong's smaller stepsister. A Portuguese colony that had once been the largest trading post on the Pearl River Delta but had recently pegged the future of its economy to a booming gambling industry. It had also had its own share of unrest and clashes between its colonial government and leftist protestors over the last year.

As the yacht neared Macau's colonnaded harbourfront, Anna could make out the Ruins of St Paul's on a hill above the city. The Catholic church, once the most powerful symbol of Europe's spread through the East, had been almost completely destroyed almost a century ago, leaving just an ornate edifice standing defiantly at the top of a grand, empty staircase.

Anna had never been to Macau before, but she'd studied her destination, and the fast but indirect route she'd take to reach it once she was back on dry land.

Once she'd established where Laing was headed in London, she'd put in motion a series of arrangements she'd worked out several months ago in case her quest brought her to Asia.

Two crewmen offered hands she didn't need to help her down from the deck to the dock. They followed her to the trishaw that was waiting to pick her up, then continued on their way without a word to her or each other. Anna guessed they were going to spend the hour they'd been told to wait for her collecting a large order of the pastéis de nata that, along with the chance to win or lose a life's savings, drew people here from all over Asia.

She decided she'd have to sample one, if she returned to the yacht.

The driver of the trishaw looked like he'd just started work for the day – his wide-brimmed hat was still perched comfortably and symmetrically on his head and the long sleeves of his loose white cotton top weren't marked with creases or sweat yet. He pedalled Anna past children in starched uniforms walking to school in small, whispering groups, and others who were just as young but alone, who appeared to have already entered the world of work in vests they'd outgrown and jackets that didn't fit yet, herding goats down to the harbour or carrying overnight catches away from it.

Anna left the trishaw by the Jardim de Lou Lim Ioc and continued the rest of the way on foot. She walked down streets where shops were yet to open, along alleys between buildings that looked only a few decades old but were already waiting to be demolished, and through ancient, perfectly circular moon gates that led in and out of temple grounds, to the door of a small silk weaver's workshop.

The workshop was a double front. For a much larger operation that produced intricate, beautiful, and incredibly expensive shawls and scarves in factories across the colony. And for someone who had once been one of the world's greatest artisans in a very different field.

A legend who might give Anna the information she'd now travelled the whole planet in search of, or try to kill her as soon as they saw her.

She knocked on the door. It was opened by an old woman. Her face was lined with deep creases, and her hair, which was black with streaks of white, was pulled back into a tight bun. She wore an emerald-green cheongsam that fitted immaculately over her thin, slightly stooped form.

The woman looked at Anna with hard eyes and the kind of gaze she herself so often cast on others. One that simultaneously took in all of a person and shot straight through them.

After a long, silent moment she turned round and beckoned Anna inside.

Anna followed her through the gloomy workshop, past its rows of pedal-operated looms, with their combs and shuttles either waiting for their weavers to arrive or wondering where they'd disappeared to, and out into a small, square courtyard where tea for two had been set on a table in the shade of a white mulberry tree.

Anna assumed the tree was mostly for show. There was no way it could sustain enough of the silkworms that fed exclusively on its leaves to produce the amount of thread needed for a single day in this workshop, let alone the others that had been quietly popping up all over Macau for the last eighteen years. She also wondered if, as no bullet, knife, or fists had been flung at her by anyone yet, the tea the woman was now pouring out for her was poisoned.

'It's jasmine,' she said, as if answering Anna's unasked question.

Her voice was more accented than Anna's, but equally unplaceable. Where Anna's could belong to anywhere on either side of the North Atlantic with a little nuancing here and there, even in just two words the woman's drifted all over Asia. However, Anna knew she was Chinese. She also knew who she'd been in her former life.

Wei Siyun. The ex-head of Chiang Kai-shek's secret police and once chief torturer of China.

Wei had been one of Chiang's closest allies since they'd both been lieutenants of Sun Yat-sen during the overthrow of the Beiyang government in 1928, and had become the invisible, feared face of the Kuomintang to Chiang's revered, public one. She'd been at his side throughout his unification of China, and the bloody purging of communists that eventually led to Mao's rise and Chiang's retreat to Taiwan in 1949.

But while Chiang and the remnants of the Kuomintang had turned themselves into a government in exile, Wei had disappeared. Some thought she'd been killed or captured, others that she'd committed suicide because of the shame of defeat. Anna knew otherwise.

Wei had completely reinvented herself with a new name, identity and past, somewhere the People's Republic wouldn't think to hunt for her but where she could still keep a close eye on what it was up to, while she built her own private empire in retirement.

'I'm honoured,' Anna replied.

'You're brazen.'

Anna smiled. 'I didn't want to surprise you.'

'I knew you were coming before you left London. And if I hadn't wanted to see you, that yacht of yours would currently be settling on the bottom of the Lantau Channel.'

Wei took a sip of her tea. Anna did the same. It was fragrant, sweet, fresh.

'Do you know why I'm here?' Anna asked, placing her handleless, opal-patterned cup back on the table.

'Because you're an admirer.'

'True.'

Wei's ruthlessness and inventiveness were legendary. Her ability to coerce confessions, extract information, destroy not just a person's body and mind but their soul as well. Anna was already supremely skilled in such techniques herself, but she'd gladly spend a few months or years refining her art at the feet of a true virtuoso if the opportunity arose.

'You should have seen me in my prime.'

Anna gestured round at the buildings that surrounded the courtyard, all of which apart from the workshop she knew had been elegantly knocked together to create the enormous mansion Wei lived in. 'Your current situation seems to agree with you.'

'I must confess I do enjoy this second life I have. But you're not just here to fawn over an old woman.'

Anna nodded. 'I come to beg a humble request, and possibly offer a warning.'

Wei took another sip of her tea. 'In case I hadn't noticed the unfortunate accidents befalling people who should know how to watch their backs better?'

Anna nodded again, and this time suppressed her smile at Wei's implicit rebuke at the suggestion that she wouldn't be aware of what had been happening all over the planet.

'At first I assumed it was my previous employers,' she said.

'But?'

'I'm still alive.'

'How egotistical.'

'It's earned.'

'Perhaps. Some of your work is impressive. Some is obvious.'

'Sometimes being obvious is the point. Sometimes people need to die in their sleep. Sometimes they need to be strung up in a square.'

Wei's left eyebrow lifted a fraction. A sign, Anna thought, that she didn't entirely disagree.

'But if not Russia, then who?'

'Neither America nor the British have the stomach.'

'So now you suspect Mao? Obvious.'

'I followed a lead. It seemed prudent.'

Wei glanced down at her cup and swirled it gently in her hands, as if she was reading the fragments of leaf nestled in its bottom. Then she looked back up at Anna and asked her, 'How do you define a nation?'

It wasn't a question Anna had expected, and she could tell from the twinkle that appeared in Wei's eyes that she'd wanted to surprise her with it. She was being tested. Toyed with. She liked it.

'A government, an economy, a population,' Anna replied. 'Power, money, people.'

Wei gave a slight nod. 'And recognition. It's no good calling yourself a country if no one else does. But we know there's another world beneath this one that isn't troubled by such concerns, don't we? An inverted world where invisibility is a more desirable state and people pay less attention to antiquated concepts like geographic borders. What would a nation look like in that world?'

It sounded like Wei was describing Line Z, or the CIA, or any other intelligence service, except that all of them in one way or another were beholden to an established, recognised power. But what if they weren't? What if there was a ghost faction operating in the world's shadows? A rogue power working to unknown ends?

Wei was right, Anna thought. She had been obvious. Shallow and arrogant. Even in the normal, surface world, nations rose and fell all the time – a global metamorphosis that was sometimes voluntary, sometimes not. The country of her birth had been arbitrarily split in two by the Americans, British, and Russians with little regard for how its citizens might feel about such an abrupt division. The Soviet Union itself had risen from the ashes of its tsarist predecessor only forty-five years ago. And the People's Republic of China was still only in its second decade.

She answered Wei's question with another. 'What would they want?'

'Some things are universal. Power, money, people.'

Suddenly Anna wondered if all those scientists hadn't been clandestinely murdered but recruited – willingly or forcibly – their demises covers for their own second lives. And how many of the murderers and torturers who had vanished hadn't ended up in a pool of their own blood but had actually been tempted to serve a new master?

She also pondered if she should be more or less offended that she hadn't been approached yet? Perhaps her curiosity had already scuppered her chances, along with her delivery of Valera into MI5's arms. Or maybe it was all connected – a test to see if she was worthy of recruitment. If that was the case then they'd also have to prove they deserved her. Anna knew the allure of wearing a leash held by a powerful hand. But she also relished operating free of restraints. If someone wanted to put new ones on her, they'd have to ask very nicely.

She took a last sip of her tea and looked up at the mulberry tree for a final time.

'Have you received any ambassadors from the netherworld?' she said.

'Why would they bother with me?' Wei replied. 'I'm just an old woman who sells scarves.'

CHAPTER 53

Atwood wasn't in Bonham Strand, and neither was Charlie. As ever, the place looked on the verge of collapse, but Knox couldn't see any indications of a midnight flight. There were no drawers with false backs or bottoms left open, no hidden safe with a few notes of foreign currency or passports left behind. There was just the normal level of unprofessional mess.

Laing and Bennett – who had picked the Avalon Logistics lock once they'd managed to get inside the building – looked shocked by the state of the place. Zhou didn't.

'This is not acceptable,' Laing said, picking his way between the main office's teetering piles of newspapers and unfiled reports.

'No, it isn't,' Knox replied to everyone. 'If he's not here but he doesn't think we're on to him, where would he be?'

Knox had explained his theory that Atwood's incompetence was actually a meticulously crafted cover as they'd all crammed into Zhou's Mercedes and she'd driven them to Sheung Wan at breakneck speed. He could tell Laing and Zhou hadn't been completely convinced until Bennett had also told them about a high-ranking rogue CIA operative she'd been investigating, along with the walled city group. The possibility of an unidentified radical organisation including two spies with access to some of the West's more sensitive local secrets was a sobering one.

'A party,' Zhou replied.

'I guess wherever he goes will be safe,' Bennett added. 'I doubt he'd put himself in harm's way.'

'It's too early for a drink, though,' Knox said, 'even for him. Which means he'll probably still be at home, getting ready. Do we know where he lives?'

'Of course,' Zhou replied. 'Conduit Road.'

'Huh,' Bennett said, 'fancy.'

Both Knox and Laing raised eyebrows.

'Conduit Road has actual houses on it,' Bennett said. 'Home to the island's most rich and important.'

'It does have some grander old properties,' Zhou said. 'Atwood's is not one of them.'

The group trooped back out to the street, and, five minutes of more extremely aggressive driving later, they were partway up the refined northern slope of Victoria Peak.

Zhou and Bennett were both right. Conduit Road was a row of mansions that looked like they'd been scooped up from the edges of Regent's Park and deposited on a mountainside six thousand miles away. They were all columned porticos, double-height floors, wide driveways and terraced gardens with uninterrupted views.

And then there was Atwood's home.

It was an aberration. It couldn't even be called a folly. Set back and between two palatial properties, with high fences on either side of it, it was a squat, rusting, and peeling flat-roofed brown box, a failed gesture towards modernism that hadn't accounted for Hong Kong's subtropical climate, and which its neighbours obviously preferred to pretend didn't exist at all.

Zhou parked directly across from the short path that led to the house and she and Bennett stayed with the Mercedes, engine running, while Knox and Laing went to see if Atwood was home.

He was, and he looked surprised to see Knox and a stranger at his door. But he still invited them in, his mask of puzzlement morphing into one of welcoming, if rushed, conviviality.

'Come in, come in,' he said, waving them through the door as he slipped on a wide-lapelled, loose linen pistachio jacket. 'Just caught me, as it happens. On my way to a neighbour's for the festivities. I'm sure you're welcome to gatecrash, Richard, and your friend too.'

Somehow Knox imagined that Atwood was already going to be gatecrashing himself.

He scanned the interior of the house. It seemed to be entirely open-plan, one single wide, low-ceilinged room with a modest kitchen, dining area, bed and single armchair, all pressed up against its sides so as not to get in the way of what, Knox had to admit, was a spectacular view through floor-to-ceiling windows that stretched the whole width of the rear of the building.

There was no decoration, no clutter – the complete inverse of Bonham Strand. It was as if Atwood had never really settled in here. If Knox had dropped in on the SLO two days ago he might have wondered if the man hadn't filled the place up with trinkets and personal touches in the hope that he might be recalled to Leconfield House at any moment. Today, he thought there were different reasons for the sparseness of the man's accommodation.

'This is Simon Laing,' Knox said, 'from headquarters.'

Atwood's confusion returned. 'Another European sales representative? Is something else afoot? Another errant child gone missing?'

'He was looking for me.'

'Well, it seems he found you,' Atwood replied, patting his pockets and checking his watch. 'Now, how are we doing for time? Dr Ho doesn't appreciate tardi—'

'He was looking for me, because you told London I'd left the city,' Knox said, interrupting him. 'When I'd actually been abducted at knifepoint.'

Confusion became shock. 'Good God man, are you alright?'

'A few bruises. And more questions. Why did you lie?'

'I did no such thing,' he blustered. 'I simply said your business here had concluded and you'd be heading home.'

'That's not what was in the message,' Laing said, pulling Atwood's attention to him properly for the first time.

'You can blame Charlie for that,' Atwood replied. 'The boy's bloody useless with even the most rudimentary code. A simple miscommunication. And I wouldn't complain about getting a free jaunt round the world out of it.' He turned to Knox. 'I'm sorry you've had a rough time of it, Richard, but you can't blame me for not riding to your rescue when you didn't tell me what you were up to. So if you're done impugning my character I have a party to attend. And I rather think it would be for the best if you missed it after all.'

Knox was impressed by the man's performance, but he didn't buy it. And he could tell Laing didn't either. But they both let him storm past them and open his front door, where he found Zhou blocking his way.

She stepped forward, he stepped backwards, quickly retreating past Knox and Laing, with the same mix of fear and irritation spreading across his features Knox had seen when Zhou had appeared in the restaurant on top of the peak on his first day in the city.

Zhou was followed by Bennett, who closed the front door behind her. Knox, Laing, Bennett, and Zhou fanned out into a semicircle as Atwood finally came to a stop in the dead centre of the house.

'It's time to tell the truth,' Zhou said.

'I don't know what you mean,' Atwood replied.

'Yes you do.'

After a long, pregnant pause, Atwood's expression changed again, a sneer spreading across his lips.

'You want the truth? The truth of this place? A place given over to smugglers and criminals, where Chinese encroachment goes unchecked. A place the Empire spent a century building into a beacon of civilisation but has been left to decay into a haven of corruption and shirked responsibilities.'

'Protecting Hong Kong was your job,' Knox replied. 'The very thing you were meant to be doing.'

'With what? A pokey office and barely enough budget to pay for somewhere half-decent to live and one moronic assistant. Don't come out here on your first-class jolly and tell me what my duty is. I know full well, and I've done what I have to. What London is too lazy, incompetent, or impotent to.'

'By throwing your lot in with communists? Bombing Hong Kong is no way to protect it.'

Knox wanted an explanation from the man, to understand his twisted logic. But he also wanted him to explicitly admit his guilt. And Atwood obliged.

'Isn't it? A bomb that will be blamed on the leftists and China, force Britain to actually defend what she swore to. They get the short-term scare they're after, I get something bigger. Rather elegant really, but perhaps too clever for someone used to pushing papers around Mayfair instead of actually getting their hands dirty doing what needs to be done.'

Knox let the insult bounce off him, mostly – he had to let a little bit of it stick because, after all, Atwood had entirely outsmarted him until an hour ago.

'You're right,' he said. 'And I've seen first-hand that there's more that can be done here, but we can make that case without blowing things up. There's no coming back from that, or way to control what could come after. You could spark an all-out war with the People's Republic.'

There was a flicker in Atwood's eyes, but it was brief. A sudden worry that he might be about to unleash Armageddon on a scale he hadn't imagined, maybe; but it passed.

'You've made your point,' Knox continued. 'But we need to stop this now. Tell us where the Blue Peacock is.'

Atwood looked at Knox, then at the other three people. Then he made a show of checking his watch again and said, 'No, I don't think I will.'

CHAPTER 54

For ten minutes Atwood stood silently at his window, looking out over the fiefdom MI5 had entrusted him with and to which he was on the verge of delivering a potentially mortal blow, while Knox explained to him in increasingly grave terms exactly what would happen to him if he did.

Atwood had transformed again. His posture was proud, his face serene. He seemed at peace, content in the knowledge that he was doing the right thing. Whereas Knox was finding his anger harder and harder to control, any relief he might have felt about his deductive instincts finally kicking in paling in comparison to his frustration at the intransigence of the man next to him.

When his suggestion that it wouldn't take much legal gymnastics for a QC to persuade a judge that Atwood had engaged in a form of high treason and could face hanging didn't even prompt a flutter of an eyelid, Knox marched over to the other end of the room, where Bennett, Zhou, and Laing had congregated.

'It's like he can't actually hear me,' he said.

'Are we already too late?' Laing asked.

'I bloody hope not. But we need to do something to get him to talk.'

'We should take him to Victoria Prison,' Zhou suggested.

'Or I could just beat it out of him,' Bennett added. 'Maybe a bullet through a kneecap would persuade him to open up.'

Knox shook his head. 'A foreign agent assaulting an MI5 officer, even this one, would only muddy things further, and might result in him never talking. But we also might not have the time for the jurisdictional wranglings handing him over to the police would entail.'

'If he's managed to get this far without anyone clocking what he's up to then he probably knows that too,' Bennett said. 'We need a third option, and it might have to be one you need to ask forgiveness for later.'

Knox knew Bennett was right. Holland had sent him to Hong Kong to step on some toes in the first place, and the danger of what might happen now if he didn't far outweighed any penance he might have to offer up if he did. The question was, what morally and legally dubious next step had the best chance of helping him avert disaster?

Laing gave him a possible answer.

'How long would it take for a taxi to get here from the Mandarin Oriental?' he asked Zhou.

'Less than ten minutes, if they're fast,' Zhou replied.

'Then I might know someone who can help.'

With a curious nod from Knox, Laing went to the phone that was bolted to the wall next to the kitchen counter, picked up the receiver, asked to be connected to the Mandarin Oriental, and then to be put through to Miss Gutierrez's room.

Exactly seven minutes later, they all heard a car pull up outside. Laing and Knox went to meet its passenger.

'The spa staff are furious with you,' Anna said to Laing, as her cab did a three-point turn and sped off back towards Central. 'They'd opened early for me.'

'I'll send flowers,' Laing replied, earning a smirk. Then he gestured to Knox. 'This is Richard Knox, a colleague.'

'Yes, it is,' Anna replied, giving Knox his own smile. 'But I assume you didn't request my urgent presence just to show me off to your boss.'

'There's a man inside who knows something he won't tell us,' Laing said.

'Something that might interest me?'

'In terms of self-preservation, perhaps. He's hidden a bomb somewhere in the city and we need to know where before it goes off.'

'Unless it's under the Mandarin Oriental's steam room it's none of my business.'

'I'd owe you a favour.'

'Well, I do like the idea of that. Who is he?'

Knox, who had been trying and failing to place the woman who seemed to know who he was, answered, 'Our SLO.'

Anna's smirk returned. 'MI5 is full of dark horses, isn't it?' I assume you haven't left him in there by himself.'

Knox and Laing both shook their heads.

'Good, then clear your people out and give me a little time alone with him.'

Knox summoned Bennett and Zhou. As she passed them, Anna gave Bennett a wink, which prompted a quizzical frown in return.

'Am I supposed to know her?' Bennett asked Knox once Anna had shut Atwood's front door behind her.

'No idea,' Knox replied.

'She likes to knock people off-balance,' Laing said.

'Who is she?'

'A free agent.'

'She better be a persuasive one.'

The four of them then fell into an anxious silence. But it only lasted two minutes, then Anna opened the door again.

'Bad news, I'm afraid,' she said to the group.

'Don't tell me he doesn't know where the bomb is,' Laing said, as Knox looked past Anna into the house, where he saw Atwood now sitting rigidly in his armchair, knuckles white as his hands gripped at its sides, staring unblinkingly at the opposite wall.

'He does,' Anna replied. 'Your problem is that there are two bombs.'

The four faces that were now firmly fixed on hers all dropped in shock.

'Where?' Knox asked.

'The peak and the airport.'

'How long do we have?'

'An hour.'

Knox turned to Zhou. 'Is that enough to get to both?'

She shook her head.

'So we split up,' Bennett said.

'The fastest way to the peak is the tram,' Zhou said to Knox after a few more moments' consideration. 'I could drop you and Bennett there, then pick up an interceptor for me and Laing.'

The division made sense to Knox: one person on each team who knew Hong Kong well, one who didn't. 'Agreed.'

'What about Atwood?' Laing asked.

'No need to worry about that,' Anna said. 'I'm not done with him yet.'

CHAPTER 55

The group sped across the city again, and after a few direct words from Zhou, Knox and Bennett were racing their way up the side of the peak, the only two passengers in a commandeered tram, while the Mercedes continued on its way to the Causeway Bay typhoon shelter.

'Do you trust that woman?' Bennett asked as they rose past the Kennedy Road station, without stopping to pick up the few confused people waiting in the shade of the trees hanging over its platform.

'No,' Knox replied. 'But without any other options I'm choosing to believe her. Trust can come later, if we have the luxury of later.'

'What if Atwood's an even better liar than we all think?'

Knox shook his head, remembering the glimpse he'd got of him after just a few minutes alone with Laing's mysterious contact.

'Let's hope he isn't,' he said.

He also hoped that their dash up the mountainside wouldn't be cut short by an explosion above them severing the tram's cables and sending them plummeting back down into the city.

Knox distracted himself from that possibility by recalling the layout of the top of the peak from his first day in Hong Kong and trying to work out where a car-sized bomb could be hidden without anyone noticing it.

As they got higher, neither of them could resist looking out at the harbour, hoping to see the wake of a police interceptor streaking across the water to Kai Tak.

'I'll give it to them,' Bennett said, grimly, 'they're going for maximum spectacle.'

'Fingers crossed the peak is quiet, and they don't equate making an impact with number of casualties.'

'Do you think Mason has the same motive as Atwood?'

'Maybe. He could have decided after Vietnam and Korea that it was time for Britain to pull its weight more over here. Or he's fully gone over to the other side. Or he has his own agenda too, and they just overlap.'

The tram started to slow down as they reached the top of its vertiginous track and arrived at the final station. As soon as their carriage's doors opened, Knox and Bennett sprinted through them.

As soon as they were out of the station, Knox pointed to the restaurant he and Atwood had eaten at. He couldn't imagine the man would blow up somewhere he seemed to love so much, but it was the only sizeable building within running distance.

They passed a viewing platform. There were more people on it than Knox would have liked, but at least it wasn't mobbed with crowds three deep waiting for their own uninterrupted view of the city.

The restaurant was shut, doors locked and lights off. But, peering through the windows, there was also no sign of a bomb inside. They tried round the back, in case the Blue Peacock had been sneaked into a storage room or camouflaged container near the kitchen. It hadn't.

Knox checked his watch. It felt like they'd left Conduit Road a lot longer than fifteen minutes ago.

He darted back round to the restaurant's car park, which didn't have a large van conveniently abandoned in it that they'd managed to miss a few moments ago, with Bennett in tow. He frantically cast his eye around for anywhere else the bomb might have been hidden. Then it landed on the first place he'd suspected before they'd even reached the peak – the tram station.

From where he was standing, Knox could see a ramp sloping down to a large set of doors recessed under the platform. He guessed it led to the cable motor room and repair shop. Bennett saw it at the same time as him and started running again a split second before he did.

There was a padlock across the join of the doors, but it was small and put up little resistance to the chunk of rock Bennett grabbed from the dirt next to the ramp and hammered it with. After a few strikes the lock fell to the floor and they each pulled open a door, revealing the hulking round shape of a Blue Peacock.

Knox knew what he was looking at immediately. The large, chest-high curved casing was out of place, unconnected to anything else and supported on its own thick struts. Its metal was painted in that off-duck-egg shade favoured by the British military, and one end of it had a pair of large, arm-sized hinges and set of bolted locks running around a thick seam cut into it. In short, it looked like a bomb.

Knox checked the bolts. They wouldn't move – they were fused in place.

'We need something bigger than a rock,' he shouted to Bennett over the loud whine of the train cable motor, which was still carrying oblivious passengers up and down the peak just a few feet away.

Bennett searched for something they could use to get the end of the Blue Peacock open while Knox pressed his ears against it, trying to detect any ticking or mechanical echoes reverberating inside.

She returned a few seconds later with two long monkey wrenches.

'Maybe we should hope it's atomic,' she said, handing one of the wrenches to Knox, then swinging the other behind her, 'you can't set off a nuclear bomb by hitting it.'

Then she slammed her wrench into the end of one of the bolts, dislodging it and sending it skidding across the floor.

They both held their breaths for a long moment, waiting for an explosion that didn't come. Then they started furiously hitting the remaining bolts.

'Don't suppose you know how to defuse one of these things, do you?' Bennett called over strikes.

'One thing at a time,' Knox replied.

He checked his watch again. Another five minutes had passed. That meant that if they got the bomb casing open in the next few they'd be left with half an hour to either stop it going off, remove any nuclear core that might be inside, or get the peak evacuated.

Knox smashed out another bolt, Bennett another, then Knox removed the final one, dropped his wrench and pulled hard on the handle welded onto the hatch at the end of the bomb. The hinges were stubborn at first. But then, with a series of high-pitched scraping noises, they started to move.

Knox pulled backwards slowly, waiting for Bennett to shout at him to stop in case she spotted any booby traps. But all he heard was her scream 'Shit!' when he'd swung the hatch all the way open.

He stepped around it and saw the cause of Bennett's outburst. The Blue Peacock was completely empty.

CHAPTER 56

Knox and Bennett were lucky heading back down from Victoria peak – they reached the station platform just as a tram was about to leave. However, their relief that a bomb wasn't about to irreparably change the geography of Hong Kong Island was dampened by the fear of what might be about to happen over in Kowloon. Taking a chunk out of the peak would have been a symbolic statement; crippling Kai Tak and cutting off Hong Kong from fast access to the rest of the world would be a devastating political and economic one.

Their journey down was slower than their ascent, every stop the tram made seemingly stretching out longer and longer. But it still only took them seven minutes to reach the bottom of the line in Central, and they made up the time they'd lost by telling the taxi driver they hailed that they'd pay him double his fare if he got them to Causeway Bay quickly.

When they arrived, they found the typhoon shelter clogged with boats that were either keeping out of the way of the races or picking up and dropping off spectators.

On the far side of the shelter were the police interceptors, a gap in their line where Zhou and Laing had removed one of their number.

Knox was working out the quickest way round to the interceptors when Bennett nudged him and pointed to a closer option that would require less time wasted proving who they were to the officers on guard duty.

A very merry party was stumbling up from a speedboat onto the pontoon almost directly beneath them, and whichever one of them had been drunkenly captaining their morning in the strait had forgotten to take the boat's engine keys with them.

Knox and Bennett watched the group tilt and sway their way a few more paces along the dock, then they dropped down onto it, untied the boat, climbed aboard and started the motor.

A few moments of jostling their way out of the shelter later, Knox finally caught a glimpse of the Dragon Boat Festival in full swing.

Lines of kneeling people were frantically rowing their long, narrow canoes between buoys strung with flags, to the whoops and cheers of people on junks, sampans, and the harbourfront.

It looked like a fun way to spend a day off. Unfortunately, Knox had work to do, so he turned away, pushed his boat's throttle as far forward as it would go, spun the wheel, and started ploughing through the low waves.

They sped east towards the airport and the runway spit quickly rose out of the water ahead of them.

There were no flights landing or taking off – most of the city's airborne arrivals and departures happened at either end of the day, which meant a lull in traffic in the middle of it. Again, Knox hoped that would mean that even if the worst were to happen, the collateral damage caused by a bomb exploding somewhere in the airport would be limited. Still, he had to fight to ignore his visions of trucks crashing into the terminal building or slamming into a jet full of innocent people.

'Where are we headed?' Bennett asked.

'I'm not sure,' Knox replied. 'Keep an eye out for Zhou and Laing's boat.'

Then he saw three mounds appear beyond the runway, like newly formed islands pushing up through the water. He remembered again what Atwood had told him about making the colony bigger inch by inch to spite the Chinese, and the wide barge moored on the other side of the spit that he and Bennett had seen after they'd escaped the grain silo.

He swung the boat to starboard, taking them perilously close to the end edge of the runway, and round to the far side of it. It was a gamble, and they might not have time to make another one if he was wrong, but as soon as they cleared the tip of the spit, they could both see that the barge had been moved closer to the runway and was now pressed up against its side, and there was a police interceptor anchored next to a ladder leading up the metal cliff face of its hull.

Knox brought them alongside and cut the engines as Bennett threw some ropes over to the other boat to tie them together.

Then they made their way up onto the barge.

Its wide deck was deserted, just the three enormous piles of sand, gravel, and cement in its centre. There were no structures, no bridge or pilot house, but Knox spotted an open hatch over to the left that had to lead inside the barge's bowels. They headed for it, ready to render whatever assistance they could to Zhou and Laing.

A tight, steep bare metal staircase took them back down to sea level, where it opened out into a wide, two-storey Meccano maze of gantries, catwalks, and pits where the delicate ballast calculations that kept the barge afloat and steady as its cargo was skimmed off were executed.

Caged lights hung in rows along the walkways, and in the well of one of them on the far side of the boat Knox could see the second Blue Peacock positioned against the hull, which itself was pressed up to the runway. And in another, a few yards from the bomb, was Laing, hanging upside down, a chain wrapped round his ankles, and slowly spinning. His arms and neck hung loose.

Instantly more pieces of the puzzle Knox had been trying to put together ever since he'd arrived in Hong Kong took shape in his mind and fell into place.

He'd been battling another unknown enemy all along without realising.

Zhou.

She must have been the one who'd arranged for Lady Reeve's inexplicable move to Stanley, and possibly even her death. She'd been the first person to suggest Blue Peacock was a drug, and had encouraged Knox to think Reeve had been a victim of it. She'd chaperoned him all over the colony, controlling what he saw and discovered, and guiding him to conclusions that kept him distracted and far away from what was really going on.

Just like Mason with Bennett, she'd nudged him towards Kowloon Walled City, and then when he'd emerged unscathed from his first visit she'd made sure he wouldn't after his second.

And she'd volunteered to come to Kai Tak, not to stop the bomb but to make sure that it went off while Knox and Bennett rushed up Victoria Peak on a wild goose chase.

He also finally understood Atwood's behaviour the first time he'd seen them together, and the last. The SLO wasn't jealous of her or threatened by her, he was anxious about being so close to a co-conspirator.

Knox looked at Bennett and could tell she'd reached the same conclusion as he had. They started sprinting again across the hold towards the Blue Peacock and Laing.

They were halfway when the shooting started.

CHAPTER 57

Knox and Bennett both dived for the floor as bullets rained down on them, ricocheting off girders and slamming into ballast pits.

After a few seconds the shooting stopped and they were up and running again, Knox scanning the catwalks above them while Bennett retrieved her Beretta from the back of her trousers' waistband.

They managed another ten feet before they were pulled up to an abrupt halt by a bullet lodging in the deck between them, sending them ducking in opposite directions. Knox looked up and finally saw Zhou standing above them at the edge of a light well, holding a police-issue rifle up against her shoulder. She was close enough to hit them easily if she'd had a clear line of sight, but luckily for Knox and Bennett the tangled architecture of the hold was working against her.

'We need to split up,' Bennett said. 'Divide her targets.'

Knox nodded, switching his view forward for a second to trace the fastest paths to the bomb and Laing, and then to his watch. They didn't know precisely when the Blue Peacock was set to go off, but by Knox's reckoning they now had less than ten minutes to stop it.

Zhou fired again, her bullet this time bouncing around the sides of an empty ballast pit. Knox watched her move to find a better firing angle and motioned to Bennett to run.

This time they made it halfway across the hold before the sound of three more shots filled the air. One flew wide of them, another hit the floor at a low enough angle to deflect off it and skip into the darkness. The third, however, glanced off a gantry strut and sliced across Bennett's right forearm, forcing her to drop her gun and let out a low, long grunt.

She knelt down, checking her wound, then inched forward to where the Beretta had landed and kicked it over to Knox.

'Change of plan,' she said. 'Cover me so I can get to the bomb, then go get her.'

Knox couldn't stop himself from looking over at Laing, who was still slowly turning in mid-air, hopefully just unconscious rather than dead. It was a hard, horrible call, but Bennett was right. They were rapidly running out of time, and they needed to disarm the Blue Peacock if any of them were going to stand any chance of living beyond the next couple of minutes. Laing would have to wait.

Knox shifted from crouching to kneeling, checked Zhou was still where she'd been a moment ago, raised the pistol, aimed, and fired. He didn't hit her, but he hadn't intended to. He wanted to distract her, sending her ducking and dodging to give Bennett the time she needed to get to the bomb.

He watched Zhou shift position, moving in and out of shadow, and he did the same, tracking her and getting closer with each silent shuffle and sudden dash.

He wanted to know why she'd been working against him since the moment they'd met, and whether she was acting according to the same twisted logic that had driven Atwood to betray his country, or for her own even darker reasons. But he understood that he might have to kill her before he got the chance.

Knox reached a ladder to the lattice of catwalks above him and climbed up it, figuring it would be easier to spot, and shoot, Zhou if they were on the same level.

Just before he got to the top he paused, momentarily distracted by the sound of the Blue Peacock's access hatch clanging against the hull. He was relieved Bennett had managed to reach it intact, and that it had apparently opened much more easily than the one under the peak tram station; he was also concerned because the bomb's position meant she'd be exposed, her back turned to the rest of the hold as she worked to defuse it.

As if on cue, Knox saw a length of polished black metal appear out of the gloom above him, barely five feet from the top of the ladder – the barrel of Zhou's rifle.

He fired, catching the very tip of the rifle with his bullet, then clambered up onto the catwalk and rushed Zhou while she was still trying to work out where the shot had come from. He knocked the gun out of her hands, but not out of her reach; he now saw the long strap that was attached to it and slung across her chest.

She reacted quickly once Knox had made his appearance, grabbing him and pulling him closer to her so he didn't have enough space to aim the Beretta again. Then she spun him round, rolling him along the catwalk railing before releasing him, timing a kick perfectly so her heel knocked his gun out of his hand and sent it spinning back down to the deck below.

He lunged forward, now pinning Zhou's arms at her sides so she couldn't get to her rifle. He expected her to have transformed, revealed a completely different version of herself like Atwood had, but her face was still stoic and expressionless, even in the middle of a fight.

'You were working with Atwood the whole time?' Knox said, as they twisted and stumbled back towards the ladder.

'Atwood was an idiot,' Zhou replied, her voice as measured as it had always been. 'But a useful one.'

'What about Lady Reeve?'

'A coward.'

'Is that why she had to die?'

'She had to learn that believing in a cause means sacrificing yourself for it.'

'And that's what you're doing? You care about Hong Kong so much you want to blow it up, and kill yourself in the process?'

'I'm not doing this to bring a dead empire back to life.'

Zhou shifted her weight and tried to spin her way out of Knox's grip. He held fast on to her, but not close enough to stop her landing a few jabs into his side, straight into his bandaged ribs. He had to force his mouth to stay shut so he didn't let out a pained grunt.

'Who turned you?' he said, once the worst of the sudden flash of pain had faded.

Zhou's face finally changed, a smile spreading across her lips.

'Who said I had to be?' she said. 'You're as stupid as Atwood. Obsessed with old politics and faded powers that are so easily manipulated into fighting each other.'

'So you just want war?'

'I want chaos.'

'Why?'

'Because fear drives progress,' she said.

Then she headbutted Knox, hitting him square in the face. The shock of the impact made him finally loosen his grip on her and stagger backwards, which gave Zhou just enough space to kick him again and tip him over the railing.

CHAPTER 58

After Knox fired up at Zhou, Bennett ran as fast as she could.

She checked her right arm again as she pumped the left one and both her legs. As far as she could tell, sprinting in and out of light, the injury wasn't as bad as it could have been – a thick, red groove that would leave a scar when it healed but that hadn't cut through an artery or any of the nerves that stretched down into her hand. Moving her fingers was sore as hell and clenching a fist was agony, but she could still do both.

She made it to the Blue Peacock without getting a bullet in the back. However, that didn't mean she was safe; she instantly realised that the bomb had been positioned so the hinges for its access hatch were against the hull. She didn't have time to be constantly checking over her shoulder – she had to trust Knox to keep her out of Zhou's sights while she tried to disarm whatever kind of trigger mechanism she found inside the bomb.

The bolts running around this Blue Peacock weren't stiff, fused, or rusted. They came away easily, and when Bennett pulled on the hatch's handle it moved far more smoothly than she'd expected and she lost her grip on it as it swung on its well-oiled hinges and hit the hull.

She froze for a second, waiting for the sound of a gunshot. It came, but it wasn't from Zhou's rifle. She recognised the slightly different pitch and tone of her Beretta.

Bennett let herself exhale and peered inside the bomb. Then her breath caught again. She couldn't see the telltale polished sphere of a nuclear warhead, but there was enough Semtex inside the Blue Peacock to obliterate the barge and reduce a large chunk of the Kai Tak runway to submerged rubble. And it was all hooked up to a timer that had just ticked past the two-minute mark.

She swore.

The wiring was complex, and it all looked the same. There was no easy-to-identify colouring or stripes she could use to refer back to the scant explosives lessons she'd received during her field agent training. She wanted to reach in and yank the timer out of the bomb, but she had to assume there was a failsafe that would make the whole thing go up in her face if she did. So, she crouched half inside the bomb's shell and started to trace the individual paths of the wires as carefully and quickly as she could, seeing which ones connected to the tightly packed blocks of Semtex, which were part of the timer, and which were dummies.

She worked out which ones were just there to get in her way, and removed them, but that took almost forty-five seconds, and by the end of it she was still left with a choice she didn't know how to make. There were three sets of wires: one that would disconnect the timer, one that would set the bomb off, and one that might be a backup or another, better disguised dummy.

Bennett had to make a guess. So she did.

It wasn't wrong, but it wasn't right either. The Blue Peacock didn't explode, but the timer leapt forward thirty seconds. She'd shortened her odds, and how long she had to make her next guess.

She felt her pulse getting faster and louder in her ears, and glanced behind her, hoping against hope that the sound was actually Knox racing towards her. But he was nowhere to be seen. She was alone.

Another ten seconds passed as she flipped coins over and over in her head. Then, taking what might be her last breath, she wrapped her fingers round one of the sets of wires. But before she could pull on them another hand reached past her and tugged the other one out of the timer. It stopped ticking, and nothing blew up.

Bennett looked up to see who the hand belonged to and saw Anna staring down at her.

'How?' she asked.

'I told you I wasn't done with Atwood,' Anna replied, as she turned away and started walking over to Laing's body.

'That's still a bomb,' she called over her shoulder, prompting Bennett to pull out the electrodes that were buried in the Semtex bricks. By the time she was done, she saw that Anna had managed to free Laing from his chains and was already dragging him away.

She lifted the timer out of the Blue Peacock, laid it down on the floor, and started stamping on it at the exact same moment Knox crashed onto the floor thirty feet away from her.

Knox landed on the edge of a deep, empty ballast pit, agony screaming through him as his stomach made contact with the raised lip of the void. For a second, his arms flailed in space before he realised he wasn't going to tilt forward and dive head-first another fifteen feet, and he squirmed and rolled over onto his back, sure that any ribs that hadn't been broken already now definitely had been. For good measure, the old scar across his scalp began to throb.

Zhou appeared above him, rifle hanging loose in front of her.

'My father believed in Britain,' she said. 'And China. He answered your call for help in the war. Travelled all the way from his village in Fujian to Liverpool to keep your merchant navy afloat and your people fed. And then when you'd finally won and started to feel embarrassed about the help you'd needed to survive, you expelled him and sent him back to a China that had suddenly become your enemy and didn't want him either.'

Knox tried to shuffle away from her. She kicked him in the side.

'Then why are you here?' he whispered through the pain.

'There was nowhere else for us to go. We weren't good enough to be British or Chinese. The only work my father could get was in the Kowloon docks, breaking his back for someone else's profit in the shadow of the two countries that had spurned him.'

'And it made you want revenge?' Knox said, his voice a little stronger.

'It made me realise how pointless patriotism was, and that wars aren't about politics and ideologies. They're about supply lines. And the winners are the people who control them. The people who decide which wheels get greased, which levers pulled, who gets a full belly and who's starved into submission.'

Just as seeing Laing strung up next to the Blue Peacock had made Knox's brain understand the shapes of the remaining missing pieces that made up the jigsaw of his time in Hong Kong, Zhou's words prompted it to crystallise all the invisible connections he'd been trying to resist for days.

Blue Peacock, Atwood, Mason, Kowloon Walled City. The missing scientists. Rabe's genetic tinkering that could feed the world or unleash microbial Armageddon. The infiltration of Leconfield House. They weren't disparate events. They were all part of the same thing. Strands of a single, vast web the whole world was caught in.

'How many of you are there?' he asked. Zhou leaned over him, grabbing his collar to pull his ear close to her mouth, and replied, 'We're everywhere.'

Then she hauled him up, ready, Knox was sure, to hurl him into the pit and either shoot him or let the Blue Peacock incinerate him after a few hideous seconds of knowing he had no chance of escape.

He went slack, pulling her off-balance, then he replanted his feet and pushed her backwards towards the void. Her heel caught on the pit's lip and she fell. Knox reached out to grab the strap of her rifle, but only managed to graze it with his fingertips.

Zhou rotated in space, turning away from Knox and spending the last split second of her life watching the bottom of the pit rushing up to break her neck.

CHAPTER 59

'Pretty good, right?' Bennett asked as Knox took his first sip of his coffee, perched on the low stool next to her.

They were sitting in the window of a coffee shop at the bottom of one of the steeper sections of Aberdeen Street on the edge of Central, half above ground, half under it, with an endless parade of legs walking up and down the stepped slope in front of them.

'Not bad at all,' he replied, savouring the taste of the drink, as he glanced at the bandage wrapped round Bennett's arm and felt the one tight across his torso beneath his shirt.

It was twenty-four hours since Knox had turned away from Zhou's lifeless body and looked across the barge's hold to see Bennett standing above an equally broken bomb timer. A lot had happened since then, but so far nothing had exploded and no wars had been declared.

After the brief respite of the Dragon Boat Festival, social tensions across the city were starting to bubble to the surface again. Atwood had become Victoria Prison's latest resident, pending secure transport back to London and what would no doubt be a very thorough debriefing at the MI5 interrogation centre at Latchmere House out in Richmond. Knox had arranged for the two Blue Peacocks to be quietly moved to HMS *Bulwark*. And Laing had been located in Queen Elizabeth Hospital, where he'd been treated for concussion and some blood loss and was being kept in for a few days of observation.

It had been Charlie, suddenly eager to prove his worth, who had finally tracked down where Anna had taken Laing this morning, barely fifteen minutes after Knox had explained that he would no longer be reporting to Atwood.

The street outside was busy, but the coffee shop was quiet, just Knox and Bennett and, at the back, one man filling small waxed bags so slowly and methodically it was as if he was counting every single roasted bean that went into them. Knox guessed the lack of other customers, as well as their shared love of a good cup of coffee, was why Bennett had picked here to meet.

'Any more ideas on who they are?' Bennett asked, her voice dropping a fraction even though there was no one in hearing distance.

After Bennett had rushed over to the edge of the ballast pit to see for herself that Zhou was definitely dead and wasn't somehow going to leap out of the hole, rewire the bomb, and kill them all, Knox had told her what she'd said to him before she'd fallen.

Knox shook his head. 'I need to discuss it with Holland. She may have been bluffing and this has all just been some locals with serious delusions of grandeur, or she was telling the truth and this is much, much bigger than we know. I hope it's the former, but I fear it's the latter.'

'Well, do me a favour and leave me out of the end of your report,' Bennett replied.

Knox raised an eyebrow, then nodded.

On the one hand, Bennett had saved the day as much as he had and deserved the credit. On the other, if she was still concerned about the potential blowback of her unwittingly helping the very people she'd been trying to stop she might want to limit the amount of evidence of her involvement that might crop up in an official inquiry. However, Knox suspected she had another motive for wanting her actions fudged in any records.

'They still think I'm their asset,' she said. 'And with Zhou gone, they don't know what happened after we left Atwood's house.

I could have volunteered to go up to the peak all by myself, or stayed there while you went to Kowloon.'

'You want to see how big this is from the inside?'

She nodded. 'They made me a double. Let's see how I do as a triple.'

'And you want to nail Mason?'

'I do.'

Knox had been booked on a flight back to London the next evening – enough time to check on Laing and discuss his mysterious new ally, have a meeting with Special Branch to warn them that several more would follow, and revisit some parts of Hong Kong Island he'd missed or been too preoccupied to fully appreciate first time round.

Bennett recommended a trip to Man Mo Temple, where Knox went through the motions of having his fortune read. He wasn't sure if he did it right, but he appreciated the solemn yet heady atmosphere of the place, and no one seemed to take offence as he stumbled his way through the ritual and listened to a Buddhist master tell him what his future may or may not hold.

Then, the afternoon before his flight, he'd taken a taxi over to Repulse Bay and found a bar by the beach to while away a few hours watching the waves.

The bay was calm, no dragon boats cleaving their way back and forth across it today. Knox enjoyed the peace, letting himself pretend for a brief spell that all was well with the world, and that he hadn't recently discovered a new – or possibly old – malevolent force working to foster chaos and discord across the globe.

As the sun started to dip, signalling that it was time to head back to the city and Kai Tak, this time just as a traveller heading home, Knox felt compelled to stroll down the beach, remove his shoes, and dip his toes in the South China Sea.

Then he indulged in the utter absurdity of catching a bright red double-decker bus back to the city through the jungle.

CHAPTER 60

Valera was back in MI5 headquarters, and today she was working in the office of its director general.

The changes to her life had accelerated even further since the emergency services and several black cars had sped up the drive of Rabley Heath and found her cradling White's semi-conscious body in the middle of the gravel, a few feet away from the very dead one of her would-be murderer.

White had been carefully lifted out of her arms and into the back of an ambulance, and she was escorted into one of the cars and whisked back to London and another featureless room in an anonymous building.

She was questioned by a man she'd never met before about what had happened in Hertfordshire, if she had any idea who the grenade-launching attacker was, and where Williams had gone. She repeated his last words to her, that he'd left to try to do some good. She didn't mention the gun and the knife he'd taken from the man he'd killed.

Then she'd been driven to Leconfield House and taken once more to the glass box, where she met another man. This one introduced himself as James Holland, the head of the Service.

'How is White?' she asked.

'Awake and already on the mend,' Holland said as he removed his glasses and wiped their lenses with a chamois he produced from one of his suit pockets. 'And he's fully corroborated your account of events.'

Valera nodded.

Holland gestured with his glasses at the table that was still strewn with the remnants of Valera and White's experimenting before putting them back on. 'Your assistance has already been invaluable. Would you be interested in continuing helping us?'

Valera looked at the enlarged photos, the copper coil, the bug with its removed shell, and nodded again. 'The problem hasn't been solved yet.'

'Excellent. Now, would you like us to let the Americans know that you're safe and sound?'

This was a question Valera hadn't anticipated being asked. She'd assumed the CIA would already know where she was, and a part of her was still expecting the British to try to hand or trade her back to them at some point. Given the choice, she preferred the idea that they might just one day stumble on the ruins of her cabin and assume she'd succumbed to the same fire that had consumed it, her body lost to the lake after a blind and burned stumble into its waters or carried off by a hungry bear or coyote.

'No,' she replied.

'Fine,' Holland said, then he turned his attention more fully to the table in the middle of the box. 'The situation has changed. After Williams's detective work we can assume whoever is behind these devices will think we're on to them.'

Valera explained the two options she'd already suggested to White: work out the bugs' activation frequency and piggyback off it, or change it so only MI5 would be able to hear what they listened in on.

'First things first, I want to be certain where they all are. How long would it take you to come up with something to find them that doesn't involve ripping up every wall and floor?'

'With the right equipment, the rest of the day,' she replied.

It was the director general's turn to nod, and tap the hourglass that had almost run out of sand.

The next destination on her tour of Leconfield House was its scientific heart – the research and development department.

She was impressed with White's realm, and the two technicians who were assigned to assist and assess her while she spent the afternoon constructing the world's most advanced bug catcher. They weren't as fast as she was, but they were quick learners, especially as most of their work was done in silence. And she couldn't judge their lack of specific expertise too harshly – few people on the planet had dedicated as many hours and years to understanding the intricacies and idiosyncrasies of radio waves as she had.

Now, in the middle of the following morning, she was in Holland's office, along with the director general and White, whose left arm was pinned to his chest in a sling.

She held a palm-sized box in her right hand. It had two short aerials sticking out of its top that could cycle through every radio-wave frequency between three kilohertz and three hundred gigahertz in just over a second. The aerials alternated, switching on and off in rapid sequence. The left one broadcast a signal that might activate a dormant hidden bug, the right one detected any device that had been tricked into turning itself on. If the catcher found one, a dial on the front side would show which frequency had given it away.

Valera had already found one bug. Though, given Holland had pointed to the piece of wood panelling it was buried in as soon as she and White had arrived, she considered that success more of a road test. The real challenge would be seeing if there were any others.

She was methodical, slowly moving across every surface as she worked her way around the room searching for the invisible doors she'd once imagined covering the planet. And she reminded herself as she went that not finding another device in Holland's office wouldn't mean failure. There was a whole building to sweep. And possibly an entire city and beyond.

Valera envisioned whole armies of technicians going under-cover into sensitive buildings across London and maybe even all over the West armed with her bug catchers while she and White decided what the next frontier of surveillance technology would look like.

She swiped the detector around the frame of a painting of a castle on a wave-wrapped headland and noticed the dial wobble, then she took the picture off its hook and ran the aerials over the wall behind it. The dial jumped to the same frequency it had when it found the first bug.

Valera turned to the two men, confirming her discovery. Holland frowned, but White looked like he was trying to suppress a proud smile.

CHAPTER 61

The next day, Knox found himself staring at a painting of a magpie resting on a rickety old gate in the snow-covered French countryside.

He'd arrived in London just after midday, and gone straight to Curzon Street to deliver his initial report to Holland. It had covered Atwood's betrayal and Zhou's death in bare terms, but made no mention of Zhou's last words or Bennett's plans.

Now, an hour later, Knox was sitting on a padded maroon bench in the National Gallery on the north side of Trafalgar Square, waiting for the director general to appear and for his proper debriefing to begin.

Leconfield House was busier than it had been when he'd left, which made him wonder if the failed attack in Hong Kong had made Zhou's 'we' a little more cautious. At least, the nation's best minds and biggest security risks were no longer under constant Service surveillance. But the air of the building, its underlying hum, still felt off to him. The feeling was confirmed by the look Holland gave him when he stepped into his office after being summoned by Miss Albury a moment after he'd reached his own.

They'd talked for five minutes, Holland asking open questions about his mission, and Knox answering them in line with whatever Zhou might have had the chance to pass on to her comrades. Then, once Holland had dismissed him, he went back next door and found a note on his desk, telling him to go to Trafalgar Square.

Knox was irritated that the full truth of what had really happened would never make it into MI5's official written history of his trip, but that was often the way with issues of national – and global – security. And at least he'd be able to share it all with Holland in person and they could start trying to work out what it might mean for the future of the Service, the West, and the very nature of the intelligence game.

An elderly couple paused in front of Knox, momentarily blocking his view of the painting before moving on to silently consider another impressionist masterpiece.

Once they were gone, Knox went back to studying the picture and trying to work out why Holland had chosen this particular meeting place. The exhibition was well attended, thanks to the inclusion of several works not normally on display in London, but there were plenty of other public places he could have picked. Perhaps the director general just wanted the excuse to see the assembled Monets, Manets, Pissarros, and Sisleys. However, Knox guessed there was a more specific reason.

And then he saw it.

Monet's winter scene was a triumph of delicate light and colour. Sky and snow bled into each other while remaining subtly distinct. It was measured, intricate, perfect – except for one detail. The magpie, which was so elegantly balanced on the top of the gate, was angled towards the left edge of the painting, but its shadow faced the opposite direction. They didn't match.

A mistake? Or a reminder, as if Knox needed one, that even in the most innocent situations all was not always as it seemed?

Another five minutes passed with no sign of the director general, and Knox started to feel restless and impatient. If they'd just gone down to White's glass box from Holland's office and spoken there, he could already be on his way to Hertfordshire to see how Williams had fared alone in Rabley Heath for a week.

Then he sensed a presence next to him, one he recognised without having to turn his head to confirm.

'Did you know that when the idea of the National Gallery was first announced, there were calls for it to be built on the other side of Hyde Park,' Holland said. 'Certain parties were scared the pollution in the centre of town would damage the art. The counter-argument was that the point of the collection was to enrich the lives of the whole population, and if it got destroyed in the process then so be it. It could hardly claim to be a national gallery if it retreated from the nation at the very outset.'

The director general got up, beginning a slow circuit of the exhibition. Knox followed him, briefly considering a rainy, night-time scene of the Boulevard Montmartre, a riverbank on a summer's afternoon dotted with people fishing and ambling, and, a little incongruously, Knox felt, a wide avenue in springtime Sydenham. They were all beautiful, and a slight shock to the system after the neon and concrete edges of Hong Kong.

Eventually Holland nodded to the exhibition exit, and Knox fell into step behind him as he strolled through gallery after gallery until they reached a locked door to which the director general happened to have the key.

Inside was an enormous room, crammed full of canvasses. It looked like one of those old Parisian salons where every inch of wall would be covered in oils and watercolours. Knox didn't recognise any of the pieces, so didn't know if this was an overly grand storeroom for minor works, or if he just wasn't educated enough on the old masters to appreciate the trove of which he'd suddenly been granted a private view.

'The infiltration?' Knox said, half-asking the obvious question.

'We're making progress,' the director general replied.

It was a half-answer. Knox pushed further. 'Has White made a breakthrough?'

'Of sorts,' Holland said. There was the briefest pause before he added, 'with assistance from Irina Valera.'

Knox felt as if the old bullet wound in the middle of his chest was reopening itself, muscle and long-removed sutures unknitting themselves, pulling the flesh inches from his heart apart.

'That's not a name I expected to hear again,' he replied, keeping his voice level and stopping his eyes glancing down to his shirt to see if it was blooming red.

'Nor me,' Holland conceded.

Knox wanted to ask where she'd come from, how she'd appeared in London, what had happened while he was away that meant someone with her past relationship with MI5 was suddenly welcome in its upper echelons. But he settled for the most pertinent question: 'Can we trust her?'

'White's vouched for her. So have I.'

The director general explained the technique Valera had developed for locating the listening devices hiding throughout Leconfield House, including the second one she'd discovered in his office.

'They're being removed?' Knox asked.

'Some. Some are staying in place a little longer so as not to give the game away completely. White's also working on upgrading his box, and in the meantime I get to visit some of my old haunts for more sensitive conversations.'

Knox took the hint and told Holland the full story about Hong Kong. That the Blue Peacock plot wasn't just the workings of a disgruntled man whose morals had gone to seed, that Lady Reeve's death wasn't a tragic accident, that Zhou had been working against him from the off. He told him too about Laing's connection to an ex-Line Z operative, Bennett's belief that her boss was working for the same organisation as Zhou, and her plan to let them think she was still their mole. And his theory that Rabe and the infiltration of Leconfield House were linked to what had almost happened in Hong Kong as well.

'A single faction we didn't even know existed,' Holland said when Knox was done.

'That might have tried to take advantage of the unrest in Hong Kong or may well have created it in the first place,' Knox replied. 'Has there been any progress on where the Blue Peacocks came from or how they got to Hong Kong? And how many more there might be out there?'

'The army are looking into how they managed to misplace at least two old bomb casings. We think a Dutch merchant cargo ship called the *Tasman* might have something to do with it.'

'Why?'

'It arrived in Hong Kong last Friday. On Tuesday its captain reported his chief mate missing to the police.'

'He might have just overindulged at the Dragon Boat Festival.'

'Perhaps. Still, we traced its route. It left Rotterdam in April, stopped off at Gibraltar and Athens before reaching Suez. Two days after it entered a canal the body of a young sailor washed up on a beach outside Port Said. I asked Special Branch to take a discreet look at the captain's logs last night and we think the body belongs to a crew member who supposedly jumped ship mid-voyage. Not much to go on, but something. And at least no one will be smuggling anything through Suez in the near future with the Egyptians blocking both ends of it.'

Knox had caught up on the aftermath of the brief Arab–Israeli war that had raged across the Sinai peninsula for six days while he'd been in Asia care of a newspaper he'd scooped up in the lounge shortly before boarding his flight out of Hong Kong. A ceasefire had been agreed, the Egyptian, Syrian, and Jordanian militaries had been crippled, but the canal's entrances remained choked with scuttled ships and sea mines. Now, he found himself remembering something else Zhou had said in the belly of the barge and wondering if regional politics and tensions were the only thing behind Suez being cut off.

'What if this faction was responsible for that as well?' he said. 'Blowing up Kai Tak's runway, disrupting global shipping. It's the same ploy, just different scales.'

'Then we really would be up against a true fifth column,' Holland replied, 'operating within and across nations, whose agenda is as opaque as their identity.'

The director general's voice, which had already turned serious, had now become grave. Yet Knox sensed it wasn't out of sudden shock, but more likely the confirmation of the set of suspicions that had sent him to Hong Kong in the first place.

'Rabe told me I wasn't on his side. Zhou said their aim was chaos. Take advantage of a whole world kept off-balance.'

'If the game has changed,' Holland replied, 'then we'll need new ways to play it.'

'Laing will be keen to come up with some when he's cleared to fly.'

'He's not coming back.'

Suddenly Knox was worried something had happened to Laing while he'd been making his own return trip to London – something the doctors at Queen Elizabeth Hospital hadn't spotted.

'Hong Kong needs a new SLO,' Holland continued. 'I think he's the perfect candidate, and thankfully he agrees. If this new challenge is a global one, we need people we can trust in the spheres around the world where we have some influence. I also imagine his new associate is more likely to remain friendly the further away he is from Leconfield House.'

Knox was relieved, and both surprised and not that Holland was already in the process of moving his pieces around the board.

He was sure that it would only take Laing a few months to make Bonham Strand a jewel in the Service's crown. It was the kind of assignment he might have fought for himself a decade ago – the chance to shape MI5's presence in a crucial intelligence theatre – or might even now, if he didn't have responsibilities at home he couldn't shirk for longer than a few days at a time.

'I'm sure Jack is eager to come back in, too,' he said, hoping he might be able to deliver some good news to Rabley Heath to make up for his extended absence.

'That may not be an option,' Holland replied.

'But he was the only one who knew what Blue Peacock was. He's too valuable to be cooped up any longer.'

'It may not be an option because Williams is gone.'

Knox was stunned. And not just by what the director general said, but by his tone. It was as if he was sharing good news.

'What?' Knox managed to reply.

'There was an assault on Rabley Heath. Williams subdued the attacker, who we're in the process of identifying but I think can quite confidently assume belonged to this clandestine organisation. Then he left.'

'You let him go?'

'I couldn't stop him, as he finally realised.'

Knox opened his mouth, then closed it again, then said, 'He only ever wanted to serve, to prove his loyalty to you.'

'And now he can, in his own way,' the director general replied. Then he handed Knox the key to the gallery and added, 'Opening gambits have been played, first strikes launched. Retreating from this is not an option.'

CHAPTER 62

Holland left Knox alone with the paintings and his thoughts.

Knox couldn't believe Williams would have just left without even a word. Of course, he hadn't been there to say goodbye to, and he had been busy stopping a catastrophe that could have been the spark of another world war. But these two facts didn't make him feel any less sad or guilty.

Knox lingered for a few minutes, ignoring all the monarchs, lovers, and laymen staring down at him from every wall. Then he left the gallery, locking the door behind him. He made his way outside, across the top of the glorified roundabout that was Trafalgar Square, then over Leicester Square and up Wardour Street.

In the past, when he'd returned from a mission a walk through Soho would be all he needed to readjust to London's beats and tones, but today he was too distracted, and they seemed too slow, too quiet compared to the frenetic syncopation of Hong Kong. Even the market in Berwick Street, which was still in its full middle-of-the-day swing when he turned in to it, seemed subdued.

He cut his way between two stalls, one selling cut-price dinner services and the other bolts of lace in every conceivable pattern, and reached Kemp House.

Knox took the lift up, grateful that it was at least three times the size of the one in Bonham Strand, and opened the door to his apartment. He had only let himself hope very slightly that

Williams would be waiting for him inside, so he was only a little disappointed that he wasn't.

There was no message from him either, and also no people floating in mid-air, mawing and cooing at him. There was, however, another key resting on his kitchen counter.

He showered, changed, and poured himself a generous measure of ten-year-old Ardbeg from his drinks trolley. He hadn't eaten since the last leg of his flight, so his body instantly set about absorbing what nutrients it might be able to extract from the whisky, along with its alcohol.

He thought about what Holland had said about the great game changing and the need to play it differently. Bennett already was – several steps ahead as usual – and Laing too, busy making new allies out of old enemies. Then he thought about Lady Reeve and Atwood. Their beliefs had pushed them down seemingly unimaginable and worryingly unnoticed paths. One of them had faltered, the other had been stopped, but they both proved just how different the world had become.

Knox had wanted to prove he still knew how to follow the rules he'd operated within for almost a quarter of a century. Instead, he'd discovered there was a whole set of fresh ones to learn. Would he be able to?

Of course he would.

He was still driven by the same fundamental urge to serve as he always had been. Any dullness he might be feeling right now was temporary, a brief lethargy caused by low blood sugar and lack of sleep. And he'd fight alongside anyone willing to stand next to him, whoever they were and however strange a bedfellow they might be.

He couldn't retreat. There was work to be done. Threats to identify, understand, and defeat.

Knox drained his glass. He considered pouring out another one, but thought better of it and carried the empty tumbler over to the sink. Then he picked up the key from the counter and slipped it into his trouser pocket.

He couldn't retreat, but he did need to pay a visit to what had, in his absence, become his past.

The drive to Hertfordshire was still automatic, almost mindless, which gave Knox time to ponder what his immediate future might hold.

Perhaps he would take over from Laing as liaison to Six. At some point someone over there would need to be brought in on everything. It would have to be handled delicately – Five would need to work out if Century House had been compromised first – and by someone with enough authority to be believed. Knox knew how reticent the Service's counterparts had been to believe even in the existence of Line Z, and this, as Bennett has said on her balcony, was an entirely different level of magnitude.

He was still lost in thought as he drove down the lane to Rabley Heath and straight through its open gates, but the sight of the house brought him back to reality. The front looked almost the same as when he'd left; the only difference he noticed as he got out of his Jaguar was a thick length of wood that had been nailed across the rarely used main entrance.

He circled round to the rear, and saw more evidence of the assault Holland had mentioned – boarded-up windows, a poorly filled-in divot in the middle of the rear lawn, and a padlock bolted to the back door, which looked loose on its hinges.

Knox retrieved the key from his pocket, unlocked the door, and stepped inside. It was dark – the electricity had been turned off – and the air was stale with old, damp smoke.

The kitchen was a mess, shrapnel holes and scorch marks every-where. But, remarkably, the fridge was still mostly intact, and cool inside when Knox opened it. He found an uncracked bowl, poured some milk into it after he'd sniffed cautiously at the bottle, and then put it out on the edge of the lawn in case Stinky was hiding in a bush somewhere nearby. Then he did a quick inspection of the rest of the house, in silence – he'd been told about the listening devices that had been found throughout the building, and warned that there might be more still lurking in its nooks and crannies.

He could see the signs of another explosion in the drawing room, and the running battle that Williams must have fought on the first floor, including another sheet of wood where a window should have been at the front of the house that he'd missed when he'd arrived.

The state of the place reminded Knox of when he'd first come to Rabley Heath after the war, and again when it had been entrusted to his care years after Williams, the last of his line, had been presumed killed in action. With his best friend now absent once more, he wondered what would happen to his family pile.

Knox wasn't sure he could or wanted to become its sole custodian a second time. As much as it had been a home for Williams and him, it had also turned into a kind of prison for both of them. But perhaps it could have a new purpose, a future inspired by its history. It had been a base for the Special Operations Executive, Churchill's secret army of saboteurs and insurgents that had helped defeat the Nazis by running amok behind enemy lines. MI5 might need something similar now – a secret division within a secret service, kept off the books and away from headquarters.

He avoided glancing into Williams's bedroom as he passed it. He didn't want to see if his bed had been made or left messy. He didn't want to know what clothes were missing, what mementos he'd left behind, or whether there were any lingering signs of injuries he might have sustained in the battle for Rabley Heath.

Instead, Knox simply collected a few things from his bedroom, and made his way back out of the house and past the still-full bowl of milk. It was only then that he finally let his mind address Williams's abrupt departure from his life.

He forced himself not to feel too piteous about it. After all, a week ago he'd been telling Holland that Williams deserved his freedom while he was being given his own. And he'd lost his friend before, under much worse circumstances. At least this time he knew that Williams was alive, and more than capable of taking care of himself wherever he was.

Still, he couldn't help pondering where that wherever might be. Was he off to wreak revenge against Line Z or whoever had attacked his home? Was he going to fight the same fight as Knox in his own way, unleashed and unrestricted? Or was he just gone, never to return? Knox couldn't begrudge him if he was.

As Knox strolled back over the driveway, noting the slightly dark smudge in its gravel directly beneath the boarded-up upstairs window, got into the Jaguar and drove away from Rabley Heath, he wondered if he'd ever see him again. Then, as he glanced back at the house's reflection in his wing mirror and saw the Williams family crest flying above the eastern turret, he knew he would.

AUTHOR'S NOTE

As the saying goes, truth is often stranger than fiction. And in *A Game of Deceit* the most bizarre things are the ones that are real.

The image of a double-decker trundling past a neon sign in Chinese script may sound like a rather obvious writerly conceit about intermingling cultures. But it was the reality of Hong Kong in the sixties. It still is now. It's a place as fascinating and multifaceted as Berlin, Istanbul, or Beirut. More espionage stories should be set there.

The pro-communist protests and riots of 1967 that form the background to this novel have been intentionally forgotten by the official histories of both Hong Kong and the People's Republic of China – perhaps by the former because they happened, and by the latter because they failed to hasten the departure of the British. In fact, while anecdotal history abounds there's only one readily available academic text on them.

Even today, as Beijing exerts increasing power over the Special Administrative Region, the events of 1967 are overlooked. But they really did happen, with all their modern resonances and the curious details about loudspeaker propaganda and unwitting pop-star poster boys that feature in *A Game of Deceit*.

As for Blue Peacock, that was real too.

ACKNOWLEDGEMENTS

My greatest thanks, as ever, go to Chris. For being the reason I went to Hong Kong and knew I had to write about it in the first place, and for helping me grapple with the strange period of the reopening of society when this novel was mostly written.

Thanks must also go to my family and friends for continuing to put up with this indulgence of mine.

To Gordon Wise, Elliot Prior, and the team at Curtis Brown for their steadfast guidance.

To Jenny Parrott, Margot Weale, Mark Rusher, Lucy Cooper and everyone at Point Blank and Oneworld for their passion and enthusiasm.

To Ben Summers for designing the best book jackets out there.

To Jacqui Lewis for making sure everything I write makes sense.

To Gary Ka-wai Cheung, whose book *Hong Kong's Watershed: The 1967 Riots* was an invaluable resource. And to Vince Houghton, whose book *Nuking the Moon* led me to discover Blue Peacock.

And, of course, to all the readers, bloggers, booksellers, librarians, reviewers, event organisers and other authors who have been so kind, supportive, and encouraging.

© Mark Rusher

Tim Glister is a creative director working in advertising. He's worked for a range of famous and infamous brands, including eighteen months at the controversial political communications agency Cambridge Analytica. His debut novel *Red Corona* won The People's Book Prize. His second book *A Loyal Traitor* was a *Times* thriller of the month. He lives in London.